THE
PRISONER
and THE
EXECUTIONER

THE
PRISONER
and THE
EXECUTIONER

CATEE RYAN

atmosphere press

For Lori

Why do you stay in prison
when the door is so wide open?

Move outside the tangle of fear-thinking.
Live in silence.

Flow down and down in always
widening rings of being.

–Rumi

The words you speak become the house you live in.

–Hafiz, 1325-1390, Poet

SECTION 1

ELIZA

17 May 1989
Wednesday
Cape Vincent, New York
05:00

THE
EXECUTIONER

When I get the call, I put down the dishcloth and look out my kitchen window. I'm not supposed to be at work for another hour, but the call from Brenda, The Warden's secretary, always comes early on execution day. After I hang up I play word games in my mind to help me relax. I delight in language, the power and richness of words, all those stories that wait to be plucked from the cosmic consciousness. I laugh. I no longer want to be The Executioner.

My father, The Warden, groomed me for this work, and frankly, I was never cut out for it. I cannot be complicit in this execution. The Prisoner did not commit the crime. She is innocent. She was set up. I don't know who set her up or why. My father knows she's innocent, too, but he did not fight her execution. My father has no balls, no gumption, no free thinking or desire to say, *No, not on my watch.*

When I was five years old, my father told me, *Some people deserve to die, son. They've done horrible things. God wants them dead.*

My mother said, *God does not want people to be executed. God is all-forgiving.*

My father wanted me to bear witness to the executions. My mother did not.

It will make him a man.

No, it's deplorable, my mother said.

Necessary, retorted my father.

Uncivilized, snapped my mother.

An eye for an eye.

Turn the other cheek.

And so it had gone.

My mother saved me from witnessing the executions until I was ten. I'm convinced my mother would have continued to fight my father—and win—if she had not gotten the unexpected call in the middle of the night that her younger sister was found dead in an alley. My mother packed quickly and left. She did not take me with her. She did not remember the scheduled execution until she heard it on the news and saw the picture in the paper of her husband and me, her ten-year-old son, whose eyes were wild. I could barely stand still.

My mother came back to get me. My father would not let me go. I stood outside the wooden door of their bedroom. I heard her crying, her anger, and her resolve. She fought for me. My father shouted at her to get out. She opened the door, and I was standing there. She hugged me. Sometimes, I can still feel her hands on my head, her fingers running through my hair, and her lips kissing the top of my head, smelling me. My father came out and loudly ordered her to go. *Leave, Marjorie. Now.* She hugged me tightly, and I felt her bony shoulders and chest. She had always been thin, but after her sister's death, she was skeletal. Her sister's death broke her in some way I did not understand at the time. My father pushed her toward the door. His parting comment was, *Don't ever come back here. You are dead to us.*

She would never be dead to me. *I love you, Brian.* I silently mouthed the same words back to her. I was afraid to say them out loud. I was afraid of my father's anger.

My father slammed the door. He turned to me. *She's gone, son. It's you and me now. I will teach you everything you need to know to become a man.* I stood there with my head down. My father walked over to me and lifted my chin. *When I'm talking to you, son, you look at me. No more hanging your head. Men do not hang their heads. They face a situation and handle whatever comes their way.*

And so my systematic training began, day in, day out. School, sports, and caves were my respite from my father's rigid rules and expectations.

I stand at the kitchen sink gazing through the window at the St. Lawrence River as I wash my coffee cup. I love this view. I smile as I watch an eagle soaring and wonder what he has to tell me. I stand there for at least ten minutes. I'm sweating, too bundled up for inside the house. My hands grip the large porcelain sink. I bow my head. *It's over.*

I look around the kitchen. I have my mother's picture in my wallet. Nothing else here means anything to me. I will go in early as usual. I have gotten the call. It's execution day. I want to be with The Prisoner. I have things to say to her. I get my gun and put on my heavy black jacket. I am already wearing my black steel-toed boots. I look around my small house, the house I built from the ground up. It's a fortress. I check the windows, lock the attic door, go down the basement steps to get papers out of the safe, and then I deadbolt the basement door.

I call my buddy, Terran, while I latch the shutters and bolt the kitchen door. If they want to get in they will have to take a battering ram to the door. They can break the windows, but the wooden shutters on the inside of the house are thick. No one can see in. The eyes of the house are closed.

I drive my car to a large field outside of town. I change the license plates and walk along the fence. Terran picks me up fifteen minutes later. I haven't driven my own car to work on execution day for years.

We drive in silence until Terran asks, "You're good?"

"Yes."

"God be with you, bro."

"And you, too."

There is nothing unusual about Terran dropping me off at work on execution day. He gets out of the car and I hug him. He says hi to The Secretary as I walk through the gate. We've all been friends since elementary school. The Secretary does her cursory check-in. I'm friendly, but I'm not as focused as usual. Before I turn and walk to the cave, I hug The Secretary. And I am not the hugging kind.

17 May 1989
Wednesday
Cape Vincent, New York
06:00

T H E
SECRETARY

I watch The Executioner until he disappears into the cave. I think this is not how it normally is. This is not business as usual. I can smell The Executioner, something reckless and excited. I smelled him like this the one time we made love and he came deep inside me. I wanted so badly to get pregnant with his child. I did not get pregnant, and we never had sex again. He cried that one and only time and told me, *I can't do this. I'm sorry.* That's all he said. Then he left and I struggled to deal with myself, my hurt, and my squashed expectations. I had no one to talk to about my disappointment, no one to help me deal with my loneliness. It took me a while, but somehow we went back to being friends.

I know the execution day protocols like the back of my hand. The Executioner has written clearly defined procedures he has refined over the past fifteen years. The Cook brings The Prisoner's last meal the night before and serves it like a waiter in a restaurant. This Prisoner ordered scallops, a fresh green salad with blue cheese dressing, and a plain baked potato. For dessert she requested a brownie sundae with vanilla ice cream, hot fudge sauce, nuts, and whipped cream. No cherry on top. She asked for strong coffee with half-and-half. After the final meal, The Executioner leaves. He returns early the next morning and spends three to five hours with The Prisoner before he walks them to the death chamber. He never discusses what happens in those hours before the execution. His protocols say time and space are important for both The Prisoner and the witnesses, to reflect upon the upcoming death, to remember that every life and every death is important and deserves to be taken seriously. The Executioner holds each death in sacred space.

While The Executioner spends time with The Prisoner, I check the witnesses in and Prison Guard Eight admits them into the viewing room. At 11:00 a.m., The Executioner walks The Prisoner into the death chamber. He helps them get situated in the chair and straps them down. Throughout the process, he quietly talks with them. When they are securely fastened, he nods to PG Nine who opens the curtain that covers the glass. The witnesses can see The Prisoner and The Prisoner can see the witnesses. In the back of the room The Warden stands, observing his son's every move. The Executioner stands next to The Prisoner and holds their hand throughout the entire procedure. He never looks at the viewers. He is completely focused on The Prisoner.

When The Prisoner is dead, PG Nine closes the curtain and The Executioner unstraps The Prisoner and lifts him onto a gurney. He places a white cotton sheet over the body, and PG Nine wheels him to the elevator. The Executioner returns to Cell Block Z and remains there in silence until his shift ends at 3:00 p.m. When he leaves the prison, he does not speak to anyone. He walks until Terran picks him up. Executions are usually on Fridays, but if they are on a weekday, like today, The Executioner always takes the next day off.

17 May 1989
Wednesday
Cape Vincent, New York
06:45

T H E
PRISONER

I am surprised when The Executioner gives me a headlamp and signals me to follow him. He is dressed all in black—black pants, boots, jacket, and hat. He looks like an executioner or the devil incarnate. Except he isn't a devil; he is a good man. I have seen his goodness. The color change from his usual grey uniform to black throws me for a loop. In an instant I become the researcher and the participant. My boundaries get murky. I don't like murky. I want things clear and crisp and clean. I usually have clear boundaries.

Then the lights in the cave go out and it is pitch-black except for the tiny beacons of light from our two headlamps. The Executioner does not stop at the elevator to the death chamber. I must have made a sound because he turns and looks at me. He does not say anything. I remain silent, too.

I was so different when I first got to the prison. I talked incessantly those first nine months. The Executioner and I fell into a routine. Each day he asked me what I needed, and although I lashed out at him with angry words, he continued to calmly ask. He read out loud to me and we played games. He brought me books and paper and pen. He told me, *The Warden approved the books. I can give paper and pen to you, but each night an hour before my shift ends, I have to collect them. I can lock up your words at my house if you want. I can't get approval to leave paper and pens. It's not allowed.*

Why not?

The Warden has determined it's a safety issue.

Bullshit.

Yes. Bullshit it is, and if you want paper and pens, then you must give them back at the end of my shift.

I'll think about it.

The next day he brought me a photo of where he would keep my words. *It's a safe in my basement. Only two people know the safe is there.*

I looked at him. I got it. And the "it" I got was that he would take care of me. Maybe I could trust him.

Before he left that night, I blurted, *Okay. I want paper and pens. I'll give you my words one hour before your shift ends.*

Thank you for trusting me.

I thought, *Not on your life, buddy,* but I held my tongue. I remembered his words were the same words I used to say to women delivering their babies at home without a doctor. Trust—it's a funny thing. I had nothing to lose by trusting The Executioner. The women I asked to trust me put their baby's lives in my hands. They had much to lose.

That day I started calling him TE, short for The Executioner.

How strange it was to be locked in an underground cell for three years and nine months. I adapted to the dark and the smallness. The outer world mattered very little. I became comfortable with my womb-like existence where very little crossed the placenta. I was in a fishbowl. I read philosophical and spiritual essays, and poetry to help me come to grips with being imprisoned and ultimately to deal with dying. These books had strong words that brought me solace. I tried to read novels, which I had loved reading before my incarceration, but found I could not get engaged in someone else's story.

This last year The Executioner brought in movies that we watched together. Sometimes I'd laugh, which was surprising to me. Sometimes I laughed so hard, I cried. I didn't understand the setup. Why did The Warden approve of The Executioner being with me day in and day out, alone, with no cameras? PG One, Two, Three, and Four, the other guards, were distant but not unfriendly. They sat in the glass-windowed office where they always had a view of me, but I rarely saw them look at me. The Executioner only sat in the office at the beginning and the end of his shift. He turned his chair and faced away from me when he did paperwork. He seemed to consciously give me privacy.

Early on, I asked The Executioner what he wrote about when he turned his chair away from me. *You,* he replied. I looked at him questioningly. *Do you want to see?* I nodded. The paperwork was a checklist that included my eating, hygiene, sleep patterns, what I did, and what I said. There was space to write brief descriptions. He showed me what he'd written the day before, which was not at all reflective of what had happened. Those were the early days when he read to me six hours every shift, before he got approval from The Warden to have books in my cell, before we had that nasty interaction about paper and pen that I regretted.

After PG One gave me the details about executions, I calmed down. I no longer believed I was getting out. I no longer had hope that anything would change. If The Executioner read my writing, he would see how I worked my way through the death process and moved to acceptance. I didn't like that my life was going to end prematurely, but most days I accepted it. I did not talk to The Executioner about losing hope. I wrote. I captured my stories in words. My life was my topic of interest. I began to write my memoir. Every day at the end of his shift, TE took my papers and put them inside his coat pocket, carefully protected in a blue-green plastic envelope. Last night I gave him my final pages. I made a cover sheet: *TE, I want you to read all my words. I hope you will get them published. They might be helpful to others.*

I'm quiet as we walk in the caves below the prison. After we pass the elevator, I don't know where we're going. I follow TE closely, although he never says to do this. I am confident he knows the way. He told me stories about when he was a boy and wandered underground in spite of his father's rule that he was not to go into the caves. He told me these caves were his playground. In my mind I added, *Your kiva, your underground spiritual life.* I imagined this because the caves were my sacred place. I was a caver. I liked to go through small openings in the earth that I found in fields and the woods. I pushed myself down through these openings, and sometimes I found myself falling like Alice in Wonderland, except my falls were short. I usually ended up in a large open room where I was surrounded by glorious stalactites and stalagmites. Often there was a small creek or river running through the cave. I turned off my light, sat in the dark, and put my feet in the water. If the water was deep enough, I immersed and cleansed myself.

My mind wanders as I walk quickly behind The Executioner. I don't know his name, but he seemed to like it when I gave him the nickname TE. He never calls me anything, never addresses me by my name, Elizabeth Jacobs. I don't even know if he knows that Eliza is what most people call me, not Elizabeth, which is the name on my paperwork. I am Eliza to my mother and father, and especially to my younger twin siblings, Mari and Oliver. That was so long ago. I don't want to get stuck in my mind and my memories. We are moving quickly. I run every few steps to keep up with him.

17 May 1989
Wednesday
Cape Vincent, New York
07:00

T H E
EXECUTIONER

I hear her running to keep up with me, and part of me wants to stop and say something to her, but I cannot afford to do this. *Time is of the essence.* We must get to the cave with the iron steps, a ladder that will lead us out into the field where I parked my car. It's about two miles from where Terran picked me up earlier today. He knows. He's the only one who knows, although Brenda knew something was up. I could see the look in her eyes after I hugged her, my way of saying good-bye.

I wonder when my father will call in the missing Executioner and Prisoner. I am banking on my father not reporting us missing until at least twenty-four hours have elapsed. He will want to have confirmation that both of us are actually missing, that it isn't merely an electrical failure. He will want to be able to announce that the execution will proceed tomorrow.

If all goes according to plan, Eliza and I will have not only crossed into Canada, but be on an international flight to Europe before the authorities begin looking for us in the United States and at the borders. I have our route seared into my brain. I have the passports that Billy Williams made. I met Billy at a law enforcement training, and we got to talking. I liked him. I found out he was an identity changer, FBI profiler, and name finder in their Witness Protection Program. They don't know he still has a side business, one that he started in high school long before he got his job at the FBI. He helps people disappear. He told me that over the years he has disappeared many people, and had once given five names to one woman. I wanted to hear more, but he wouldn't give me any. He's private like that. I know he will not tell anyone about Eliza and me. Billy has given Eliza and me new names, Wendell and Wendy Falls. Nice names, names of dead children.

I worry I haven't prepared enough. Along with the directions and the passports, I've got two small duffel bags in the trunk containing clothes for both of us. We will look like a couple who is out for a drive on a Wednesday afternoon, just going to Canada for a couple of days. Except we are not going for a couple of days. We're crossing the border in Vermont and then we're going to the airport in Toronto. Tomorrow at 6:30 a.m. we will fly to Frankfurt.

In the four-hour drive to the border, I will tell Eliza the story. *Which story?* I wonder. There is certainly more than one story here. There's the "I've fallen in love with you story." Do I tell her that story?

We come to a creek. I hear her breathing change and

an *ahh* as she stops briefly to put water on her face. She's smiling, radiant. I feel her joy, her energy. The water has made her come alive, a thread has been loosened. I look at her. She looks at me. Still no words. I nod and we are off again. I imagine she feels my urgency. She is an energy reader, as am I. When you are one of the sensitive ones, you have to be careful. This is what got her into trouble. People can use your sensitivity against you. My father used mine against me, but he wasn't entirely able to shut me down. When Eliza came to the prison, my heart broke open.

17 May 1989
Wednesday
Cape Vincent, New York
07:15

ELIZA

I have not spoken in three years. I took a vow of silence after being in prison for nine months. I knew if I didn't, I would say things I regretted. I read about silence before I went to prison, but I never imagined myself completely ensconced in it, totally cocooned in my own inner world. I have had many revelations. I have made connections. I see how I ended up in prison, convicted of the murder of Lydia Garth, a crime I did not commit. At first, I fought. I was not one to keep my mouth shut. I had opinions. I spoke them, not loudly, but I spoke. People knew where I stood.

I was Lydia Garth's school counselor. She was a girl who was being sexually abused. She did tell me *yes*. She never told me who. Her *yes* came out twisted and gnarled, like the roots of a hundred-year-old oak tree. Lydia hung her head in shame.

You are not to blame, I told her.

But I don't stop it, Lydia said.

How can you?

I could run away.

Where would you go?

I don't know. I have nowhere to go.

Do you want to go?

Yes, she said. A strong *yes,* and I knew I would find a home for her in another state, far away from whoever was hurting her. I contacted Billy Williams, and we made arrangements. That afternoon, I walked Lydia out to a cab and hugged her good-bye. Poof! She was gone.

Bob Bruce, Cape Vincent's police chief, questioned me the next day, and I lied, said I had no idea where Lydia had gone. In fact, this was not a full-on lie. I didn't know, and would never know exactly where Billy sent Lydia, what name he gave her. Maybe one day I would know, maybe Billy will tell me, but it wasn't safe for Lydia or me to know.

Two days after the police chief talked to me, Lydia's father, Dr. Peter Garth, came to the school. My principal asked me if I was willing to meet with Dr. Garth to talk about his missing daughter. The principal added that I was under no obligation to do this. I told the principal I wanted to talk with Lydia's father. I did not tell the principal that I wanted to see who this man was. When I saw, I knew I had done the right thing. The father was guilty. He'd been using his daughter and possibly he allowed other men to use her, too. I felt his slimy energy as his eyes moved up and down my body. It made me sick. I wanted to spit on him, but instead I sat calmly in the principal's office talking with him while the principal sat quietly and bore witness to our conversation. His secretary took notes. There were things I didn't like about the principal, but in this instance, he protected me. He did not leave me alone with Lydia's father.

I am lost in my thoughts when I bang into TE's back. He has stopped and is shining his headlamp on metal stairs. I watch him climb up the ladder, hear the hatch groan open, and see the tunnel of light.

He returns down the ladder quickly and clips a cable to me. "This will protect you if you start to fall. Let's go."

He is right behind me as I start climbing the steep ladder. At another time in my life I would have fought being attached to a cable, but I'm weak. I haven't had this kind of exercise in almost four years. I follow his directions. When I stumble, he catches me. I rest briefly in his arms, and when he nudges me, I continue climbing. As I begin to make my way to the open hatch, I am focused on TE's gallantry, but I do not let my mind linger long there. If I'm going to make it up and out, I need to focus on the task at hand.

At the top of the ladder, TE unhooks me from the cable, and I climb out into an open field where the light is so bright that I can barely keep my eyes open. Tiny yellow and purple flowers cover the ground. It's spring. I've forgotten how beautiful spring is. I feel the cool breeze on my face. I start to feel woozy and fight to remain standing. TE is breathing hard as he finishes pulling up the cable. He closes the hatch and covers the cable and the hatch with debris. I am completely still with my hands clenched at my sides. He quickly comes over and guides me to the car. My legs are shaky. I climb in. He gives me sunglasses and hands me a water bottle.

"Drink this. You're dehydrated."

It's true. I drink what he gives me. He could be

drugging me. When you've been locked up as long as I have, and had so little contact with anyone, your mind plays tricks.

"I brought some clothes for you. You need to get out of your prison blues." He thrusts the yellow bag into my hand and walks to the back of the car.

I unzip the bag and bury my face in the clothes—pants, shirts, and new underwear. I breathe in the smell of clean laundry. Images flood my mind. I am giddy and teary at the same time. I strip off my blue pants and the old, holey, misshapen underwear, and put on new, soft, white, French-cut undies, a style I like. I wonder how he knew, but he couldn't have known. I could make up a story: he likes a French cut or he thought I would like them, but the truth is, it doesn't matter. They fit. And they are soft and precious and pure white and I love them. I tug on the black stretchy pants and put on the black bra and aqua T-shirt. There's another shirt, a red blouse with white stars on it, which I'll save for another day. I put on a grey cardigan, soft heavy cotton. I don a black hat. I'm a hat person. I take off my old, dirty, prison-issued Velcro sneakers and lace up my new, tri-colored Nike Air running shoes.

I'm perspiring, something I haven't done since I've been in prison. I'm broken from my reverie when TE gets in the car. He passes me a black trash bag. I stuff my prison clothes into it. I give him the yellow duffel, which he tosses onto the back seat.

"We'll dump the trash in a garbage can when we get to Vermont. Let's roll. Time is of the essence."

He starts the car and puts on a hat and dark sunglasses.

"Eliza, put your hair up inside your hat."

"What's happening?"

"What did you say?"

I look at him questioningly. I have broken my vow of silence.

His voice gets softer, and his laugh is deep and guttural.

"We're escaping."

"Where are we going?"

"We're heading to the Canadian border. Open the glove box and get out the passports. I suggest you memorize your new identity."

I see my picture and my new name, Wendy Falls.

"When we get to the border, they'll ask us what we're doing. I'll tell them we're on a road trip to celebrate our three-year anniversary."

I stare at him.

"My new name is Wendell Falls."

I'm paying close attention now. *He's changed his name, too? What's going on here?*

"At the border, they may want you to tell the story. We're going to a motel in Montreal, The Blue Goose. I have reservations, but of course we're not going there."

I start to speak, but the only word that comes out is, "Confused."

"Yes, that's not surprising. You've been locked away for three years and nine months, and for most of that time you've been silent. That's a long time."

I nod and turn away. I feel the tears right behind my eyes.

After I was convicted, my lawyer, David Drysden, visited me at the prison a few weeks into my sentence. He told me he was working on getting my charges dropped and would visit me again in two weeks. When he didn't return, I asked to see him. I wrote him letters. I got no response. He never came. I don't know if he even got my letters. They threw me away and lost the key. After that I had no visitors. The underground cell was where I would be until they killed me. TE came five days a week. He never took a vacation. I wondered if he had a life.

I look at TE. "Why didn't you go on vacation?"

"I was afraid you wouldn't be taken care of."

My throat is tight, and I feel like crying. Early in my incarceration TE went to a conference for five days and I missed him. Ironically, it was a conference that both of us had attended the previous year, although our paths did not cross. While TE was away, I had a conversation with Josh Candry, PG One, about what happens in the death chamber. I got calm, almost content. Soon after this I took my vow of silence.

TE says, "We're going to Toronto tonight. We'll stay at a hotel near the airport. We leave on a six thirty flight to Frankfurt tomorrow morning."

"You're full of surprises."

He glances at me. "We're probably good for at least the next three to six hours. They won't be able to get into Cell Block Z because I changed the codes. They'll be dealing with that for a while. They won't actually know what's happening until they get in there. When they see we're gone, all hell will break loose. I wanted to cross the border in Cape Vincent, but too many people know us. We can't risk it. We're crossing the border in Vermont where it's less likely someone will recognize us."

"You've been busy."

"Yes. I've been busy. Today's the day. Execution Day.

A day of freedom for you and for me."

"Do tell."

He looks at me and smiles. "It's good to see you relaxed and regaining your sense of humor."

I reach over and touch his shoulder. "I'm okay, TE. I'm tough. You know that."

"I do. And I'm hitting you with a lot of information. Cell Block Z was not a stimulating environment."

I laugh. "That's an understatement. Thanks to you, I read like a fiend. You brought me magazines so I could keep up with the world. I wasn't as isolated as I would have been if you weren't there. PG One, Two, and Three rarely spoke to me. For sixteen hours a day I had stillness and quiet. Half of that was black, lights out. Sometimes I'd hear PG One's music. He liked rock and roll. I was grateful to hear that."

"So PG One was breaking the rules. Huh. I'm surprised Josh had it in him."

"He also worked out, lots of running in place. He used the dictionary as a weight. I watched him in the guard room and heard him grunting. I know his wife and kids. I delivered his daughter, Shell. She and I went caving together."

"I guess many of us have another life, a hidden life."

"So, that being said, I am now Wendy Falls."

"Pleased to meet you, Wendy. I'm Wendell."

We both laugh and I touch his shoulder again. This time he leans his head into my hand, and I touch the side of his hairy face.

"I'm going to shave tonight in Toronto."

"I'm going to cut my hair really short. By the way, what's your name?"

"Brian Stafford," he says softly.

And so it begins. Except I realize it began the day I walked into the prison, when TE walked into The Warden's office and got between me and his father, who was furious with me.

We drive to the border, mostly in silence. The windows are open, and I take in all the sights and sounds. I open and close my eyes and try to comprehend this man: The Executioner, TE, Brian, and, at the border and forevermore, Wendell. He is taking me to freedom, a new life. I think about the children who I sent to new lives and wonder how they managed. I hope Lydia Garth made it safely to her new destination. I wish I could have prepared her better. I look at our passports. We're married.

I wake up with a start to rain, thunder, and lightning. I am disoriented and scared. *Are you fucking kidding? Scared?* I say this to myself once I gain my bearings. I'm in a comfortable car where I've slept like a baby for I don't know how many hours. This is the safest environment I've had in three years and nine months. I'm with a man who has taken care of me this entire time. TE told me the plan, said we'd probably make it to the border in three or four hours. He gave me my passport with my new name, Wendy. Five letters, just like Eliza. I like that. The numbers work. The mathematical beauty of his plan makes me smile as I try to process what is happening. I am no longer in Cell Block Z, underground, buried alive. I had reconciled that I was going to die today. I had hoped my parents would be there so I could see them one last time. I didn't like that my life was going to be taken from me, but I could not change my external circumstances, only my internal reality, and that is what I did when I took my vow of silence.

The lightning flashes and the thunder booms, bringing me to the present. We are waiting in line to cross into Canada. I keep my eyes closed.

"Eliza. We'll be at the border soon, so it's Wendy and Wendell Falls now."

I nod and place my hands in my lap. My breathing is shallow.

"It's going to be fine. Everything's in order," TE says reassuringly.

I say nothing. What is there to say? He's saying all is well, and I want to believe him. He is calm and alert, careful and assured, yet I see the tension in his shoulders and feel his heightened vigilance and diligence. His voice has a slight edge when he asks me to get the passports out of the glove box. I put my hand on his hand and look at him. I am completely still. I learned to be still in prison.

"Thank you."

I take my hand away and see that he has relaxed—not fully, not one hundred percent, but his shoulders are down now. TE takes a small envelope out of his pocket and hands it to me. I open it and see two rings, a single diamond in a princess-style setting and a plain silver band.

"Will you be my wife?" I laugh, but my eyes are filled with tears.

I touch his face and nod. He puts the ring on my finger. I put his ring on his finger, and he says, "I do."

There isn't time to take it all in.

"Identification, please."

I hand TE the passports. I sit with my relaxed hands in my lap.

"What's the purpose of your trip to Canada?"

"We're celebrating our anniversary."

"Where will you be staying?"

"The Blue Goose in Montreal."

"How long do you expect to be in Canada?"

"A few days."

I listen carefully. I hear every word they say, but I'm not much interested in the interaction. It is part truth and part lies. It's all pleasant, not like the night that I let the police into my house and got screwed over by Detective Serge Valentino. I find it hard to believe that I'm four hours away from the prison and I'm already beginning to feel fury, fury that I had squelched, feelings that I did not allow myself to feel, experiences that I stopped revisiting because whether I revisited them or not, I wasn't getting out. The system condemned me to death on a trumped-up murder charge, and what I wonder now—again, after I thought I'd let it go—is, who wanted me gone? I never figured that out, not in the first year that I kept revisiting the series of events. When I took my vow of silence, I chose to silence some of my own voice for my survival.

The official peeks his head in the car window and says, "Okay, sir and ma'am. Have a wonderful trip. Montreal is beautiful this time of year and a great place for celebrating anniversaries."

"Thank you," I say with a smile.

He hands our passports to TE, who passes them to me.

17 May 1989
Wednesday
Cape Vincent, New York
11:15

T H E
WARDEN

I get the call.

PG Nine says, "Sir, The Executioner has not brought The Prisoner to the death chamber."

"Give him five more minutes, son. If he doesn't show up, call me."

I know The Executioner's protocols. My son is orderly and punctual.

"Brenda, did you check The Executioner in this morning?"

Brenda comes to my door. "Yes, Warden, at six. He always comes early on execution day. Terran dropped him off as usual. Is something wrong, sir?"

My phone rings and I take the call. As Brenda begins to walk out I tell her, "Call PG One and have him go down to Cell Block Z. Let's find out what the holdup is."

"The holdup, sir?"

"Yes. The Executioner is late, and you and I both know he is never late."

Twenty minutes later I hear PG One say to Brenda, "I need to speak to The Warden."

Brenda knocks on my closed door and says, "PG One is here, sir."

"Send him in."

When PG One enters the room I see his flushed red face and hear his heavy breathing. "I can't get in, sir. I tried the code ten times and then I went to the backup code. There's nothing."

"Nothing?"

"No power, sir. No electricity. All the lights are out. It's pitch-black down there. I had to get a flashlight."

I am silent and still.

"Thank you, PG One."

After PG One leaves, I sit at my desk looking out the window at the line of visitors waiting to be checked in so they can view the execution. I denied Elizabeth Jacobs's parents' request to talk with their daughter the day before her execution. I have the right to deny access to the prisoner, but this is the first time I have ever denied any parent this privilege.

I know this denial is not going to look good, but, I got pissed off the first day she came to my prison. I didn't like her standing up to me, not doing what I told her to do. I wanted to hurt her. I hated her boldness and her mouthiness. I made a split-second decision to put her in Z Block even though we had prepared a cell for her in A Block. I can justify it, though, because the statutes allow me to do this. There is, however, no justification for keeping The Prisoner in Z Block for three years and nine months. I never thought anyone would look at her paperwork.

After Detective Valentino arrested her, the governor asked The Board of Corrections to push through legislation allowing a men's prison to house five women, if necessary. The Board approved it because of the overcrowding issue in the women's prison. The Board members did not know that the governor's request was about Elizabeth Jacobs specifically. She never should have been sent to my all-men's prison, but Peter Garth wanted her close. *We need control over who visits her and what communication she has with the outside world. She was the last person Lydia saw before she disappeared. Lydia may have told her something.* We all agreed with him, I just didn't want her to be in my prison. I tried to get out of it. I brought up the possibility of housing her in another men's prison. I told them, *I don't like women all that much, and I certainly don't want them in my prison.* The governor, the judge, the detective, and the accountant agreed with Peter. I was the only dissenting vote. I had to go along. I got stuck with her.

I buzz Brenda. "Call Sam Davis and tell him I need him pronto. The electricity is out in Cell Block Z."

A few minutes later Brenda knocks on my door. "Warden, Merry says Sam's in Buffalo, been there a few days. He's doing a big job. He won't be back till late tonight."

"Is there any way to reach him?"

"Merry said she'll make some phone calls and get back to me."

"Let me know when he's on his way. And Brenda, get

the governor on the phone. I need to let him know that the execution will be delayed. We need a plan for the witnesses."

Brenda buzzes me ten minutes later. "Governor's on line two, Warden."

I take a deep breath and pick up the phone. The governor is not pleased. "Alright, Arthur. Tell them Z Block cannot be accessed at this time due to an electrical failure and that the execution will most likely proceed later today or tomorrow. Call Betsy's and have the visitors treated to lunch on our dime. We should know more after lunch."

I ask Brenda to call The Cook. When The Cook arrives he tells me, "Everything was normal last night, Warden. I served The Prisoner her last meal. She was calm. The Executioner did what he always does. He brought The Prisoner out of her cell, and they sat together at a small table that he covered with a white linen tablecloth. I served the food on the china that he always uses."

I know all this. My son ritualizes each death. I don't like it, but I've allowed it because I don't want my son to walk away from the job. "Did The Prisoner speak to you?"

"No, Warden, she did not."

I think about how my wife betrayed me when she left and wanted to take Brian from me. I didn't let her take him. Even though he lived with me, Brian was always more attached to his mother. He obeyed me except when it came to exploring the caves. He had some sort of fascination with them, and even though he knew I would punish him, he continued to wander around in the dark, underground. I never understood that, and I didn't like it.

When Brian's friend Derrick died, Brian walked the caves all the way to Vermont and emerged near the northern tip of Lake Champlain. Terran picked him up. The local paper did a story on him. When he got home, I went to put my hands on him, and he blocked me. He said, *No more. That's it.* I could not free myself from his grip. I felt afraid. *When had Brian gotten so strong?* I saw his strength in his eyes. He reminded me of Marjorie. She had a backbone of steel, too. I saw this same strength in Elizabeth Jacobs. My mother had this strength. My father did not, and it was my father I wanted to please. My father did not treat my mother well, but my mother stayed with him. When my father died in a car accident, my mother's lover moved in. My life got different. I left for college six months later, but the damage was done. I could not stand my mother's happiness. She reeked of sex. I hated her.

17 May 1989
Wednesday
Cape Vincent, New York
11:30

BRENDA

I call Betsy and explain the situation. She and I make a tentative plan to meet after work and take a walk along Svenson's Creek. I sit at my desk. The Warden's door is shut. I knock and bring him a cup of coffee. He's sitting in his big brown chair staring out the window. I've only seen him like this once before, when his wife called and told him she wanted a divorce. The rumor was they'd had no contact since she left, and he wouldn't let her take Brian. They had not bothered to get a divorce. I set his coffee down and leave the room quietly. I know when he needs something he'll holler.

My phone begins ringing off the hook. I field the calls. The Warden takes none of them.

"No call back from Merry or Sam?"

"Not yet, Warden. Merry said she'd call me as soon as she gets ahold of him. PG One is down in Cell Block Z trying to get the lights working."

"If they're still in there, they're not getting out anytime soon."

My stomach clenches when The Warden offers up the possibility that Brian and The Prisoner might not be there. I think about Brian hugging Terran and me earlier this morning.

The governor intervenes in the middle of the afternoon. Sam Davis and his son arrive at the prison by helicopter. The local news reporters are waiting outside the prison gates. The Warden lets them know that he will hold a press conference after Sam deals with Cell Block Z's electrical problem. He reminds the press that the governor issued a statement, that due to an electrical problem, The Executioner and The Prisoner are trapped inside Cell Block Z.

The Warden walks away as one reporter shouts, "Are you worried about your son, Warden?"

The Warden doesn't turn around, and leads Sam and his son into his office. He explains the problem and lets Sam know that PG One and Two are available to help. Sam asks for big lights so he can work through the night if need be.

The Warden tells me, "Let all the PGs know there's a mandatory meeting at shift change here in my office. I need you to take notes, Brenda. Call the graveyard shift and let them know I'll be sleeping in my office tonight. If there's an emergency, they can knock on my door."

At the meeting, The Warden says, "As most of you know, we have an electrical problem in Z. Your job is to keep the prisoners from getting agitated. The Cook will give them a meal with dessert tonight."

PG Seven says, "The prisoners are asking if she might

have escaped."

I sit completely still. Everyone does. You could hear a pin drop. The Warden says, "That's not likely."

I am glad The Warden doesn't say escape is not possible, because of course it is, especially because The Executioner knows the cave system, grew up playing there despite his father's warnings and beatings when he disobeyed his father's orders.

I continue to field calls. When Sam comes up from Cell Block Z, I direct him to The Warden's office.

I hear Sam say, "It's a work of art, Warden."

"You know Brian. He's got a mind like a steel trap."

"Well, he certainly knows about electricity. Never seen anything like this. It's backup system after backup system. It's complicated."

"Can you get in, Sam?"

"Oh, yeah. I can get in. It's just going to take time. Hopefully Brian and The Prisoner are not getting too hungry in there."

The Warden laughs a restrained laugh which is more like a snort. "There's a fridge in the office that they keep stocked with drinks and snacks. Brian should be fine. Tonight I'm sleeping in my office, Sam. Come get me if you need me. The Cook will bring you and your son dinner after the prisoners eat."

The Warden tells me, "Go home and get a good night's sleep, Brenda. I need you to come in a couple of hours early tomorrow. Sam thinks he'll get in Z sometime in the morning. I'd like you to be here when he does."

"Of course, Warden. I'll be in at four."

The Warden walks back into his office and closes the door.

I leave the prison and go directly home. I call Betsy and cancel our walk.

I'm tired but I don't want to go to sleep. I'm worried about Brian. I pick up the phone more than once to call Terran. Finally, I call and get his answering machine.

Terran, this is Brenda. Can you call me? I don't care how late it is.

He calls me an hour later.

"Have you heard about what's happening at the prison?"

"Yup. I've been at Bandy's all evening listening to the scuttlebutt. It's all people are talking about."

"Do you think he's locked in there, Terran?"

"How would I know, Brenda? Your guess is as good as mine."

"He hugged us both today. He never does that."

Terran laughs. "Maybe he's getting soft in his old age."

"Come on, Terran. Be straight with me."

"Brenda. I picked him up and brought him in just like I always do on execution day."

"You're telling me something wasn't different?"

"I'm telling you I don't know anything. I think we should wait until Sam gets the goddamn door open."

"What are you so angry about, Terran?"

"You're pissing me off, Brenda."

I sigh. "I'm scared, Terran." I hear him take a big breath.

"Let's see if he's in there, Brenda. If he isn't, then we'll go from there. And if he is, there's nothing to talk about. Get some sleep. No matter what happens, you've got a busy day tomorrow."

"Okay. Will you call me tomorrow? I'm having a hard

time being by myself."

Terran hesitates. "Yeah, I'll call you tomorrow after work."

17 May 1989
Wednesday
Canada
12:00

WENDY

Once we're through the border TE's shoulders get farther away from his ears and he breathes deeply.

He says, "It's a little over an hour to Toronto. We've got a hotel room near the airport. We'll take a shuttle in the morning. I've got to drop this car off after we get settled in our room, so I'll be gone for a while."

"I need scissors to cut my hair," I blurt.

"You got it."

We stop in a small town for scissors, razors, and water. We're quiet on the drive to Toronto. Silence. I don't want to collapse, but there's a lot to process. I thought I ate my last meal less than twenty-four hours ago. I looked The Cook right in the eyes and let him know how much I liked his delicious food. I didn't say anything. I was determined to go out of this life honoring my vow of silence. I took it seriously. I was fully committed. It was the only thing I could control. I wasn't giving the system anything. I did not want the people who put me there to know how much they harmed me. They tried to take away my humanness, but they were not successful. I read Viktor Frankel's book *Man's Search for Meaning*. Actually, The Executioner read it to me before I started calling him TE, before he got approval to give me books. Was he trying to give me hope? I don't know.

After nine months of verbal processing, I asked TE to bring me a book about vows of silence. He found me more than one and I read them with relish. I learned that taking a vow of silence meant I would make a promise it would kill me to break. I would commit to cultivate awareness and clarity. The system was not getting any more of me, not that they wanted anything. Silence was a way to fight for myself.

I told TE I was taking a vow of silence. He nodded and said he would miss our conversations. Life went on. TE was comfortable with silence. He continued to read out loud to me. He was a good reader, really good at dialogue. He asked me regularly if I had any book preferences. Usually I shook my head, so he picked the books. One time I wrote a request for *Love Story* by Eric Segal and books by Scandinavian authors. I don't know why I asked for *Love Story*. It had always made me cry. And cry I did when TE read it to me. I felt like he wanted to touch me, to soothe me, but he didn't. He was already breaking the rules. He never imposed himself on me, although I didn't trust that he wouldn't take advantage of me. Any of the guards could have, but none of them did. I began to doubt that I was attractive. Then I dealt with the question: Do I need external validation from men? I saw things about myself and my character that I had seen before but had not understood. I did not like seeing them now, however I did gain some peace of mind as I healed from these revelations. Aah, the joys of clarity!

I made a deal with myself that if I ever got out of prison, I would live the life I love. I asked myself, what would that life look like? The answer was no giving in, no settling. I would help women deliver their babies in a way that New York state laws did not allow. I would write children's books, short stories, novels, and my memoir. In these past three years I wrote and wrote. Every afternoon TE took my words and placed them in a blue-green plastic envelope. The next day he returned with the same envelope full of poems that I took to memorizing. In prison I learned I was a writer.

I wonder if all those words are lost, gone. I tell myself a writer has to let go of superfluous words. I regret I didn't get a chance to edit mine. I wanted TE to bring me the words I'd written, but he never did, and I never asked him to. Actually, it was almost like he could read my thoughts when he said, *It's not safe to bring your pages back in, I'm sorry.* I thought, *No problem. I am grateful for paper and pens five days a week.* I went through a lot of pens. I don't know how many. I wish I'd counted them. When a pen ran out of ink, I tapped on the metal cell bars and TE brought me a new one. He put the old inkless pen in his uniform pocket. He did not throw it in a garbage can. I don't think there was a garbage can in the guard station.

On my once-a-week shower day, I walked by the glass guard station. There a desk and chair, one filing cabinet, a coffee maker, a small fridge, and a bulletin board which was mostly empty, although TE, when he first arrived for his shift, often put things up on it, a changing collage of pictures and poems. I could see the images from my cell. The last hour of his shift he took the collage down. PG One, Two, and Three never put anything up. PG One did pull-ups numerous times throughout his shift. Each time he collected my dinner plate he asked me if I needed anything. He always used the same five words: *Do you need anything, Eliza?* I always looked him right in the eyes and shook my head.

The lights went out nightly at nine thirty, so when PG Two came on at eleven he and I had no contact even though most of the time I was awake. When PG One and Two talked at shift change, I pretended to be asleep. I was envious of their easy conversation and laughter. One time they agreed to meet at Bandy's, the local bar. I'd been to Bandy's, but I wasn't a regular there. My haunts were the caves and rings of tall trees that seemed like someone had planted them for a sacred purpose.

After PG One left, PG Two would read for a while and sometimes do crossword puzzles. He used the dictionary. Then he turned off the lights. I assume he slept. His alarm went off thirty minutes before TE arrived. On the weekends, PG Three worked doubles and PG Four did the night shift. There were no blinds in their office. I couldn't imagine these guys liked me being able to see them. I wasn't the only one who was in a fishbowl.

The Warden visited Cell Block Z twice a year at TE and PG One's shift change. The Warden never made any contact with me. I don't know what he was doing, what he was looking for, but TE got stiff, like he was encased in a steel box or behind a brick wall. He didn't seem to like his father. I wrote a story about them. I figured I'd never know if it was true. I just wrote, and trusted that TE didn't read my words because he said he didn't, wouldn't. I also figured if he did, so what? What would it matter? I'd be dead soon. I spent many hours pondering why TE was so generous, but I never asked. I had lots of time for mental masturbation on such topics.

I'm grateful for our silence in the car because my mind is busy trying to keep up with how fast everything is happening. I'm glad we're staying at a hotel near the airport. I look forward to room service and quiet. TE told me he wants to watch the news.

Check-in at the hotel is uneventful. People are nice. I forgot that people could be so friendly, and these Canadians are especially kind and accommodating. I hear conversations in the lobby. People are animated. I feel the immense energy. I have been in an environment where mostly what I responded to was my own energy, my own internal processes. The caveat was that I was locked in a six-by-nine cell. I am grateful TE let me out so I could do yoga postures and walk around. Movement. Over time, I got less and less enchanted with movement and more engaged in meditation, stretching, and writing. I embraced calm, quiet stillness. I read books about people's experiences on death row. I was the only one on death row in Cell Block Z, which meant I was essentially in isolation, the guards my only human contact. I am grateful I didn't have to deal with other inmates.

I wait for TE as he uses a phone in the lobby to make arrangements for the car. We take the elevator up to the fifth floor.

When we get in our room, he says, "I shouldn't be gone more than an hour. Do you want to order dinner while I'm gone or wait until I get back?"

"I'll wait for you."

And then he's gone, and I'm in this room with an amazing view of a river and airplanes coming and going. Tomorrow I will get on one of those planes. I feel excitement moving through my veins.

I stand at the open window for a long time and feel the breeze on my face. I wonder what my life is going to be like now. I have contemplated death for so long and now I might actually be free. But there are self-imposed prisons.

I have not been physically alone in over three years. I pull a chair over to the window and look out. The lights, airplanes, and sky are beautiful. The sunset's colors are spectacular and ever-changing. Only in my mind's eye did I remember the wonder of these colors, but I actually stopped remembering because my world was grey walls, grey bedding, and grey underwear. I imagined the underwear used to be white, but not anymore. TE and the guards all wore grey uniforms.

In prison I rarely saw color. Sometimes the covers of the books that TE brought me were colorful. I'm surprised they didn't take off the book covers and give them to me colorless. One Halloween TE brought me a tiny pumpkin and set it on the floor outside my cell. I scooped it up and delighted in its color. I had missed orange. I love Halloween. Before the twins were born, when I was an only child, I loved trick-or-treating and dumping out the candy on the floor in the living room. Mom and Dad watched as I bartered with my cousins. *I'll give you five Tootsie Roll Pops for one Reese's Peanut Butter Cup.* One cousin always said no. He liked chocolate as much as me. His sister usually traded—more was better. She loved Tootsie Roll Pops. One for five worked for her. The pumpkin took me back to carving pumpkins with my mom and dad on the green linoleum kitchen floor covered in newspapers. My parents were smiling.

I held the small orange pumpy next to my aching heart. I asked myself, *How does someone live in a colorless world? How do I live in that world?* The answer: *You read. You write. You meditate.*

I hated the weekends. I read a lot of books once The Warden approved them. The Librarian, if there actually was one, wasn't allowed into Z, but PG One brought in the cart and I got to pick three books at a time.

The first time I saw The Warden was the day I arrived at the prison. He was a tall man with closely cropped hair. He was big-boned, overweight, and looked as though he used to be fit.

I didn't kill Lydia Garth. I will get out of here.

He looked me in the eyes, and in a dead-calm voice, said, *You've been convicted. You're not getting out of here.*

Convictions can be overturned.

Not yours. It's not going to happen.

He was so assured, so self-righteous. I hated him. I wanted to spit at him.

You don't know that.

He said nothing, but looked me straight in the eyes with his hard, cold, piercing blue-ice eyes.

Brenda, call The Executioner.

The woman came to the door. She was wearing a matching green skirt and jacket, black pumps, and nylons. We looked at each other. I saw compassion in her eyes. I heard her soft, melodic, kind voice.

Yes, Warden.

Sit down, The Warden ordered me.

I prefer to stand.

Sit down.

I said nothing and continued to stand.

He took a step toward me.

I stood my ground and thought, *Really you bastard? You're going to hit me?*

A man walked in and he placed himself between me and The Warden. The Warden stopped moving.

Take her to Cell Block Z.

The man looked surprised but said nothing. He gently led me out of the room. I saw Brenda at her desk. She stared at the man, and she and I made brief eye contact. I saw her clenched hands by the sides of her typewriter. She handed the man some paperwork, and we were off. We went through three locked doors and when we got to a landing, before we went down the stairs, the man unlocked my leg irons so I could walk more easily. He also took off my handcuffs.

We're going down three flights of stairs. You might want to hold on to the railing. The stairs are steep.

Who are you and where are you taking me?

I'm The Executioner, and we're going to your cell.

It's underground? I asked incredulously.

Yes. Prisoners who are going to be executed are housed downstairs.

In the bowels of the prison? My voice was squeaky now.

Yes. He looked at me then. I saw the same blue eyes that The Warden had, except this man was gentle, kind, and fit.

As I headed down the stairs, I couldn't believe that all this was real, that this is what my life had become. *I have* to get out of here. *How can this be happening? I'm a counselor and a midwife. I did not kill Lydia Garth.* I still believed I would get out. At the same time, there was something foreboding about that walk down those dimly lit stairs. I did not know that I would not see the sky again until TE and I walked through the caves and climbed up the metal ladder three years and nine months later.

I am not the same woman now. I turn from the window and go into the bathroom. I shut and lock the door. I look at myself in the mirror. My skin is pasty white. I have lines on my face and my eyes remind me of the living dead. I don't look healthy. They fed me well in prison, but they starved me of sunlight and fresh air. I'm thin, and my hair is thick and grey. I take the scissors and begin to cut my hair. I have towels on the floor, and I put the hair in the laundry bag. I keep at it. It's a slow process.

I hear the door open. TE must be back. I open the bathroom door and he looks at me.

"Wow! You look different."

I stand there, unmoving. I hand him the bag with all my hair, just like I handed him the black bag with my prison blues at that gas station in Vermont. He threw it into a dumpster.

I go back into the bathroom, lock the door, and start the bath water. I shave my legs and pits. I take in the room as I relax in the warm water. There is a soft, thick, white bathrobe on the back of the door. I hear TE on the phone ordering room service. In an instant, I'm hungry. I get out of the bath and look in the mirror. I like my closely cropped hair. It's shorter than I've ever worn it before, but that was another life. Now I have this life. I put on lotion and then the bathrobe.

TE is sitting at the table waiting for me. I go and sit across from him. He has the slider open and has moved the table near the balcony. The breeze caresses my face and legs. It feels good. I sit down and look at him. I want to say something, but I'm not used to talking.

"Well, It's official. I've broken my vow of silence."

"How are you feeling about that?"

"Weird. Surprised. Hungry."

He laughs. "I ordered you fish, scalloped potatoes, and a salad. I don't really know what you like except for what you ordered for your supposed last meal."

I laugh through my tears. I like his use of the word *supposed*. "Perfect."

He has a filet mignon, baked potato, and vegetables. There's bread and butter on the table. I help myself to the bread and put the cold, hard butter on it in really thick chunks. I love how it melts into the warm bread.

"Mmm."

He smiles.

We eat in the quiet of that room.

"Getting rid of the car went as planned."

"Good."

He hands me a box. "I bought them at that gas station in Vermont. The woman who made them is a local artist."

I put on the earrings. They are purple, faceted, glass-crystal orbs with a tiny green glass bead above each ball. They are beautiful. They work with my short hair.

"They look good on you. You like them?"

"I love them." There's so much more I could say, that I want to say, but I don't say. Not now. Not yet. I'm not used to saying. There's time, I think. There's no hurry. I breathe.

"I'd like to watch the news," he says.

He moves to the couch and turns on the television. I sit in the chair. There is nothing about The Executioner and The Prisoner.

"This is good. I didn't think my father would call it in until he had confirmation that we were actually gone."

"You know your father."

"Yes. Unfortunately, I know him all too well."

We watch the rest of the news. I think of all the nasty things I said as I vented about The Warden when I first arrived at the prison. TE listened to all of them. He never once gave any indication that this man was his father until after I stopped venting.

When the news is over, TE says, "I'm going to shower and shave and try to get some sleep. Our airporter leaves at four."

When he's in the shower, I take the cart with our plates and put it in the hall. I don't see anyone and I'm glad. I go into the bedroom: two beds. My yellow bag is on the bed near the window. I dump it out and look at what I have—three pairs of underwear, two bras, two pairs of black pants, three shirts, the grey sweater I wore today, a black down jacket, a pair of tennis shoes, three pairs of socks, the black hat, and pajamas. The pajamas are light green with dark green leaves all over them, vines. As I examine them more closely, I see hummingbirds sitting on nests and flying to get nectar. I love them. I quickly put them on and put everything back into the duffel except the clothes I'm going to wear on the plane tomorrow. TE has put *A Wrinkle in Time* by my bed. I smile. It's a book I read many times to my brother and sister. When he comes into the bedroom I look up. His beard is gone, and he has on maroon-and-green plaid lounge pants and a white V-neck T-shirt. His eyes are shiny. He looks sexy.

He gets into the other bed and picks up his book, an Agatha Christie mystery.

"Goodnight," he says. "Sweet dreams, Wendy."

"To you, too, Wendell."

I lie awake in bed for a long time. Many thoughts cycle through my mind. I am Wendy. TE is Wendell. I think I can still call him TE, as only he and I know him as that. I won't have a problem dropping Brian because I never knew him with that name.

I broke my vow of silence today. That's the biggest thing that happened. No! Who am I kidding? I escaped from solitary confinement and my death today. That's bigger than breaking my vow of silence. I don't want to compare them because it's like apples and oranges. Both of these events are huge, life-changing. I wonder if TE's awake, but I don't think so because I hear his soft, even breathing. I'm glad to be by the open window where I can see lights and airplanes and feel the cool breeze.

I don't feel normal. I'm not used to being around people and sounds. I think about spending a lot of time in the basement as a child. The piano was there, as were my father's bookcases, full of novels and his professional books. I liked the subterranean feeling of being underground. I felt protected, although there were high windows that could be accessed and opened. I could tell if it was day or night. In prison there was grey. I only knew what time of day it was by the coming and going of the guards and mealtimes. TE let me out of my cell so I could more fully do the yoga postures. He was careful, always making sure I was back in my cell an hour before the next shift came on. I could tell he didn't like making me return to my cell, but I went willingly. Sometimes I walked around the small space like it was a miniature track.

I adapted, as much as anyone can, to a neutral, non-stimulating environment. Over time I accepted my fate. I read about Edith Bone, a Romanian doctor who was in solitary confinement for seven years. She wrote about how she took care of herself by nurturing her inner life so she remained mentally and spiritually fit. Her book, along with Viktor Frankel's, gave me a solid structure to be able to not only survive and endure, but to thrive. They both walked out of prison free, something I never expected to do.

But here I am in a comfy bed by a window with TE in a bed next to mine. I can get up anytime I want and wander into the living room, which I do because I can't sleep. I meditate, which helps calm my busy mind. TE's going with me tomorrow to Frankfurt, but I don't know if he's staying with me or just getting me to a sanctuary city where I'll be safe. I haven't asked him. One step at a time. My heart beats faster. I'm overwhelmed. I'm exhausted and overstimulated, simultaneously. Every sound, every light, draws my attention. My nervous system is firing quickly. I focus on my breath, and my heart rate returns to normal.

We haven't been gone from the prison twenty-four hours. In fact, if we get on the plane when we're supposed to, it will be exactly twenty-four hours that we've been missing. I come back to my breath and replay how I felt when TE gave me the headlamp. When the lights went out and it was pitch-black, we walked right past the elevator to the death chamber. My body clicked into the darkness and exploring. The air got cooler the farther away we got from the sterile environment of Z and its poor circulation.

There were no dank smells, no dirt on my feet, and no sounds of water trickling. Cell Block Z was an underground tomb where people might go if they were trying to survive a nuclear explosion, buried, below ground, where they could have the illusion of being safe. Except it never felt safe to me. But here in this hotel, in this fifth-floor suite, the top floor, I feel safe. My breathing is calm and steady.

18 May 1989
Thursday
Toronto, Canada
01:13

WENDELL

I hear her leave the room and can only imagine what she's going through. I look out the window and this morning's eagle comes to mind. It's been quite a day. Something big is happening, and it isn't an execution, at least not in the classic sense. I am executing my plan.

Nine months ago I began to grow a beard which I'd never done before. I found out I didn't like facial hair, but it served a purpose. I gradually changed my appearance. I wanted people to get used to me with a beard. My father commented on that. I told him I wanted a new look. He asked me if I had a new lady-friend. I smiled and played along with my father's supposition. There was no way I would ever tell him anything about any of my relationships.

Other people commented on my new look, too, said I looked like a mountain man. At work the other guards told me I looked wild and reckless, which to them meant I was less in control. How wrong they were. I never felt more focused. I was more alive than I'd been in a long time. When I left the prison after my shift, I worked out for hours every night in my basement gym while I watched the news, listened to music, and lifted weights. Sometimes I did treadmill runs, but mostly I did nighttime runs on trails in the woods that I accessed right from my house.

My nearest neighbor, Celeste Gordon, saw me go out at night which I would have preferred her not knowing, but I wasn't concerned. She and I have a long, intertwined history. She's the woman who was a mother to me after my own mother left. When Celeste was sitting on her front porch swing in the early morning, which she often was when I drove by her house on my way to work, I slowed down and called out *Hi* as I went by. She's a sturdy woman, a woman who's had a lot of tragedy and loss in her life. Most recently, her husband Cal went hunting and never came back. It was months before they found his body. She shared with me that she would rather he had run off with another woman—which she did not believe he did—than have something happen to him in the woods. When they found his mangled and half-eaten body, it was clear he'd broken his right leg which made it impossible for him to get back home to her. Celeste believed he slipped and fell. She told me there was something going on with his balance.

When she invited me to lunch on a Saturday, my day off, we talked about Cal's accident and death. She didn't cry, but she told me she missed him. She told me she was going to a grief group once a week in Cape Vincent led by SueBeth Kingsley. I wasn't surprised she told me this, but I was surprised she was doing it.

I knew SueBeth, and liked her. She went away to college but came back and settled in Cape Vincent down the street from her parents who were still living in her childhood home. She bought a house and brought a husband home with her who was not from the area. Jeff was a likeable guy. The Warden recently hired him to work at the prison. It was part of my father's new policy to hire men from out of town. He did not want the prison guards to fraternize outside of work anymore. When the prison first opened, most of the men who worked there grew up in Cape Vincent, went to school with each other from kindergarten through high school, graduated, and drank together at Bandy's. The Warden wanted to change this. He banned the use of personal names as an attempt to even the playing field, reducing each person to the job they did. This did not really work because everyone had a history of multiple connections. His next step was to hire outsiders who did not want to live in Cape Vincent. The result of his new hiring practices was that the prison culture was changing.

I told Celeste, *Years after my mom left, SueBeth came up on me when I was running around the high school track. She told me she was sorry I lost my mom. I didn't want to talk about my mom leaving, so I picked up the pace. She picked up hers, too, and we ran side by side. We increased our pace for a mile until I couldn't do it any longer and we both stopped to catch our breath. I was exhausted. She thanked me for a great workout, and off she ran. The thing that got me was when she said my mom must have been in a lot of pain to leave me.*

Celeste said, *It seems like SueBeth came to her profession honestly.* I agreed.

Then Celeste asked me, *So, what's up with your new look?*

I laughed and said, *I don't know. I just stopped shaving one day. I wanted to see how I looked with a beard.*

She laughed and had that twinkle in her eye. *Perhaps it's a woman.*

I told her, *No. I don't have a woman in my life right now.* Then I started talking about Eliza, the woman prisoner. *The Warden put her in solitary from the very beginning, which was strange. It doesn't usually work that way. Eliza talked a lot at first. She was pissed off. She's a fighter. I started bringing her books and announced at a staff meeting that I was doing that. The Warden looked at me because it's not something we normally do for people in solitary, but my father approved it. Well, not exactly approved it, but he didn't disapprove.* I did not tell Celeste that I gave her pen and paper, too, which was against the rules. My father would have taken a hard line on that. There would be the *blah, blah, blah* about safety, but it wasn't really about safety. It was about repression and control.

I told Celeste about a recent conversation I had with Eliza that bothered me. *Eliza told me it seemed strange that I talked about my father as The Warden. I told her it was a prison rule. She challenged me. Said it seemed distant. I agreed with her that it was odd, and she said it was more than odd. Then she asked me if I liked my father. The silence after her question was the kind you could cut with a knife. I sat there completely motionless, not one twitch. I'd never been like that with her before. I saw her observing me. I didn't want her to see my struggle. We sat there for thirty minutes in silence with her question*

hanging in the air. Finally, I told her I didn't like my father.
Then I got up and did my shift documentation. It's the one
and only time I didn't say good-bye to her. I just left. I felt
bad about that.

Celeste said, *My, my, my. This is quite a complicated*
relationship you're having.

That stopped me dead in my tracks. I wanted to say,
I'm not having a relationship, but I didn't. I tried to
remember what got me started. Oh, Celeste commenting
on my new look. She asked the same question as my
father, but my response to her was like a son who wanted
to talk things out with his mom.

As I lie awake in the motel in Toronto, I'm happy I
didn't take Eliza to her death today. I walked the familiar
caves with her, climbed the metal steps, cut the chain that
someone put there long before I discovered it, and got
through the first international border. I wanted to walk
these caves to Vermont like I did when I was a boy, but
there was no way she could do that. It required stamina,
and it was enough to ask her to walk for an hour and climb
the steep ladder, drive four hours to the border, and then
an hour to the hotel. Human beings can only be pushed so
far. It was enough that she's been deprived of fresh air and
sunlight for three years and nine months.

I must have fallen back to sleep because I wake up
when I hear Eliza walk in and quietly get into bed. It's 3:13
a.m. The alarm goes off seventeen minutes later and both
of us get up.

"Places to go and people to meet," I say.

She laughs as she puts on her black hat and picks up
her yellow duffel. I pick up my black bag and we race each
other down the steps. She wins.

We get in the shuttle and then we're in the airport security line. As a married couple we go up together. It goes easy and we are through security with time to spare. We get some coffee and sit quietly in the terminal until we board. I hear Wendy breathe a big sigh when the cabin doors close at 6:43 a.m. I am relieved, too.

18 May 1989
Thursday
Cape Vincent, New York
06:43

T H E
WARDEN

Brenda says, "You certainly earned your keep last night, Sam. Coffee?"

She buzzes me and I open my door. "Well?" I ask Sam.

"Nobody there, Warden. Staff office and cells are locked up tight."

What a fucking nightmare.

"No note?"

"Not that I saw. Her bed is made, and her books are arranged in alphabetical order. In the office three coffee mugs are lined up next to the coffee pot. There's a dictionary on the desk. Nothing on the bulletin board except colored thumbtacks made into a smiley face. I recoded the keypad."

Sam hands me the number. I slam the door. *Fuck.*

Minutes later I bark at Brenda, "Get the governor on

the phone."

The governor tells me what I already know. "It's officially a crime scene, Arthur. When any inmate escapes it's a big deal, and she was on death row. No one will be allowed to go in until law enforcement does their investigation. We've got to be prepared. It's your town, your prison, Arthur. Call the local police and sheriff. Put out a press release. My people will release a statement, too. Once that's done, wait for the wagons to circle. This'll go nationwide quickly. I'll come up tonight and we'll have dinner at Betsy's and come up with a plan about how to proceed."

I want to slam down the phone, but I don't.

It's exactly like the governor predicted. The press swarm outside the prison. I brief my staff and call the editor of Cape Vincent's local paper. I tell him Brian and The Prisoner are gone. He'll send a reporter to interview me later this afternoon. Brenda fields the calls, arranges dinner at Betsy's, and handles the flood of law enforcement officials. I announce over the intercom that the lockdown will continue. The inmates already know The Executioner and The Prisoner are missing.

In the afternoon I get the call from the FBI.

"Good afternoon, Warden. I'm Special Agent Robert McCauley. I'm leading the investigation of Brian Stafford and Elizabeth Jacobs in conjunction with Chief Bruce and his team. I'll be there tomorrow morning to set up interviews with you and your staff. A local police officer is on his way now and will be stationed outside Cell Block Z. I've been informed that local deputies left Brian a note yesterday and drove by his house every hour. An officer will be stationed there until we go inside. We want to maintain the integrity of a possible crime scene."

My body stiffens. I don't want the goddamn Feds involved.

18 May 1989
Thursday
On airplane to Frankfurt, Germany
22:00

WENDELL

We sleep, eat, and watch movies during our nine-hour flight to Frankfurt. When the stewardess wakes us up an hour before we land, she offers us coffee, a German pastry called Milchbroetchen, and apricot jam. We walk to the hotel where I have reservations and check us in. The clerk hands me an envelope that I casually put in my inner jacket pocket, and she tells me that two boxes have been put in our room.

When we get to our room, Wendy asks, "What's in the envelope?"

I open it and hand her a different passport. She stares at me.

"So, I'm no longer Wendy Falls? Now I'm Alice MacFarland. Born six March 1951 in Minneapolis, Minnesota. I'm a Pisces. I've been a Virgo my whole life. And you're not Wendell?"

"No. I'm Mason MacFarland. My birthday is thirty

August 1949. I'm a Virgo now. I used to be a Pisces."

I wonder if Billy did this purposefully, found dead children who had the astrological signs of Pisces and Virgo. It's not beyond the realm of possibility.

"Well, Mason. I guess you're going to find out about being a Virgo. I can give you some hints, you know, my experience, strength, and hope."

"Okay, Alice. I look forward to that."

"Did you know?" she asks.

"Yes. Not the names, but that we would have another name change in Frankfurt."

"Is this the last name change?" she asks wearily, testily.

"I believe so."

"Who did them?"

"A person who specializes in finding people new names and identities."

"Who?"

"Billy Williams."

"Billy Williams? I know him."

"Yes. We all know each other."

"Why's he helping us? He's FBI."

"He works for them, but he still has his private business changing people's identities."

"But I was a death-row inmate. Why would he take the risk?"

"He knows you're innocent."

Those four words sit there like a ticking bomb about to go off. She is shaking as she turns and heads to the bathroom. She slams the door. I hear the lock click and the sound of running water.

I can only imagine how out of control she feels. Hell, I

feel out of my comfort zone, too, but I know the plan. I told her the plan in stages because I didn't want to overwhelm her. Perhaps I made the wrong decision.

When she comes out of the bathroom, I'm sitting at the table. "I ordered room service."

She ignores me. "I don't like getting things piecemeal, TE. I can deal with things changing, but I want the big picture."

"Okay. We're here tonight. Tomorrow morning, we take the train to Salzburg. It's approximately a six-hour train ride. When we cross into Austria, we'll use our new passports. We're staying two nights in Salzburg, then we fly to New Zealand, our new home."

"That's it?"

"That's it. We'll choose where we live in New Zealand—North Island, South Island, city, rural." I emphasize the *we*.

"So, you're staying there, too?"

"Yes. I'm staying there. We're in this together."

"Good to know," she says sarcastically.

"You didn't know that?"

"No, TE. I don't assume anything. I obviously knew you were going with me, but you never said, *I'm changing my whole fucking life, too.* Why would you do that? Why would anyone do that?"

"Well, I haven't liked my life all that much," I say quietly.

"What does that mean?"

"I never wanted to be The Executioner."

She stares at me like she's daring me, begging me to say more. But really, do I want to have this conversation right now? I don't think so.

"So that's it? One line."

"How many lines do you want, Alice?" I ask wearily.

"How many do you want to give me, Mason?"

I look at her and am reminded of my parents and their fights about me and the executions and my mother leaving.

"Bottom line: I couldn't stand up to my father. I couldn't walk away."

"Why not?"

"My mother left when I was ten. Walking away isn't my strong suit."

"Thank you for telling me. At some point I would like to hear more, if you want to tell me more, but this feels like enough for now."

"I agree."

We eat our meal in silence. It's a good silence, the air has been cleared.

18 May 1989
Thursday
Frankfurt, Germany
23:00

ALICE

After our quiet dinner, I excuse myself and take a shower. My fury that was zinging around the room and inside of me like electricity and hot wires, sizzle-sizzle, has calmed.

"What's in the boxes?"

"Let's open them and see," TE says excitedly.

He passes me the scissors and I slit open my box. On the very top, there's a sheet of paper with tally marks on it and the number 267 circled. I laugh. "Is this how many pens I used?"

"Yup, I kept track. I figured you might want to know. I would have wanted to know."

When I pick up the white cotton cloth, I look at him with wide-eyes. "TE, my writing." It's not a question. Tears roll down my cheeks and I can feel the smile on my face. "Thank you. Thank you so much. And yours?"

I pass him the scissors and he rips open his box. He holds up a drawing.

"It's the drawings and writings of all the prisoners I've executed. I kept files on each man, each death. I couldn't leave them. I also brought the cards and letters my mom wrote me after my father pushed her out the door."

I am touched by TE's care and holding of people's history. Fifteen years of deaths. I don't know how he can hold all that pain, grief, and loss. I held my pain, grief, and loss for the past three years by living one day at a time, remaining curious and accepting my fate.

I look at the label. "You shipped the boxes from Boston?"

"Yeah. I couldn't ship them from Cape Vincent or any of the surrounding towns. I had to be careful. Actually, Terran shipped them."

"Who's Terran?"

"My best friend. He's like a brother to me. We used to be three, but Derrick died when we were sophomores in high school. Now we're two." He sighs a long sigh. "I have to go out and buy two large suitcases so we can take all of this on the train tomorrow. There's a luggage store close by. We passed it on our way to the hotel."

"I saw it. So many different colors of luggage. Beautiful."

I stand up and walk over to him. I take his hands and lightly squeeze them. He squeezes mine back. I put my right hand on his face. He closes his eyes briefly. Then he's gone.

It doesn't take him long to get the bags. I am sitting quietly in a chair when he gets back.

He got a green suitcase for me and a black one for him.

"What time do we need to leave tomorrow?"

"Our train leaves at ten. I'm thinking, up at seven, eat

breakfast here at the hotel, and then walk to the terminal. It's a ten-minute walk."

"Sounds good, TE. Do you have a preference about which bed you want?"

"No. You?"

"Yes. I'd like the one by the window."

"You got it. And Alice, I need to destroy Wendy's passport tonight."

"How are you going to do that?"

"I'm going to cut up the pages and flush them down the toilet. I'll burn the covers in the sink."

I am showered and packed when TE awakes startled to the sound of the alarm clock. I'm wearing my new purple earrings.

"Good morning, sleepyhead."

"Good morning, Alice."

"How'd the passport burning go last night?"

"Good. I'm Mason MacFarland now. I like my new name. Billy did good."

"I like my new name too. Alice suits me. It has the same five letters and begins and ends with a vowel, just like Eliza, except Eliza has a Z and Alice, a C. TE, I'm wondering if you're up for getting breakfast in the terminal instead of here at the hotel? I want to be doing normal things, like drinking coffee and people watching, even though I don't feel normal."

"Let's do it."

We check out and find a small café near the train station. I sit, watch people, and write. I'm out in the world now. I like watching the women in particular, how they're dressed, their fashion and the colors of their clothes. I cannot understand the German words, which is a relief.

There is no expectation that I have a conversation. You might think that after so little contact I would want to connect, yet there's a part of me that misses the snail-slow, mouse-quiet life. In prison I only had to take care of myself, make it through each day, one day at a time. I got into a rhythm.

They say the vow of silence is about awakening. For me this is true—I awakened to myself and saw myself clearly. I still see myself clearly, but now the playing field is larger. I can see how things could get cloudy fairly quickly. There is much to draw me away from my center. People have conversations that are filled with chatter and words. I see a lot of people wearing headphones, listening to music or a book. I wonder if this is the way people block out the busyness and the noise of the world. I love to sink into a book, too, yet right now I want to take in all these sights and sounds.

"Is there anything in *The New York Times* about us?"

"Nothing," he says.

We board the train to Salzburg as Alice and Mason MacFarland. Wendy and Wendell Falls are gone. Another short-lived life. I think about their ashes going down the drain and of dead people I have loved.

19 May 1989
Friday
Cape Vincent, New York
08:00

BRENDA

The FBI Investigator, Robert McCauley, arrives at the prison at eight in the morning. After he talks to The Warden, I am instructed to go into the private interview room.

"Do you want a fresh cup of coffee, Mr. McCauley?"

"Yes. Thanks, Brenda. I'm told you're the check-in person on execution days."

"Yes."

"How did check-in go on Wednesday?"

"Fine. Terran dropped off The Executioner like he always does."

"And who is Terran?"

"A good friend of The Executioner. They've known each other their whole lives."

"You know him, too?"

"Yes. We all went to school together. I've lived here my whole life."

"Terran's a friend of yours?"

"I don't see him that much anymore, but yes, he's a friend."

"Are you nervous, Brenda?"

I look at him. "I am. You're the FBI."

"I'm here to gather information about Brian and the prison. I hope to get information from you that might help us figure out what happened and ultimately to find out where Brian and Eliza are. Do you have any questions you'd like to ask me before we proceed?"

"No. I'm good."

"So, once again, did you notice anything unusual at check-in?"

"No. There was nothing unusual. Terran dropped him off and I watched The Executioner go into the cave to Cell Block Z." I do not mention that he hugged me and Terran, or that I'm in protection mode. I know how to play dumb, which I'm not, but The Investigator doesn't know me and no one else is in the room. I'm glad The Warden isn't here because he would see right through me, and I don't want to be seen right through. I'm pleasant, although The Investigator's right, I'm nervous. I know he's priming me for something, but I don't know what. Finally, the question comes.

"What's your relationship with Brian like?"

"We're friends, been friends for a long time. I don't call The Executioner 'Brian' here at work. No one calls him by his name anymore, at least not here at the prison. He's always called The Executioner."

"Why's that?"

"The Warden's policy."

Robert McCauley looks at me.

"Kind of like how everyone's calling you The Investigator."

"Okay. So people here don't use personal names? People don't call you Brenda?"

"No. Only The Warden calls me Brenda. There's The Warden, The Executioner, and I'm The Secretary. There's the prison guards, PG One, Two, and Three through Eleven. There's The Cook and The Nurse. We're a small prison. The inmates don't know our names and we don't tell them even if they ask."

"Do you know all the employees' names?"

"Yes. I do the checks, but the rule is to not call anyone by their personal name at the prison, ever."

"How long has that been in effect?"

"Around five years, I think. I could look it up for you. I have the memo."

"Why did The Warden institute this policy?"

"I don't know."

"You don't know? Or you don't want to say?"

"I have my thoughts about it, sir, but The Warden never gave a reason."

"How long have you worked here, Brenda?"

"Seventeen years. I got hired after Louise retired. She'd been here twenty years. She was hired when the prison opened. I came back to Cape Vincent after secretarial school and got this job."

"How long has Brian Stafford been working here?"

"Fifteen years. He came back after college and The Warden immediately hired him to be The Executioner."

"Do you like your job, Brenda?"

I hesitate. "It's fine. It pays well."

"Is there a but?"

If I was going to be honest, I would tell him that now that Brian's gone, there's really no reason for me to stay. I get overtime, double time, which I'm grateful for. I live alone in the house I grew up in. My parents are both dead, and I have no siblings. My parents left me everything, a house completely paid off and a bundle of money, money that only the local bank officers and Brian know about. The townsfolk don't know I'm a wealthy woman. Brian knows because I told him, but that didn't change anything, and I didn't expect it to. I wanted someone to know, because more and more I am disconnected from people. I find connection difficult, nearly impossible. I make small talk at Perry's with Beth who has a husband and four kids. All my high school friends are married with shitloads of kids. At some point I stopped going to the parties, the gatherings. I felt too alone. The children are easier for me to be with than the adults, but I cut myself off from them, too, because I can't bear not having a husband, children, and parents. It's all too much of not having. I have money. I have a job. I had The Executioner, but during the past year he drifted away. I now wonder if that's connected to Elizabeth Jacobs. I never thought of that, but now both The Executioner and The Prisoner are gone. I believe they're together. Did The Executioner plan in advance to leave with her?

The Investigator interrupts my thought process.

"Brenda. I seem to have lost you. We were talking about whether you liked your job and you drifted off."

"It's fine as far as jobs go. I feel stressed now, so it's hard to stay focused."

"Is your stress connected to Brian's disappearance?"

"His disappearance? He left with The Prisoner. I have

no idea where they went, but he helped her escape and I imagine they're together."

"Did he talk about The Prisoner with you?"

"Only that she wasn't guilty and he could not be complicit in her execution."

"He used those exact words?"

"Yes. He used those exact words and not just with me, with The Warden, and with all the PGs in more than one staff meeting."

"When did he last talk at a staff meeting about not being able to be complicit in her execution?"

"I'd say about nine months ago. I've got the minutes. I can get them for you."

"Yes. I'd like all the staff meeting minutes since Elizabeth Jacobs got here."

"I'll make copies for you, sir."

The Investigator says, "I appreciate that. We're done for now. I may have follow-up questions in a few days, Brenda. If you think of anything that seemed unusual let me know."

He slides one of his cards toward me and I pick it up.

"Will you call Josh Candry for me, please?"

"PG One," I say.

"Yes. PG One."

"I'll have the minutes ready for you when you finish your interview with PG One."

"I'd rather get them now before I see Mr. Candry."

As I make copies of the staff meeting notes I think about how no one knows about my relationship with Brian. We agreed to tell no one, and I trust we both kept our commitment. Still, Robert McCauley's a federal agent, and I don't like lying. But really, what difference does it make? I can't kid myself about that. I know the difference it would make. I'd be more likely to protect The Executioner, my old friend and one-night lover. I don't think my disappointment shows, but I also know this FBI guy is trained in nuance. I want to talk to Terran. I want to get our stories straight, alike. But I don't want the phone records to show that I contacted him after my first interview. Terran begrudgingly said he would call me. If he doesn't, I will just have to wait until we run into each other, which is unlikely, although at Bandy's or Perry's we could easily meet by chance. I don't know Terran's patterns anymore. High school was a long time ago.

"These are all the staff meeting notes since Eliza Jacobs arrived, sir."

"Thank you, Brenda."

19 May 1989
Friday
Cape Vincent, New York
09:30

ROBERT
MCCAULEY

I interview Josh Candry in Cell Block Z in the glass guard station for two reasons: I want to see him in his work environment, and I want privacy. I can tell he doesn't want to meet there, but he doesn't ask to meet somewhere else.

"How long have you been working down here?"

"Three years and nine months, sir."

"How long have you worked at the prison?"

"Seventeen years."

"Do you usually work with the death row inmates?"

"No. This is only my second time, sir. The first guy was here for two weeks. Then he was executed, so I went back to B Block. When Eliza Jacobs came, none of us thought she would go directly to Z."

"That was unusual?"

"Yeah. She was supposed to go to A Block, but she

never did."

"Do you know why she didn't go to A Block?"

"I heard she pissed off The Warden, so he sent her down here the day she arrived."

"Have you had other women in A Block before?"

"No. We never had a woman in this prison before. We specifically prepared the cell for her. The Warden told us we were getting a woman because the women's prison was full. But the strange thing was a friend of mine works at that prison, and she told me something was off because the women's prison was not full."

"What do you think about that?"

Josh is quiet for a bit and his left leg bounces up and down.

"Is this interview confidential, sir?"

"Yes. Only the FBI has access to the content of these interviews."

"It's not right, sir. Cell Block Z is supposed to be a place where prisoners stay for two to four weeks, tops, before they're executed. Eliza was there three years and nine months. It's a tomb. That's what we call it, The Tomb. It's like being buried alive. Nobody wants to work down here. Well, maybe The Executioner feels alright about it. I don't know. We only passed each other at shift change. We never talked much about The Prisoner or anything."

"When it was a male prisoner, did The Executioner talk about what happened during his shift?"

"Not much. With Eliza he made it seem like she never said anything. I found that hard to believe."

"That someone could be quiet?"

"Yeah. I mean early on she and I had a conversation about how the actual execution went."

"What did you tell her?"

"The truth. You get strapped down. Then you're hooked up to the drugs. They open the curtain and you can see the people in the viewing area. She asked me who could come. I told her there was a list that The Warden approved. She wondered if her parents could get on the list. I told her they could, but I didn't know if The Warden would approve them. She asked me why he might not approve them. I told her he was quirky, that it was hard to know what he would do. She smiled at me and said, 'Quirky. I like that word. Don't know that I would describe him like that.' She used the words *unpredictable, controlling, and power-hungry.* I agreed with her but I didn't say anything."

"Why not?"

"Not protocol to talk about The Warden with an inmate."

"And you always follow protocol?"

Josh is silent.

"I usually follow protocol, sir, but not always. After four weeks of being down here I was having a hard time breathing. I'd go out into the cave many times during my shift to try and catch my breath, but it wasn't really helping. I didn't want to come to work. My wife got me a little tape deck so I could listen to music. I'm not supposed to have it, but the music helped me."

"You felt panicky?"

"I don't know about that. I found it hard to breathe, so I went outside Z into the cave. On my two twenty-minute breaks I'd go up the steps and stand outside and be in the fresh air."

"Did you have other conversations with The Prisoner?"

"Yes. We talked about my kids. Eliza was the counselor at their school. Shell was upset when Paula Langdon got taken out of the school by paramedics because she had some kind of a breakdown the day before Lydia Garth disappeared. Soon after that Eliza got arrested for Lydia's murder. Shell was scared. My kids knew Eliza and liked her, said all the kids liked talking to her. For my son, AJ, to say she was cool goes a long way with me because he reads people good. I trust his judgment. My wife and I liked her, too. She delivered Shell. She was our midwife."

"Was Elizabeth concerned about Shell?"

"Yes and she was happy to hear about how both my kids were doing. She stopped talking soon after our conversation about how the execution went."

"Did you think she was bothered about what you told her?"

"I do. It would be a hard thing to hear, but she thanked me for telling her the details."

"So it seemed to calm her down to know what would happen?"

"Yes, but she stopped talking soon after that conversation. I asked her every time I collected her dinner plate if there was anything I could get for her. She always looked me right in the eyes, smiled, and shook her head. PG Two told me she took a vow of silence. When I asked him what that was, he said it was some kind of spiritual thing. I went home and talked to my wife about it and ended up at the library. I also talked to my minister."

"So you wanted to understand what Elizabeth was doing?"

"Yeah. I wanted to understand the point of it. It seemed a little out there."

"A little?"

"Well, I couldn't imagine it. I'm a guy who likes to bullshit with my friends. It was hard enough for me to be down there five days a week. I didn't like it. She seemed pretty peaceful, though."

"You watched her?"

"Sometimes. I watched her read. She read a lot of heavy stuff, Thoreau, Emerson, Nietzsche, Rumi, Sartre. And she sat on her bed for hours with her eyes closed. She didn't move a muscle. She was completely still for hours. I can't imagine what she thought about all that time. Me, I did pull-ups and push-ups and walked around. I was restless down there."

"Did you and Kevin talk about The Prisoner?"

"PG Two? Yeah. But he told me he never said a word to her the whole time, that she was asleep when he got there and asleep when he left. We used to joke around that they were sleeping together, him in the office and her in her cell."

"Did Brian ever talk about her?"

"No. Not to me. PG Two told me The Executioner told him she'd taken a vow of silence."

"You were bothered by what was happening to The Prisoner?"

"My wife got on my case, said it was wrong that Eliza was underground with no light and fresh air. I knew she was right. My wife wanted me to say something to The Warden, but I couldn't do that. I didn't want any problems, and I knew The Warden would not take kindly to me saying anything."

"Do you know what she was charged with?"

"Murder."

"Do you know any of the details?"

"I read about the murder in the paper. There was almost nothing about Eliza in the paper. Her lawyer only came once. That was weird, too. The scuttlebutt was she wasn't guilty."

"Do you think she was guilty of killing Lydia Garth?"

"I found it hard to believe. She was an advocate for children."

"What do you think happened to The Executioner and The Prisoner?"

"He helped her escape. He didn't think she was guilty. Everybody knew how he felt. He was the only one who stood up to The Warden in staff meetings. He was the one who got her books. The Warden never let anyone have books in Z."

"How do you think they escaped?"

"Through the caves, sir."

"The caves?"

"Yeah. There's a massive cave system here. It goes all the way to Vermont. Brian was really into the caves. During high school he walked them by himself all the way to Lake Champlain. The local paper wrote a big story about him. He and my daughter, Shell, did that very same hike. Eliza and Shell went caving together a couple of times, too. Shell loves the caves. She's got a big map of the caves on her bedroom wall. Personally, I don't like them. I don't like her going down there by herself, but I know she goes anyway. She tells me it's safer than hiking in the woods, says she never sees anybody down there. To each his own, I guess. She could be drinking and having sex and she's not doing either one of those. She's a straight A student. Got her sights set on a four-year university."

"Did Brian and Elizabeth know each other before she came to prison?"

"I don't think so. The Prisoner wasn't a Cape Vincent girl. I think she grew up in Alexandria Bay, but I don't know that for sure."

I thank Josh and tell him I might need to talk to him again and that I might want to talk to his daughter.

"Her mother will want to be with her if you do. She's only fifteen."

19 May 1989
Friday
Frankfurt, Germany
10:00

ALICE

Fifteen minutes after we board the train it leaves the station. We're off to Salzburg. I'm excited and relieved. I've never been to Austria before. I pull my thick grey cotton sweater around me. TE picked this grey sweater and the red-and-white starred blouse. What a contrast of color. I hear the steady clicking of the wheels. I look out the window at the beautiful countryside.

Last night TE told me he was not going back to the United States. I don't know what that means about us. I loved our ceremony in the car. I've never been married before. I remind myself that I'm not really married now, but some part of me feels married. I like this diamond ring on my finger and that TE wears the silver band on his hand. We could take them off, but we haven't. Well, we're still travelling.

We haven't reached our destination and we won't for a while. New Zealand. I asked TE, *Why New Zealand?* He told me, *Extradition to the United States is limited and they speak English.* So extradition and English, two E words. I can build a life there. I could practice midwifery. I am going to write. I won't use Alice MacFarland as my pen name. I need to cover my tracks. I don't want to be found. I don't ever want to have to deal with the possibility of being incarcerated again, locked up against my will, waiting to be executed for a crime I did not commit. I thought that shit only happened in third-world countries or in big cities, not in small town America, land of the free, home of the brave. What a fucking farce.

For years I maneuvered around and through the establishment's limits and rules. When I saw children who were being abused I called and wrote a report to Children's Protective Services. I did steps one, two, and three through fifty. I was supposed to be done, but often I wasn't done because the system added another set of requirements. Months later I'd get a piece of paper in the mail saying the case was closed. Many times the same children were still being abused. They were coming to school with bruises and fear. Writing a report did not make the children safe. I grew weary. I began to cut out steps in the process. I began to circumvent the rules. I came up against barriers where I found alternative ways to help these children. I attended seminars to learn about the law, and by extension I learned ways around it. I called Billy Williams, the FBI identity changer I met at a criminal justice conference. We talked about each child and their situations. He found them new names and homes. They were good to go. Simple. One, two, three. Not forty-nine, fifty, and then twenty-five more hoops to jump through. I got done. I subverted the system I worked in, until the system swallowed me up. I would have died if TE hadn't rescued me.

The train wheels go round and round and it lulls me back into the clinks and clangs in the prison, the loud flushing sound of my toilet, the buzzing of the door when the guards changed shifts, and the beeping when the guards came in and out of the glass guard station. They kept me on a schedule. I never asked why. I had no reason to ask. What was the point? Why would it matter? I was facing death. My life was going to be taken before I was ready, before God would naturally take me. Perhaps a person's process is different when it is not a natural death. I don't know. What I do know is, I lost my curiosity, my desire to know certain things, my willingness to engage in conversation. Once I found out I was going to be executed I read about vows of silence. Was this my protest? Was this my opportunity to go inward and develop a relationship with myself in a way that I had never deemed possible before? Is this the monastic life of some nuns and monks, to be silent, to make a commitment to silence? Did I ever feel passionate about silence before I knew I was going to be executed?

I did have an interest in, and a desire for, silence. I went on two ten-day silent meditation retreats. We meditated ten hours each day. The second retreat was physically easier. In both, I got bored on day six. I wanted something to read or paper and pen to write, yet what they allowed was the figure-eight walking path. After a silent lunch I took a forty-five-minute determined walk. I needed to vigorously move my body and sweat. My energy was focused and purposeful. I was committed. I developed a routine. The path was my track. Surprisingly I did not count the laps, just like I did not count the pens I used in prison, and for some reason I wish I had, although it doesn't matter because TE counted them for me. I am grateful. I did count the days I'd been at the silent retreat and was acutely aware of how many days I had left. I did appreciate when we broke the silence on Saturday because booksellers were there and I could borrow books. I went to my room and read. I drank in words. I was not interested in the words of the other participants. I did not want to engage in conversations. I did not like hearing snippets of conversations that felt like a din of noise. I yearned for the silence.

Will Alice be different from Eliza? I am already different. I do not live in the United States anymore. I doubt I ever will. I don't care about that, but I am sad that I may not see my parents and my brother and sister again. TE told me The Warden approved them to come to my execution, so I knew I would see them. TE smuggled letters in and out for me, so I did have ongoing communication with my parents. I am grateful for this.

I want to believe Billy Williams will contact my parents. He and I have the same ethics about how to help children—remove them from the abusive situation and place them in a safe home, a sanctuary. In prison I thought a lot about what sanctuary meant to me. Writing. Reading. Meditation. Yoga. Silence. I enveloped myself in these five practices. They gave me comfort. I had a place to hang my hat. I did not have to please anyone. I did not have to spiritually or emotionally feed anyone. I wrote stories where my characters fed me and I fed them. We had a mutual relationship. I helped them come to life and in that process, I became more alive.

I got unsettled yesterday. TE and I are now Alice and Mason MacFarland. He tells me these are our permanent names. Maybe that's true. I don't know. I want to settle. Yet I am not settled, not yet. TE got rid of Wendy and Wendell Falls. They are gone. In a way I feel bad because these dead children helped us get across two borders. They served a purpose and now they're dead, again. I feel like I used them and then betrayed them. I wonder if Billy feels like this. I know he honors dead children by giving their names to someone else, so having them die again so quickly seems harsh. If I see him, I want to have a conversation about that. But first, when the time is right, I'll ask TE if he wants to talk about any of this. I hope he does.

19 May 1989
Friday
Cape Vincent, New York
13:30

ROBERT
MCCAULEY

I let The Warden know I'm going to lunch at Betsy's and that we're going into Brian's house today. I ask him if he has a key, and he tells me he doesn't. After lunch, my team and I meet Chief Bruce and some of his police officers at Brian's house. The chief introduces me to Charlie Barrett, Don Nichols, and Serge Valentino.

Chief Bruce says, "Detective Valentino arrested Eliza Jacobs and found evidence in her house that made her a suspect in Lydia Garth's disappearance and subsequent death. He was instrumental in getting her convicted."

I look at Detective Valentino and he looks at me. We size each other up.

"Who's the woman on the porch?" I ask.

"Celeste Gordon, sir," Charlie says.

The chief asks Don, "Will you let Celeste know what

we're doing here?" He turns to Charlie. "Still no key?"

"No key, sir."

"Don, while you're at it, ask Celeste if she has a key. It's going to be a real bitch to get in the house without one. Brian built a fortress."

"Why would Celeste have a key?" I ask.

"They're close, like mother and son."

I don't ask any questions.

The chief asks, "Has Terran called back about the key?"

"No, sir."

"Speak of the devil," says Serge.

I turn and see a man getting out of a classic blue and white '57 Chevy.

"Got your call, Chief. Wanted to be here when you went in. I've got a key. Has somebody let Celeste know what's going on? She's worried sick."

"Don's talking to her right now. Terran, this is Agent Robert McCauley. He's helping us with the investigation."

"Hi, Robert. Good to meet you. Heard the Feds had been called in."

I'm sure you did. "Good to meet you, Terran."

We shake hands. I can tell a lot about a man by his handshake and if he looks me in the eye. Terran looks me right in the eye. I think I see a flicker of amusement.

I go into the house with Chief Bruce and Detective Valentino. Terran sits on the porch bullshitting with Charlie. The house is spotless and organized. We find the safe and the file cabinets in the basement. The only thing in the safe is an envelope for Terran. It's the deed to the house. The file cabinets are full of papers. I ask my men to put them into a box so we can go through them. I hold onto the deed.

"Why would Brian leave the deed to Terran?" I ask the chief.

"Friends all the way through school. The three of them were tight: Brian, Terran, and Derrick, Celeste's son. Derrick died in a snowmobile accident in high school. Since then, the two of them have been inseparable."

"Looks like I need to set up interviews with Terran and Celeste." I don't say I need to look at all the evidence from the arrest of Eliza Jacobs. I want to get Detective Valentino's file and interview him. I'll talk to the police chief about this privately.

19 May 1989
Friday
Salzburg, Austria
16:00

ALICE

Our train arrives in Salzburg around four o'clock. When I get off the train I feel the cool, clean mountain air. The Alps tower over the city. Altstadt, Old Town, is picturesque with its Baroque architecture and backdrop of mountains. I feel like I've entered a magical world, the world of the Von Trapp Family in *The Sound of Music*. We walk on the Getreidegasse, the main street of Old Town Salzburg, until we come to our hotel. From our window we have a view of the Salzach River. We decide to explore Old Town and TE suggests we go to the hat shop that we walked by on our way to the hotel.

Before we go, I say, "I'm uncomfortable with you paying for everything, TE. I think we need to talk about money."

"Alice, let's talk about money when we get to New Zealand. I have enough money for both of us. I want us to enjoy being here together. Let's think of it as a vacation, a respite. Can you let me give that to you?"

I look away and quietly say, "Thank you."

When I put on the purple hat I feel like a million bucks. I can't remember the last time I felt lighthearted. Being locked up in solitary confinement, I forgot what lighthearted felt like, not that I was a woman who felt lighthearted very often. I tend to take things seriously and ask questions about the deeper meaning and how something fits into the greater picture. I want to understand the universe and I wonder again, who and why did someone want me gone? I can't think of anyone who didn't like me or at least tolerate me. I'm friendly. I'd say most people don't know me that well. I need space, maybe more than most people. Some people might say I'm distant, but distance and space are not the same thing. Distance implies something negative. I need space so my soul can sing.

19 May 1989
Friday
Salzburg, Austria
17:00

MASON

I watch her try on hats. She twirls and models them for
me. She picks the purple one. It suits her. She's beautiful.
I'm watching her come back to life. What a treat! She
literally went underground, and now she's resurfacing. I
went underground five days a week, but I emerged into
the light each day. I had that privilege. She did not.

Eliza sank into, dove deeply into the depths of her
being, like each death row inmate I worked with as he
made his way through time-space to the death chamber.
Initially I saw these death-row inmates weekly in the
general population. We chatted and I got to know them. In
the last two to four weeks of their lives when they were
transferred to Cell Block Z I helped them identify where
they got off track and what work they wanted to do. Some
did more work, some did less. Every man reckoned with
himself in his own way, and the reckoning helped him deal
with his fears and disappointments and afforded him the

ability to look his family and the victim's family in the eyes before I administered the drugs.

I had the privilege of sharing these last weeks with these men. I had the privilege of hearing their words, seeing their art, and holding their tears, outrage, and fear. I was not a priest or a minister. I could not give them that kind of absolution, but I allowed them to come to terms with themselves, to find and follow their final path. I was a listening ear, the one who accepted them for who they were, the one who heard their goodness and where their goodness went awry. Each man took stock of himself and each often wrote a letter to his family and the victim's family. I gave those letters to the families after the execution, to help them tie up loose ends.

Sometimes the dead prisoner's family wanted me to sit with them and read his letter out loud. The victim's family usually did not ask me to read them the letter. I don't know what the victims' families did with their letters. Only once in fifteen years did a victim's family contact me, a mother whose daughter was raped and murdered. She thanked me for the letter and told me it helped her have closure. Close the circle. Always close the circle. She told me she started a group in her community for families who lost a family member to some kind of violence. She asked me to come and speak to the group. I drove to Westchester, far away from the north of New York. I talked about the prison program and about loss, hope, forgiveness, and the hole in your heart that may never fully get filled. I spoke about energy and love and goodwill. I held people's tears and anger.

After Alice picks the purple hat we go to a shop where she gets a simple, elegant, black dress and a purple shawl that she can wear to dinner and a concert at Mozart's house tonight. I get a sports coat. We both get dress shoes and hiking boots for tomorrow's adventure to the ice caves. When we get to our hotel, we shower and get ready for our evening out. She puts on the purple earrings. We walk arm in arm to Mozart's house.

"For the first time in a long time I feel normal," Alice says.

"I'm glad you're feeling more normal. I loved watching you try on hats and twirl around. The shopkeeper was kind of flirting with you as he brought you different hats to try. It was fun to see you playing around with him. On a more serious note, I'm sorry I couldn't get a room with two beds. I requested that, but they couldn't accommodate me. I don't want you to think—"

Alice puts her finger on my lips and traces my mouth. "I'm glad to be here with you, TE. You have gone to great lengths to make me, us, safe. The life that I had before has been gone for three years and nine months. Now I get this amazing opportunity to create a new life. I'm grateful. You have made this possible. I love walking and exploring Salzburg. It's heartwarming. There is only a little hustle and bustle. I love the pace. It feels right."

I hug her and say, "I tell my friends I'm not the hugging kind."

"You could have fooled me."

19 May 1989
Friday
Cape Vincent, New York
18:00

TERRAN

"Yoohoo," I call out from the back steps. I promised to call Brenda, but on a whim I dropped by like I used to do in high school. I always used the back door then. Old habits die hard.

Brenda says in a low voice, "Come in, Terran."

She's sitting at the kitchen table in one of the green chairs that her dad and I made when I was in high school. She doesn't look up or say anything. I take the seat I used to take when I came to visit her and her folks. I liked her mom and dad. They were good people. Her dad was a master furniture builder and teacher at the town trade school. He could build anything. He taught me how to build things. From the start I liked working with wood. I was able to focus, and focusing had never been easy for me. I compared myself to Brian and always came up short. Brian was the king of focus. I wanted to be more like him. Brian told me there was a downside to being focused, like being less flexible, getting stuck in a routine, not being able to see an alternate perspective. At the time I didn't see these as problems. I was tired of ripping and roaring.

Brenda breaks into my musings. "Do you want a cup of tea, Terran?

"Do you have whiskey?"

She looks at me, then turns and goes to the cabinet where her dad kept his Jack Daniel's.

"I love this table and chairs. I remember when your dad asked me if I wanted to help him make it. He was a great teacher. I owe my career to him."

"I got to pick the color," she says. "My mom was standing at the door smiling at me when my dad asked me what color I wanted him to paint them. I said, 'Daddy, I like that pine green color.' He said, 'Green it is, pumpkin.' The three of us went to the Ace and bought two gallons of paint. Then we walked to Betsy's Diner. It still had the old-fashioned red cushions on the barstools, and you could watch Betsy's mother make sundaes and cut those big thick slices of cherry pie."

"I'm a fan of the cherry pie. So, you wanted to talk, Brenda?"

"Yeah. I had my interview with Robert McCauley today."

"How was it?"

"Alright, I guess. I felt protective of Brian. Then I got pissed off that Brian took The Prisoner and walked away from his life. Why, Terran?"

I look at her. Do I tell her the whole truth and nothing but the truth, so help me God? I take the simple route. "He believed she was innocent."

She looks at me. "What aren't you saying, Terran?"

I sit there. I don't want to hurt her, but she's already hurt. Telling her the truth is what I need to do. "He loves her."

She stares at me, then pours some Jack into her teacup. "Is that why he started growing a beard nine months ago? Was that part of his plan?"

"Yes," I say quietly.

"He got more distant and secretive then, and we stopped having dinner once a week. He avoided me. I chalked it up to the fact that we had sex. Did you know we had sex, Terran?"

I shake my head and act surprised. She glares at me.

"After we had sex Brian put the kibosh on any hopes I had of having a relationship with him. I waited so long for him to come around, Terran. He's why I took the job at the prison in the first place. He was coming back to be The Executioner. I would see him five days a week, so it didn't matter that the job meant nothing to me. I've been betrayed, Terran. He picked The Prisoner over me."

Terran says, "Brenda, he's your friend."

"Friends don't have sex with each other."

"Sometimes they do, Brenda. Sometimes it works out and other times it doesn't."

"The first day she arrived at the prison I heard her stand up to The Warden, Terran. She defied him. When he moved toward her, she stood her ground. I thought he was going to hit her. I called Brian and told him we had a situation with the new female prisoner. He intervened and took her to Z. I read her paperwork that afternoon. Her case was controversial. They found a burnt body that Lydia Garth's father, Dr. Peter Garth, claimed was his daughter's, but there was no real evidence that Elizabeth

Jacobs had anything to do with that. Later, Detective Valentino discovered Lydia's locket in Elizabeth's house. They convicted her of murder even though she claimed the necklace was planted. They condemned her to death and sent her to our all-male prison."

"So you questioned whether she was guilty?"

"I did. Her file was small. The evidence was slim. In all the other death row convictions the charts are thick. When Brian returned to The Warden's office after his shift he and his father fought, Terran. He told his father, 'Her case is on appeal. She should not be in Z. It's way too early.' The Warden said, 'She isn't getting out, son. Her appeal will be denied.' Brian questioned him about how he could be so sure. Then Brian said, 'She's been set up.' It wasn't a question, Terran."

"Did The Warden say anything?"

"He said, 'Look at it however you want, son. She got convicted and condemned to death.' He never said, 'She's guilty,' Terran."

"What did Brian do?"

"He shut The Warden's door quietly and walked out of the office. He didn't say anything to me. I don't think he was aware I was there. Fury and determination were all over his face. Do I tell Robert McCauley any of this, Terran? Do I make myself vulnerable? Do I betray The Warden like Brian betrayed me? Where did he go, Terran?"

"I can't tell you, Brenda."

"Are they together?"

"They're travelling together. He wants to be with her. He doesn't know if she wants to be with him."

"He gave up his whole life in the hopes that she'll want

him?"

"That about sums it up," I say.

I think about the conversation I had with Brian a week before he left.

What if you come back? You'll want your house.

No, Terran. I'm letting it all go. I have to.

She means that much to you?

It's not just about her. It's about breaking free from my father. I'm done doing what he thinks I should do. I'm done being a child trying to please daddy. I can't please him. I've sold my soul, and still he isn't pleased. It's time to please myself. This whole situation with Eliza and the legal system failing her, it's not right. It's ugly. I can't stop thinking about how many people get set up.

So it's about escaping from an unjust system?

Brian laughed. *There's a lot of unjust systems, bro. Bottom line, I'm in love with her. I don't know why or how. It's not logical. I felt it from the moment I saw her standing in my father's office, not moving a muscle, with a look on her face like she was daring him to hit her. I inserted myself between them. I got her out of there. That first nine months I listened to her talk nonstop. She was desperate to make sense of a situation that you couldn't make sense of, Terran.*

Brenda says, "Terran, I'm going to quit my job."

"Brenda!"

"I have to. I can't stand being there anymore. The only thing that made it tolerable was Brian and my hope that he and I would get together. That's not going to happen. I need to get on with my life, whatever that means. I can't go on like this."

I breathe deeply. "What are you thinking about doing,

Bren?"

"I don't know. I'm going to give my two-week notice tomorrow. I've got a lot of sick time. I'm taking tomorrow afternoon off. I've got an appointment with BethAnn Kingsley."

"BethAnn Kingsley? Wow, that's a flash from the past."

"As I recall, you liked her for a while."

"I did, but I wasn't her kind of guy. Brian was. She liked focus. Seems that a lot of the ladies like that in a man."

"Terran, you're a hell of a lot more focused than you let on."

I smile. "It's nice to be known, my lady."

We sit in quiet silence. She gets up and fills her cup with tea and I pour myself another shot of her dad's whiskey.

"Will you stay the night with me, Terran? I'm not talking about sex. I don't want to be alone tonight."

I'm hesitant, but I say I will.

She reaches out her hand and I take it. She puts her head on the table and cries.

As she cries my mind wanders to Brian, Derrick, and me. Derrick and I were the wild ones, but he was always pushing the edge, going over the edge, always wanting to see what just a little more was like. You killed yourself, bro. I watched you do it. I'll never forget the look on your face when you were sinking. I saw your surprise and watched you almost instantaneously move to acceptance. You turned and saluted Brian and me. There was nothing any of us could do. You shouted, 'Tell my mom and dad I love them.' Then you were gone, glued to the machine you loved. You didn't seem afraid. Perhaps you were glad your run in this life was over. You couldn't focus worth a damn in school, but in your wild and crazy escapades you were completely focused on going to the edge and beyond. It was who you were, and your mom and dad both knew this and accepted you. I don't think either of your parents were surprised when Brian told them what happened. It's like you'd been flirting with death your whole life, not that you had a death wish, but you did have a desire to go beyond the normal limits. If it meant your demise, your ultimate destruction, then you were game to take it on. You would have made a great firefighter, or a pilot in the military doing reconnaissance missions or dropping bombs. You needed something daring. You were always daring Mother Nature to take you. I'm like that myself, but not as much as you. You were full-on. I admired you.

Brenda has stopped crying. "I'm exhausted, Terran. I thought I was done with The Investigator, but at the end of my interview he told me he may have more questions. I need to go to bed. I'll straighten up in the morning."

"I'll put things in the sink and come up, Bren."

19 May 1989
Friday
Salzburg, Austria
18:30

ALICE

When we get to Mozart's House, we share a table with two Austrian couples who speak excellent English. They visited the Hohensalzburg Fortress's executioner's house today. The last official executioner lived there alone in the 1700s. People in the village avoided the executioner the day before an execution because they were afraid he might sleepwalk and kill them.

During this conversation, TE's facial muscles get tight and his shoulders move closer to his ears. I take his hand, and he gives me a startled look. The conversation moves on to capital punishment. Each of us express our opinion. TE talks about theoretically not believing in capital punishment, but wonders if there is justice in an eye for an eye—if you kill someone, then you get killed to balance the equation. All four Austrians express compassion for the aloneness of the executioner and how he gave up his life to be the one who tried to bring justice and rightness to the world.

TE seems to be trying to make peace with his fifteen years of being The Executioner. I make a decision during this conversation that I'm not going to call him TE anymore. I do not want to remind him of this time in his life. I want to support him in moving on. His name is Mason, a person who works with stone and builds things. He told me he likes his new name, that it was a strong name. I replied I also liked his new name, that it suited him.

Mason does not tell these four strangers that he has been an executioner, and our conversation ends when the concert begins. Almost immediately I am transported to another world by the music. The acoustics in Mozart's house are remarkable. At the end of the concert we say our good-byes to our tablemates and thank them for the wonderful conversation.

19 May 1989
Friday
Salzburg, Austria
22:00

MASON

Alice takes my arm as we quietly walk back to our hotel. Although the evening was good, I was disturbed by the conversation about the executioner's house and how he attached a noose around the prisoner's neck and pulled the lever so the body dropped and the prisoner's neck was broken. I dripped numbing drugs into a prisoner's bloodstream and watched his body relax as the drugs circulated throughout his body. I prayed I got the balance right. It was important to me that the prisoner did not suffer. I wanted his death to be painless. Can death be painless? I don't know. Perhaps if it is natural it can be, but being put to death is a whole different ball game. Most of the men I killed did not want to die, even though most of them believed they deserved to. Most of them embraced an eye-for-an-eye type of justice.

I want to shake off these thoughts and feelings, but I can't. Justice is such an arbitrary thing. Men and women make up rules, and then they break them. One rule for me, a different rule for you. People manipulate the rules to suit their own purposes.

I feel Alice squeezing my arm. I say, "I've got mixed feelings about going to the executioner's house tomorrow."

"We don't have to go."

"No. I want to go. You don't know this, but my house in Cape Vincent was just like the one here. It was literally The Executioner's House—I was The Executioner, and my house was on a five-acre parcel of land. All the houses on my road were situated on five acres. Spacious. Isolated. And beyond the isolation, people stayed away, knowing who lived there. Except for my two friends. Celeste had the five acres right next to me, and Terran and I built my house. It was a fortress. Why did I need a fortress? Protection? Was I trying to protect myself, or others? Was I guilty of something? Am I wanting absolution for my own sins? Can an executioner be good?"

"Mason, you have a lot on your mind. I'm glad you're talking to me about it."

"I'm finding it hard to believe that you're the one listening to me after spending all that time in solitary confinement."

She laughs. "Stranger things have been known to be true."

"Like what?"

"Like you risking your job to mail my letters to my parents and bringing in their letters to me for three years."

"Yeah, well, the biggest risk was that my father would find out and he would take me out of Cell Block Z. Then I would not have seen you five days a week. That wasn't likely, but it was possible. What was more likely was that you would bear the weight of my punishment—the guilty, manipulative woman, the object of my father's disdain and hatred. You must have reminded him of my mom. He believed and told people my mother abandoned him and me. But really, he kicked her out. When she filed for divorce, he raged. I didn't understand his fury, but I knew it had something to do with power, power that my father wielded over me and others. This power made my father feel good about himself. My father is a lonely, wounded, man, but he's a fighter. It's not my way, but I see how it worked for him."

"It's clearly not your way. I'm glad for that."

"Me, too. I doubt I will ever see him again, not that I saw him that much even when we both worked at the prison. By working in Z, I lived in the cave forty-plus hours a week. I liked it. Often at my lunch break or after work, I walked the caves and the passageways that I explored as a boy. I entered the silence, a place where I feel at home. I connected with myself. My jumbled thoughts came together. Actually, I did doubles whenever I could to save money. I created our escape plan in the underground passageways."

Alice takes my hand. She looks beautiful and sexy in her purple hat and black dress.

"I want to forget about The Executioner, but The Executioner is me. There is no forgetting."

"No. There is no forgetting. There is accepting and moving on."

I pull her into a hug, and we stand on the street. I hear our beating hearts.

20 May 1989
Saturday
Salzburg, Austria
06:30

ALICE

I wake up early. Mason is asleep. I sit on the balcony overlooking the Getreidegasse and the Salzach River. The fishermen chatter as the tour boat operators prepare for their day. I am bundled up; it's cold here this morning. I love the coolness. I love the river. I love watching the city wake up. There's a woman sweeping her stoop. She did it yesterday afternoon and now she's doing it again this morning. I see another woman hanging her colorful laundry. I'm happy to see the cornucopia of colors, like a kaleidoscope. The changes in the sky and the shadows as the light takes over from the dark are breathtaking. In prison I had color deprivation, and the plethora of hues now is overwhelming. A man pushes his wooden cart with milk. He stops and gives milk to a woman and her son. Another boy on his bike delivers bread. A cyclist straps his briefcase onto the back of his bike and waves to a dark, curly-haired woman who is in her pink bathrobe picking out the weeds in the flower box. He walks his bike over and kisses her. She leans into him. I almost have to turn away, it's all so poignant and intimate. I can barely stand the intimacy.

For the first time in a long time I miss my old life in Cape Vincent and Alexandria Bay. Six months before I got arrested, Stephen and I separated. He found my travelling intolerable. He wanted me to give up my midwifery practice. I loved him. I tried hard to make it work, but I wouldn't give up my practice. I moved from town to a small cottage on Svenson's Creek surrounded by national forest. I was far enough out of town to have quiet, that utter stillness I required and the connection to nature that filled my soul. I had miles and miles of trails where I hiked and never saw anyone. I needed space.

In prison I stopped going to my cottage in my mind because this was where my pain lay. I made a home there on Svenson's Creek, something I never expected to do. In fact, until I did it, I didn't even know I wanted a home. It was more than a want—I needed a home. I had my office there, but my meetings with clients were at their homes. I was close enough to get to the women promptly when they went into labor.

Six months after I moved there the police came en masse. I heard them coming. I don't know how they found out where I lived. It was not an easy place to find. My nearest neighbor was three miles away. I regret that I didn't go into the basement and into the caves, but I had no reason to believe anything was wrong, not at first anyway. It was the amount of law enforcement that got me concerned. It seemed like overkill. They knocked on the door and I answered. They were polite at first.

Detective Valentino told me they had a search warrant. I looked it over. I couldn't imagine what they were looking for. I watched them toss my house.

Where is it? asked Detective Valentino.

What are you looking for?

He looked at me grimly. *You know what we're looking for, Elizabeth.*

No, I said with my hands on my hips. *I can't imagine.*

Come on. Don't play stupid.

The truth is I had no idea what they were looking for. What could I possibly have that they might want? My mind ran through the list of non-narcotic analgesics and herbs that I had for women who were having trouble in their labor. I used western medicine sparingly. I had a license. I did home births. I'd been doing them for years. It was my calling. I was good at it. I'd only lost one baby, and that was a long time ago.

When they cuffed me, dragged me out of my cottage, and shoved me into one of the police cars, I knew I was in trouble, but I wasn't really worried because I thought they'd made a mistake. I replayed the scene many times. When my lawyer did not show up, I considered telling TE that I helped Lydia Garth disappear and that Billy Williams gave her a new identity, but I did not want to put either one of them in jeopardy. Finally, in my last year in custody, I stopped playing those tapes. Acceptance came. I did what I did and didn't do what I didn't do, and still there I was, locked in a cell in the bowels of a prison with six different guards, one with whom I had a heavy relationship. Strange.

How come we never met, Mason? We went to the same criminal justice conferences. We lived in the same area.

You were a caver. I was a caver. It took prison for us to meet. As horrible as it was to be locked up, I got the space I'd been craving. I would never have chosen such a stark existence. But now my freedom is important to me, in a way that I've never experienced. To walk with you by the Salzach River, to go to a dinner concert at Mozart's house, to order a coffee and sit outside at a cafe and listen to conversations in German that I don't understand. A mother buttons up her son's jacket and hugs him. It's these things, these mundane acts, that remind me of the life I lost.

I hear Mason stirring. I want to snuggle up to him in bed. Do I risk it? What's to lose? I go into the room and get under the covers. I want to spoon up to his back. He puts his hand on my butt and pulls me closer. I must fall asleep, because when I wake he is dressed, smiling, and brings me coffee.

"I liked you getting into bed with me."

"I liked it, too. I'm glad to be here with you."

"Me, too," he says.

I get out of bed and walk over to him. I put my arms around him, and he holds me. I feel the electricity between us. He takes my face in his hands. We kiss. My legs feel weak. I can barely keep standing there.

"Okay," I say.

"Okay," he repeats.

I lean into him. He pulls me close. I feel our beating hearts.

20 May 1989
Saturday
Cape Vincent, New York
10:00

CELESTE

Robert McCauley knocks on my door at precisely ten o'clock. I like a man who's on time. He's a nice-looking middle-aged man. He sounded younger on the phone. After we get settled at the kitchen table, he begins the interview.

"Did you notice anything different about Brian recently?"

"Well, he was bothered about the upcoming execution of Eliza Jacobs. Said he knew for a fact that she was innocent, and that innocent people do not deserve to be murdered by the state."

"He said that specifically?"

"Yes, he did. Brian and I are close. When my son Derrick was killed in a snowmobile accident in his sophomore year of high school, Brian was the one who told me what happened. The police were not forthcoming."

"What happened?"

"The boys were out on the ice and spring was just around the corner. The ice was beginning to melt and was thin in places. Brian and Terran got off the ice, but Derrick continued to play until his snowmobile broke through and sank with him on it. They never recovered his body."

I must look stricken, because his eyes are full of sympathy. He seems sincere.

"I'm sorry for your loss, ma'am."

"Thank you. It was a long time ago, but you never really get over losing a child. And now Brian is missing."

"The FBI has been called in to help your local police find out where Brian is and what happened. Did Brian discuss any other executions with you?"

"Yes. He talked about how the prisoners did or did not come to terms with death. He tried to help them see that they had a choice."

"A choice?"

"In how they looked at dying. He helped them review their lives if they wanted to do that, and go over some of the sticking points in their lives. He made timelines with some of them."

"Aren't the inmates on death row there for only two to four weeks?"

"Yes, but death row was the culmination of weeks or months of personal exploration. When the prisoner's execution date was set, the prisoner was transferred to Z. Brian worked intensely with these men until they were executed. He was very engaged in the process."

"The process?"

"Like I was telling you, reviewing their lives, discussing death, and talking about their fears and any other unfinished business. He read poems and stories to the prisoners. He gave them diaries and encouraged them to write. He gave them art materials to express themselves."

"Where is all this material?"

"In his basement in a locked file cabinet, or in his safe."

"Have you seen it?"

"No. Brian told me about it."

"What was the nature of your relationship with Brian?"

"The nature of my relationship? What does that mean?"

"It means, what kind of relationship did you have with him, ma'am?"

"I was like a mother to him. Brian's mother left when he was ten years old. His father kicked her out. Brian's father spent a great deal of time at the prison, so Brian spent most weekdays and nights with us. My late husband Cal and I took Brian under our wings. He became our second son. The boys were best friends. Do you know what it's like for a boy to lose his mother?"

Robert McCauley strikes me as a man who does not usually share anything about himself, but he says, "Yes. I do."

Still, I'm not going to talk to you about Brian's changes over the last nine months. I'm not revealing anything about Brian and his relationship with Eliza Jacobs.

"It seems that Brian was more like a spiritual counselor than a prison guard."

"Yes, that's true. Brian is a trained spiritual counselor. He's not your typical executioner. In fact, there are no other spiritual counselors who also carry the title of executioner in the state of New York. When he sees a true turning around in a prisoner—which is unusual—he believes there needs to be an alternative to death. He's spoken at criminal justice conferences about this and to The Warden personally, but he's gotten little support for his position."

"Are you saying that Brian doesn't believe in the death penalty?"

"I'm saying Brian believes in redemption. He's a kind and gentle man. He did not like being The Executioner. He is sensitive and believes capital punishment is overused. The counseling part of the job made it acceptable to him. He felt he was being of service to the inmates on death row. He liked the one-on-one contact with the prisoners and told me they responded positively to him." I do not add that Brian told me that the best discussions he ever had about this subject was with Billy Williams. I'm giving this FBI agent as little as I can while still seeming cooperative.

"When did you last talk with Brian?"

"Two days ago. He always visits me before an execution. He needs to talk."

"What did you talk about?"

If I were to be entirely candid—which I'm not—I would tell him that Brian was calm in a way I had not seen him in a long time. "He was resolute regarding The Prisoner. He told me he could not be complicit in her death. I asked him what he was going to do. He repeated that he could not be complicit in her death. I took this to mean that he had gotten someone else to administer the drugs. I never in my wildest dreams imagined he would escape with The Prisoner, take the woman and flee."

"So you think he planned this escape?"

"He must have." *And good on him.* I don't say this to Robert McCauley, and I will not say this to anyone. Well, maybe Terran. The only other person I can imagine saying this to is Cal. We would have talked at length about Brian's disappearance right here at this kitchen table.

"How do you think they escaped?"

"Oh, it has to be the caves. Brian knows those caves like the back of his hand."

"His father mentioned that he didn't allow him to explore those caves."

Something about this statement gets under my skin, and I snap at Robert McCauley. "The Warden is not a nice man."

Robert McCauley looks surprised. I need to rein myself in, so before he gets out another question, I say, "My husband and I did not like The Warden, Mr. McCauley. We did not like the way he treated his wife and son. He was hard on Brian. He expected total compliance in everything. Of course, he didn't like Derrick and did not like that the boys were best friends, along with Terran. The three of them were quite a trio. After Marjorie got the boot, I was surprised The Warden allowed Brian to hang out with Derrick and our family. The Warden usually got home from work late, so Brian was with us until well after supper. Of course, the boys had sports after school, then they came here, ate, and did their homework." I laugh. "Well, let's just say they were supposed to do their homework. Brian was a good influence on Derrick. Brian was a good student. Derrick had difficulty focusing, but he got better when Brian joined our family."

"He joined your family?"

"Like I said, he was a second son to us. He spent many

a night here and we took him to our camp for a month in the summer. The Warden was consumed with running the prison. Only one time did he say that he did not want Brian to be a burden. My husband and I both set him straight about that. Brian was never a burden to us. The boys were like brothers. They were always wrestling around and playing. I never told The Warden that because I don't think he would have liked it. He expected his son to be loyal to him and him alone. But Brian was part of our clan. He spent holidays with us. We always invited Arthur, but he never came. I don't know what he did. To me, he always used the prison as an excuse, like he had to be there. Brian spent one Thanksgiving at the prison and told us he never wanted to do that again."

"The only other question I have for you now is, do you have any idea where he might have gone?"

I shake my head. *And if I did, I wouldn't be telling you, Mr. FBI Man.*

"Okay. Thank you for your time and information. I may need to meet with you again as we proceed with the investigation. If you think of anything relevant, give me a call."

He hands me his card. We shake hands and I walk him to the door.

After I shut the door, I wonder why the hell I picked the kitchen to do the interview. I should have gone with the living room. I probably shouldn't have said as much as I did. But that's just it, the kitchen is the beating heart of my house and I wanted to be where I was the most comfortable. I hear Cal's voice. *You did good, honey-bunny. You were friendly and you gave him a lot of background information. You gave him little to nothing about the present. You did a good job of protecting Brian.* I walk back into the kitchen and put Mr. McCauley's cup in the sink. I turn on the stove to heat water for another cup of tea. When I sit down, I put my head on the table and cry. I go over the conversation I had with Brian two nights ago when he dropped by after his run in the woods. He hugged me hello and good-bye. He told me he was tired and wasn't looking forward to Wednesday, execution day. *Where are you Brian? I miss you. Please let me know you're safe.*

20 May 1989
Saturday
Salzburg, Austria
11:30

ALICE

When we come out of the executioner's house, Mason's shoulders are tight.

"Are you alright?" I ask.

"I'm feeling uptight. It's hard to be here. I'm interested in the history of the house and the executioner, but I keep thinking I'm one of these men, part of this club. I don't want to be part of this club. I never wanted to be an executioner."

"Mmm. It must be hard."

"Yeah. I've been an executioner for fifteen years. Fifteen years of killing people. Fifteen years of deaths. I'm out now. No more. I don't know what's next. I'm scared, excited, and hopeful all at the same time. Being in Salzburg at the executioner's house with you is perfect somehow, although I must say I felt dread at the thought of coming here today."

I take his hand and lead him to a bench. We sit outside the executioner's house and stare at the beautifully manicured grounds and green grass.

"I wonder if any of these men actually wanted this job. It's not a job most people want. The guys I've met who do this work fell into the position by the allure of money and power. They make enough money to support their families with ease. Most of the guys believe in an *eye for an eye*. One man didn't want to stay in his family's mortuary business, but he was fascinated with death. I've only met one female executioner and she was a law-and-order gal, a believer in women's rights. She had a vendetta about men wronging women. She didn't care much about men wronging men. I haven't met anyone who was an executioner and a spiritual counselor. In the bigger prisons, there's a minister or priest who does the counseling."

"You liked doing the counseling?"

"I loved it, although it was bittersweet. I got close to the men. I helped them grapple with their life and their upcoming death. Each man's opening was beautiful to me. Then I killed them. I was a state-sanctioned professional killer. I got rid of 'the bad guys.' Except I didn't see them as bad. I saw wounded, reckless, hurting, angry, abused men, most of whom had addiction problems. I saw the dark side of people and of myself."

"We all have a dark side, Mason. Some people claimed I kidnapped children. I believe I was an advocate for them. Different ways of looking at the same situation. Children being harmed, raped, and beaten, hurt physically and emotionally, is unacceptable to me. My mission was to save the children, to get them into a safe environment."

"You gave kids a chance to have a better life."

"I hope so. I've had mixed thoughts about this since I was incarcerated. My motives were pure. My mission was clear. I wanted to protect young people. Until I was incarcerated, I didn't really consider what the parents of a child might feel when their child disappeared." I breathe deeply and try to get ahold of myself. Mason sits quietly next to me. I take another deep breath and he moves closer to me so our thighs are touching. "I wanted to save those souls that picked a family where they were abused and tortured. Was it my right to say that a soul made a bad choice, a mistake? I don't believe in mistakes, Mason. No mistakes, only lessons. I don't get to determine who lives and dies, but I can say what is acceptable and not acceptable to me."

We sit in silence and get distracted by a bird who is chirping loudly. We laugh.

"I could say the police made a mistake the day they came to my house and arrested me. They planted evidence, handcuffed me, then carted me off to jail. I didn't like it. Who would? In my tiny cell I grappled with questions about life. You gave me old but clean sheets and blankets, and brought me a comfortable new pillow and mattress which no one else had slept on. I would have been a lady of leisure if I could forget that I lived in a six-by-nine underground container. I was a woman in a cage, like animals in a circus. Lions and tigers and bears, oh my! I came to know that for some reason I needed—my soul needed—the solitary confinement, the alone time, the limited stimulation, the grey. Like I said, no mistakes, only lessons."

"You're amazing to me, Alice. You took total

responsibility for your situation."

"Isn't that all any of us have control over—managing ourselves to the best of our ability in whatever situation we find ourselves?"

"It is. But it isn't an easy place to get to."

"No. It isn't. I got to practice what Miriam, my mentor, told me when I was training to be a midwife. There is so much joy when a baby comes into the world, and when a baby dies, there is great sorrow. Birth is a time of great intimacy and vulnerability. Death is also a time of great intimacy and vulnerability. I told people God does not rank children. They are all perfect, each in their own way. Acceptance of what is, is the key."

Mason says, "What a beautiful thing to bring life into the world."

"I feel lucky to have had this opportunity. It's a gift and a privilege. Love opens doors and breaks down barriers. I got to witness people's hearts break open. I imagine you did, too. Beginnings and endings are powerful places to share with people."

"When you came to the prison, the brick wall around my heart began to crumble. You inspired me to leave, Alice, to give up the life I was living, a life I never wanted."

"I inspired you?" I ask incredulously.

"When I came into my father's office that first day you were at the prison I saw you going toe-to-toe with him. I admired and respected you. I fought for you when my father put you in Z Block. We had prepared another cell for you, and I argued that just because he got mad at you was no reason for you to go to Z. My father wouldn't listen to any of it. I couldn't even get approval to take you outside to exercise. It was wrong. Bottom line, you should never have been put into an all-men's prison."

"That's exactly what David Drysden, my lawyer, told me when he visited me that one and only time. He had a plan to get me out. I felt hopeful. Then he never came back. I lost that hope. I did not believe I would ever get out."

"Something was wrong from the beginning. I called David when he missed his appointment with you. His secretary told me he closed his practice. A few days later I received your file in the mail."

"David sent you my file?"

"He did. That's when I got more outspoken at staff meetings. I fought for you like my mother fought for me, but in her case, my father prevailed. My mom couldn't keep fighting after her younger sister died. She broke. Her self-confidence eroded. She had to save herself. She had to pick up the pieces that were left and build herself up again. She had to get to a nurturing environment."

"Where did she go?"

"At first she went to the Georgia coast, to Tybee Island, a beautiful little place eleven miles outside of Savannah. It has a three-mile-long white sand beach and is a mecca for artists. I think you'd like it. My mom took long walks on the beach and became the lighthouse keeper. She held the beacon of light for herself and for me."

"You held the beacon of light for me, Mason. You took a lot of risks. I appreciate everything you did. Does your mom know that you helped me escape?"

"No. I couldn't tell her. I didn't want to put her in danger. I told her I couldn't leave you beyond the required work trainings because I was afraid that the PGs wouldn't take care of you if my father tried to do something to you. She understood this and came to some of my trainings so we could spend time together. The PGs were afraid of my father. I got less afraid the more I stood up to him. He didn't want me to leave the job. He wanted to matter to me, and he knew he didn't. Actually, I don't really know what he wanted besides me returning after university to become The Executioner. Fear kept me in line until it didn't."

"You were afraid of him?"

"Yeah. As a kid, he beat me for exploring the caves. That didn't stop me from exploring them. They were my safe place. The beatings actually solidified my defiance. Exploring them helped me hang on to what little there was left of me."

"I love the caves, too. I spent a lot of time in them. They're sacred to me. I'm amazed we never met."

I move the conversation back to the last executioner who lived in the house. We laugh about people being afraid of him sleepwalking. We move away from the personal for a minute.

"Like I said last night, I'm not going to call you TE anymore. Your name is Mason."

"I'm ready to be Mason. I'm ready to move on in this new life, hopefully together."

I take his hand, and he pulls me into a hug.

I say, "I think Mason's the hugging kind."

He holds me tightly and whispers, "I think so, too."

Mason holds my hand as we walk back to town. He stops and turns around and takes one last look at the executioner's house. "This house really reminds me of my home in Cape Vincent. It's alone, surrounded by trees, and is a fortress."

We come to a café and decide to eat lunch outside.

When we're seated, he asks me, "How are you doing?"

"I'm happy and a bit weary. I think I need a bit of quiet. How about you?"

"I'm looking forward to going to the ice caves this afternoon if that still works for you."

"I wouldn't miss them, Mason."

Then I am quiet. It's okay for me to be quiet with him. It's built into the fabric of our relationship, a relationship that is taking a turn here in Salzburg. My stomach tightens. I feel fear. I have not been all that successful at relationships.

When the food arrives, Mason picks up the thread of our conversation.

"I wanted to make a difference. When I found spiritual counseling, my life changed. I found a way to be The Executioner and be true to myself. I offered compassion to men I was eventually going to kill. I became the compassionate executioner."

"The compassionate executioner."

"Most people in the system teased me about this. They didn't understand what I was doing."

"I get it."

"Billy Williams got it, too. I began calling him the compassionate FBI man."

"Do you know who Wendy and Wendell Falls were?"

"They were premature twins who lived three weeks. Their lungs were not well developed at birth. Wendell died first and Wendy died a week later. Billy believed she died of heartbreak because her lungs were doing fine until her brother died. He believes she couldn't bear life without her brother, so she let go and joined him."

"What do you know about Mason and Alice?"

"Mason was three years old when he fell off the tractor his father was driving and got crushed by the tractor's wheels. His family were farmers in North Dakota. Alice, originally Alice Leigh, was six years old when she died. She lived in Booth Bay Harbor, Maine. She was walking home from school when a truck skidded on the ice and the driver hit her. They both died. The bus driver who had just dropped her off witnessed the accident. Alice was an only child. Her parents and the whole community were devastated."

"Billy told you all this?"

"Yeah. You know how he is. He's a stickler for detail. He does a thorough history of each child. He kept Alice's original name to honor her, but he wanted us to be married with the same last name. He told me that married couples with different last names are looked at more closely at the borders. He didn't want to put us in harm's way."

"I like my new name, Alice Leigh MacFarland."

"I like mine, too, Mason James MacFarland."

We're quiet as we eat. I break the silence this time. "I wanted to make a difference, too, Mason. As a counselor I listened to teenagers talk about their lives and I let them know it was possible to have a different life. I helped abused kids get out of bad situations if they wanted to. I offered them hope. I felt completely justified helping a child leave, even if that meant they left their family all of a sudden."

"Did you help Lydia Garth get out of her situation?"

"I did. During my incarceration I wondered if I did the right thing. I took Lydia away from her family. The week after my principal and I met with Lydia's father Dr. Garth,

MaryLou Garth came up to me in the grocery store parking lot. She had on large, dark sunglasses so I couldn't see her eyes. She asked me if Lydia was safe. I gave her a slight nod. She nodded back and walked away. It seemed to me she just wanted to know if her daughter was dead or alive. I never got to ask her if she tried to protect her daughter. I wondered if MaryLou's grief was different from a mother whose daughter dies of cancer and there's a funeral with supportive words and family gathered together. I wonder if her mother is still grieving. I wonder if her mother ever grieved. I justified facilitating Lydia's leaving because Lydia said *yes*. She wanted to go. I told myself I saved her from more abuse. I hope that's true, otherwise, what was the point?"

"You protected her because she wasn't in a safe situation. Do you know where she went?"

"No. Billy Williams told me it wasn't safe for her, or for me, to know. During my incarceration I began to wonder if I really did help these kids by taking them away from their families."

"I wish someone had helped me leave my father after he kicked my mom out. I felt alone. I'm grateful to Mrs. Teasdale, my school counselor, who helped my mom and me stay in touch. A few days after my mom left, Mrs. T called me into her office, and I got my first letter from my mom. We communicated for eight years through cards and letters. Mrs. T couldn't reunite me physically with her, but emotionally my mom and I stayed in close contact through letters. Mrs. T and I had conversations about how my mom did not abandon me. These were important talks for me and helped me create a story of hope and love instead of abandonment and betrayal. She never told the principal about my mom's letters because my father came to the school soon after he kicked her out and insisted that the school never let me leave with anyone besides him. He didn't say my mom's name, but everyone got the message loud and clear. *If you let my son go with his mother, your life will be hell.* My father wielded a lot of power. People who knew him did not stand up to him. Mrs. Teasdale silently crossed him. I admired her for that."

"Mrs. Teasdale worked as a counselor for the Thousand Islands Central School District?"

"She did. She travelled between schools. There weren't many counselors at that time. I went to the same school that you worked in when you got arrested and taken into custody. You had Mrs. Teasdale's job. Strange, huh?"

"It's a small world, for sure. Do you still have contact with her?"

"Yes. She retired and moved to Florida. My mom and she live in the same community now. Everyone calls them 'the Marjories.' They're quite the dynamic duo. I'm happy for both of them."

"Will you make contact with them once we get to New Zealand?"

"Not directly, but through Terran, at least at first."

"Will I be able to contact my parents through Terran, too?"

"Of course. Once we're settled you can send a letter anytime. Terran has a P.O. Box and he'll take the letter to your folks. He'll take the letter out of the envelope because it isn't safe for them to know where we are, not for them or for us."

"Why isn't it safe for them?"

"Well, if they think your family knows where you are,

your family could be in danger of having that information coerced from them. But also, if whoever wanted you gone in the first place has any idea that you're in contact with your parents and your brother and sister, all of them could be used as leverage."

I look at him. "Leverage?"

"To keep you from revealing what you know."

"I don't know anything."

"They don't believe that."

"Who's 'they'?"

"Well, the cops for one. Detective Valentino, specifically. I think my father and the governor are in it up to their eyeballs, too."

"What makes you think that?"

"You coming to an all-men's prison. My father would never have agreed to that without some big reason and intense pressure. He was highly reactive around you from the beginning and had that over-the-top cockiness that you would never be released. He didn't allow your parents or your friend Maria to visit, either. That was unusual."

"What about Maria?"

"She came for a visit with all the proper paperwork, and he sent her away."

"How do you know that?"

"Brenda told me."

"The Secretary? The Warden's secretary?"

"Yes."

"You're friends?"

"Yes. We went through school together. She told me my father had regular contact with the governor the entire time you were there. She made copies of all your paperwork and gave them to me. She said my father was frequently looking at your file and when he gave it back to her, papers were always missing. I had your complete file."

"Wow. I guess secretaries really do run the office."

"There's no doubt about that. My father trusts her. But her loyalty is to me."

I look at him. "She loves you?"

"She thinks she does."

"Do you love her?"

"As a friend."

"Did she know you were leaving with me?"

"No, only Terran and Billy Williams knew. She would have been upset. I didn't want to hurt her, although I'm sure I did."

"How so?"

"By not wanting to be with her, not wanting to be a couple."

"You had another girlfriend?"

"Of sorts."

"What does that mean?"

Mason looks at me for long seconds. "Well, there were a lot of limitations."

I raise my eyebrows, not understanding.

"Like, you were locked up."

"You wanted to be with me?"

"I did. I do."

I stare at him. I don't know what to say. Tears roll down my cheeks. He pulls me next to him and puts his arm around me. We sit in silence. Right now, in this moment, I'm not as comfortable with the silence as I was when I was in prison. I need something to reassure me, but I don't know what.

"Breathe," he says as he squeezes my hand.

I squeeze back.

20 May 1989
Saturday
Cape Vincent, New York
12:17

ROBERT
MCCAULEY

When I leave Celeste Gordon's house, I cannot stop thinking about how much pain she must be in. She never mentioned that she recently lost her husband. She mostly focused on Brian as a child, not on Brian as an adult. She was friendly in a kind of distant, northern New England way. She served tea and coffee and homemade cranberry muffins. She gave me a lot of background information, but nothing really about the here and now. That is significant, along with telling me in no uncertain terms that The Warden is not a nice man.

The prison staff and guards like their jobs. They get regular raises and can support their families here. They believe The Warden takes care of them. There is some agreement that The Warden is quirky, but the benefits of the job surpass any of their complaints. Many PGs do not like how the prison is changing, that new guys—outsiders—are being brought in and people are encouraged to not socialize with their co-workers outside of work. I believe there is a lot the prison staff is not saying.

I have a lot of questions for The Warden, whom I have not formally interviewed. I wanted to interview his guards and the other staff first to get background information before I interviewed him, the man whose son has vanished with The Prisoner. I've talked to him daily and used the excuse that his son was missing so I could wait to interview him.

Right now we do not know where Brian Stafford and Elizabeth Jacobs are. No Brian Stafford or Elizabeth Jacobs crossed the Canadian border. They could have identification or passports with different names, or they could still be in the caves. Sam Davis told me when he was a boy he explored the caves with his father, who knew them like the back of his hand. The cave system was intricate and complicated, Sam said, but he also told me Brian walked the caves all the way to the tip of Lake Champlain when he was in high school. The local press interviewed him and there was a big spread in the paper. The Warden didn't like this. He didn't like the implication that he did not have control of his boy. The whole town already knew the story of him kicking Brian's mother out of their house, and The Warden didn't want another negative incident for people to gossip about. But no one ever said a word against him, at least not to his face.

I am done interviewing The Prison Guards and The Cook. I am not done with Brenda. It is time to interview The Warden.

I know all about rural, small-town life. God help me.

20 May 1989
Saturday
Salzburg, Austria
14:00

ALICE

After lunch we go back to our hotel and get ready for our ice cave adventure. We put on our new hiking boots and bring our down jackets, hats, and gloves.

Our small group hikes up a steep incline to get to the doors of the cave. The views of the Alps are breathtaking. I love feeling my beating heart. When we go through the door to the caves there is a rush of freezing-cold air. Our guide gives each of us a glass lantern and begins to tell us the history of the caves. We explore the ice landscape of caves and labyrinths for the next three hours. I've never seen anything like this before. How can one place hold so many treasures? The large ice formations are jaw-droppingly beautiful. I love the small passageways and colors in the ice. The water in the cave is a cold blue turquoise. I put some water on my face and taste the strong limestone. I love this expansive space and the sounds of water dripping. We keep moving so we don't get cold, but Mason and I are used to this kind of cold, so the few times we stand still don't bother us. I'm aware of Mason and occasionally look at him, but we are silent. No one talks except the guide, who is sparing with his words. I am sad when the tour ends. Afterward, we gather in a warm room to drink hot chocolate and people ask questions. Most of the people are not cavers, but they are intoxicated by these formations. We thank the guide and tell him about our caves in New York. He nods. Cavers know each other. No one has to say much. Nature says it all.

I am full after the tour. My soul is singing. Mason and I hold hands on the drive back.

He breaks the silence as we head up to our room. "I'm thinking no boat cruise on the Salzach tonight. Let's pack and eat at the restaurant right on the river. We can watch the boats from there."

"Perfect," I say as I pull him into a hug. "Oops, I forgot you're not the hugging kind."

He laughs.

TERRAN

I decline The Investigator's offer to meet at my house. I don't want him here. "Why don't we meet at Brian's place, since he left me the deed to his house?"

Robert McCauley smiles and says, "No. The house has not been officially released from its crime scene status." We agree to meet at his motel office.

"I want to know more about your relationship with Brian Stafford."

"What do you want to know?"

"How long have you known each other?"

"Since we were three years old. My mom and his mom were friends.

"So, you used to play together?"

"Yup. We were both only children, so we spent a lot of time together."

"Are you close?"

"Yeah. We hang out together. Used to take winter

vacations together."

"Where'd you go?"

"Usually to one of the islands in the Caribbean."

"You said you used to take vacations together. What changed?"

"Eliza came to the prison and Brian didn't trust that she would be taken care of by the other guards if The Warden tried to do something to her."

"He was worried that The Warden might harm her?"

"Yup. The Warden has a violent temper, and he doesn't like women much. You probably already know that Eliza's lawyer, David Drysden, came to the prison to meet with her only one time. Said he would return in a week, and he never did. When Brian went to his office, the lawyer was gone. His secretary, Amanda Lewis, told him that he would be getting Eliza's file in the mail. Did you find it in the pile of papers in his filing cabinet?"

Robert looks at me. "I can't give you any information about the ongoing investigation."

"Well, hopefully you found it. He left it for you. I can give you my copy if you need it."

"So you and Brian talked about the Elizabeth Jacobs case?"

"We did. He believed she was set up."

"By whom?"

"He didn't know. He never did figure it out."

"You think that's why he helped her escape?"

"Yeah. He wasn't going to kill an innocent person."

"None of the other prisoners he executed were innocent?"

"No. He believed they were guilty."

"How did he feel about his job?"

"State-sanctioned murder."

"That's what he thought it was?"

"Absolutely. Isn't that what it is?" I want to know his opinion about the death penalty.

"Some people believe that. The protestors that come to every execution don't believe in capital punishment."

"But I'm asking you what you think, Robert."

"It doesn't matter what I think. I'm here to gather the facts and to try and get justice."

"Justice?" I ask sarcastically. "She was in The Tomb for three years and nine months. I'd say we're way beyond justice at this point."

"What do you mean by 'way beyond justice'?"

"Come on, Robert. There's nothing *just* about this case. Eliza was abused by the system. I'm asking you if you're going to go after them and get to the bottom of this."

"I'm going to do my job."

"And is your job to go after the bad guys? Because the bad guys to me are somebody who's got a lot of power in the system. Are you up for that?"

"Did you and Brian talk about what you would say to the authorities?"

"Oh, we talked ad nauseam. I am representing his voice and hers, too, even though she doesn't know me."

"Do you know where they are?"

"No." I look him in the eyes.

"And if you did know?"

"If I did know, what?"

"You wouldn't tell me."

I recognize that he is making a statement, not asking a question.

"My loyalty is to Brian."

"My loyalty is to the truth."

"Then we ought to get along just fine," I say. "I'm all for the truth."

"You think he escaped with her?"

"Absolutely. He took her and they got out of Dodge."

"You supported his plan?"

"Yup. Come on. What choice did he have? Brian isn't going to kill someone who's innocent. For that matter, he doesn't really like to kill the men who are guilty."

"Why does he do it, then?"

"I don't know what he would say to that. I don't think he really knows why he does it. But obviously, he's done doing it."

"You don't think he's coming back?"

"No."

"You think he planned this escape?"

"What do you think?" I ask sarcastically.

"I'd say by the looks of his house and his file cabinet, he's a very organized guy. He would have had a plan."

I laugh. "Brian's a guy who likes a plan."

"And you? Are you a guy who likes a plan?"

"Sometimes. I'm a guy who pays close attention to detail."

"What kind of work do you do?"

"I'm a master cabinet maker."

"Did you help Brian build his house?"

"Yup."

"Is that why he left it to you?"

I look at him. I say quietly, "He wanted me to have it."

"You wanted to have it?"

"I'm fine with having it. I like the house. I'm nearer to

Celeste. I need to look out for her."

"Your turn?"

"Yeah, my turn."

"Okay. I think that's it for now. I'll probably want to talk to you again."

"Anytime, Robert. I'm looking forward to justice being served."

20 May 1989
Saturday
Cape Vincent, New York
16:30

ROBERT
MCCAULEY

After Terran leaves, I stay at the office and write my notes. He and Brian are close friends. Terran made a point of seeing if I found the Eliza Jacobs file at Brian's house and let me know he had a copy if I hadn't. My men did find the file, although it was not in alphabetical order like the rest. Brian must have been covering his tracks. What the fuck is going on here? There is documentation about her arrest, but Eliza's account to her lawyer does not jibe with Detective Valentino's police report. Discrepancies, discrepancies. We need to interview the detective, the police chief, The Warden, and the judge. I keep asking myself who and what are these men protecting. *What did Elizabeth come upon?* There seems to be a connection with the missing girl, Lydia Garth, and her father, Dr. Peter Garth. The school principal and secretary's detailed notes confirm that Dr. Garth's loud, intimidating words were "over the top." Dr. Garth did not like being challenged. White men in power. I know all about this. I'm one of them, but I don't have the status of head surgeon and pediatrician. I want to have a chat with the head surgeon's wife without the good doctor being there. *What's her name? MaryLou.* There's another daughter, Isabelle, but she lives and works on Cape Cod, where she attended and boarded at a residential school from twelve to twenty-two. Pieces, lots of pieces. I tell myself I love to fit the pieces together.

Yesterday I talked to my boss after I read Eliza's file. I told him, *We've got a shitstorm here.* My boss laughed and said, *Do what you do best, Robert. Tear it apart and put it back together.*

It is always good to know my boss backs me. I told him, *Whatever this is, it's way bigger than Elizabeth Jacobs. After Lydia Garth disappeared, something got set into motion. Elizabeth got caught in the frenzy, stepped on somebody's toes. Somebody got scared she found out something that they didn't want her to know. The police went to three judges before Leon Corelli signed the search warrant. We'll interview all of them. I don't know who put the pressure on and why Corelli signed off. Lots of questions that lead to more questions than answers. I've got Brian Stafford's best friend and confidant, Terran Volker, in the middle of all of it. He's taken on the job of motivating us to do the right thing.* My boss laughed. *Looks like you've got a handle on it, Robert.*

After we get off the phone I sit and think. *I've known guys like you, Terran. My best friend, Tommy Crenshaw, is the Terran in my life. It's not quite time to call him, but* soon I'll be picking up the phone and running this case by him. Connor Grey's my go-to man now, but we don't have a long history. I trust him though. We're a good team.

21 May 1989
Sunday
Somewhere over the Pacific Ocean
01:00

ALICE

Mason and I are on the plane to New Zealand, a place I dreamed about going to, but after only nine months in prison I stopped thinking about going anywhere and it never came up when I meditated. New Zealand was a lost thought, a lost dream in a long list of "never going to happens" that I lived with and accepted. Mason's sleeping. I like how he looks when he's sleeping. We had a great time in Salzburg. I'm calling it my transition place, the place between prison and our upcoming arrival in New Zealand where *we* plan to live. The more I know Mason, the more I like him. We have the whole history of The Executioner and The Prisoner, the imbalance of distinct roles and rules that Mason bent as much as he could, probably more than he should have. I doubt PG One or Two would have reported him even if they'd seen me writing or found me outside my cell, but they would have noted it and it could have come up when they drank at Bandy's. Mason is careful. He tends to detail. I appreciate this. I am like that myself.

I am surprised how comfortable I am with Mason. I can be myself with him, and he accepts me. When I fell in love with Stephen, he accepted me, too. He wanted and got an independent woman. Then he tried to change me. When my work took me out of town for extended periods of time—home visits, middle-of-the-night calls, births, midwife conferences—we fought when I left, and we fought when I returned. He said he was sick of me being gone all the time, that he made enough money to support both of us. He asked me to quit my job. I didn't want to quit my job; I liked it. I stood up for myself, and we continued to fight. I grew weary of the constraints. Eventually I moved to my little cottage on Svenson's Creek. Six months later they arrested and incarcerated me. I haven't told Mason about Stephen, or my pattern with men. I don't want to jinx the relationship.

I loved Salzburg. It was comfortable and homey. It's hard to believe that I've been out of prison for only four days. Both of us are still wearing our wedding rings, and although we aren't legally wed, I feel married. Our time in Salzburg felt like our honeymoon. We have not had a conversation about this. Maybe when I wear my new purple hat I will be brave and bring it up. I am glad that I am not—and do not want to be—silent any longer.

After the quiet in prison, I notice how much people talk. Yak, yak, yak. They try to connect. That's what words attempt—a connection with self and with others. When I was alone too much my aloneness could turn into loneliness. I did not want to cross that line. Buddha, aka Siddhartha, sat by the river after he left home. He wanted to grow and learn about the world and his place in it. His parents overprotected him. Mine did not overprotect me, but they were interested in my life. I was a daddy's girl. Sometimes I think my mom didn't like this. Writing and receiving letters during my incarceration helped me heal some of those old wounds. I had a lot of time to reflect on my family and my immense need to get away so I could be myself, find myself. I did not want to get caught in the family web.

I loved my mom's letters. She shared details that helped me see pictures in my mind. *Mari tried on a beautiful, lacy, off-white fitted dress, cotton, old-fashioned, a dress you would like and look good in, too. Mari reminds me of you. She likes the old. She's smart as a whip and a good negotiator and listener. Like you, she takes everyone's needs and wants into consideration. She's athletic and a leader on the cheer squad. She runs with the popular girls, something you did not do. She tells me some of them are catty. She doesn't like catty. She's careful. She doesn't give herself away. Her first boyfriend, Zach, Zachary Mayfair, is a doll, a good hockey player, and the two of them are quite the couple.*

I miss my family. Perhaps I'll write my memoirs. My luggage is filled with letters. I wrote mine twice, so I could have a copy. My history has literally followed me. Our history always does come with us one way or another. We weave the past and present together in the stories we tell, incorporating the past into the present picture.

21 May 1989
Sunday
Cape Vincent, New York
02:13

CELESTE

In the middle of the night, I awake with a start. My heart is pounding, and my neck is stiff from sleeping in the chair. I had a bad dream. I was drowning, dying. I miss Cal. He would have held me until I went back to sleep. I look out the window and see Brian's dark house. The police car is there. I could go down and talk to Charlie, but I don't really want to. I sit in my chair by the open window and gaze out. I hear silence. It's too early for the birds and too late for the crickets and the frogs. The stillness is broken when the breeze blows and the leaves in the trees rustle as the wind rolls through them like gentle waves. My heart breaks again, this time for Brian. I can't believe he's gone.

After my interview with Robert McCauley I did not feel calm—too many questions, too many memories, too much loss. They say those of us who live in the north country are tough and strong. And God knows I come from generations of tough and strong. But losing Brian so close to my loss of Cal is testing my strength. When Cal died, I had only Brian. I need to know Brian is safe.

Every day since Brian's been gone Terran has visited me. He's not used to sitting with me. I hope he gets more comfortable and eventually tells me everything he knows about Brian's plan. But for now, I am glad for his company. I will bake chocolate chip cookies with nuts today for Terran, his favorite. I haven't baked in a long time.

ROBERT
MCCAULEY

"Thank you for coming."

"We're glad to meet with you," replies Alan Jacobs, Elizabeth's father.

Arlene, her mother, agrees and says, "We want to find our daughter, Mr. McCauley. We are not happy she's disappeared."

"How did you learn about Eliza's disappearance?"

Alan says, "We were in the visitor's line at the prison waiting to be checked in for a ten o'clock scheduled visit with our daughter right before her execution. We wanted to see her face and hear her voice one last time. The Warden's secretary called us late the day before and told us The Warden approved the visit. Better late than never."

"My heart was breaking," Arlene adds. "I could barely contain myself, but we stood stoically in line, surrounded by the noisy protesters."

Alan hands me an envelope. "This is David Drysden's file. He was our daughter's lawyer when she got convicted and then condemned to death. When we went to his office to get her file, his secretary told us Mr. Drysden was gone. He left a note in her file recommending we hire Lucas March, a lawyer from out of town. First we tried to hire a local lawyer, but none of them would take her case. When Mr. March looked at the size of the file, before he even read it, he told us the information was too sparse for a conviction and death row determination. He said he would help us find out what happened to Eliza before, during, and after her conviction.

"Now she's missing, Mr. McCauley. We know our daughter. We do not believe she did anything wrong, although we know she has strong convictions about children's rights, and it is possible she could have crossed some line."

"What line might that be?" I ask.

"Helping a child get to safety if they were being abused, taking them away from their family without parental permission. She was a child advocate. She would never murder a child."

I say, "I want you to know that we have been able to track your daughter and Brian Stafford to Frankfurt, and now the trail has gone cold."

"Do you think they're still alive?" Arlene asks.

"We have no reason to believe there's been any foul play, but since we have no idea where they are now, we don't actually know their status. Has your daughter made any contact with you since her escape?"

"No, we haven't heard from her. We're worried. When

she was in solitary confinement, we heard from her once a week."

"I didn't think you had any contact with her."

"We weren't supposed to, but we did." Alan hands me a box and says, "Here are copies of three years of letters between us. We received weekly letters from her, and we sent two letters to her every week. Arlene and I wrote to her separately. We didn't tell anyone we were doing this; it was our family secret. Eliza wrote that TE, short for The Executioner, was going out of his way to help her, and if we told anyone about these letters it would not only put him in harm's way, but it could mean we wouldn't get any more letters from her. We were not willing to take that risk."

Arlene chimes in. "The whole situation was like a bad soap opera, Mr. McCauley. We know our daughter received our letters because we were having ongoing written conversations with her."

"Our current plan is to send her letters to the press, one at a time," Alan says. "We discussed this with Mr. March and asked him if this would serve our daughter's cause. He told us it would not hurt her now that she is missing. We want to expose the system that harmed her. We are ready to brave this fight. We have always believed that America honors basic human rights, but hers were completely denied."

The envelopes in the box have a Vermont address, P.O. Box 397, Burlington.

"When did you get her last letter?" I ask.

"Two days after she disappeared."

Her father takes it out and reads it to me. "The Cook prepared me an exquisite meal. I had scallops and a hot fudge sundae. TE talked with me. I continued my vow of silence. I feel immense grief and sadness that tomorrow my life will be over. I also have a sense of relief that I will finally be done with this bare, minimal existence. I have accepted that, for some reason still unknown to me, I am being asked to die, to have my life taken from me, hopefully for some greater purpose. Otherwise, what has my life been worth?

"I love you Mommy and Daddy. Tell Mari and Oliver I love them, too. Please know my heart is full and that I will have been glad to see your faces one last time.

"Your loving daughter and big sister, Eliza."

"Mari and Oliver are her brother and sister?"

"Yes. They're twins. They miss her terribly. We've tried to keep things as normal as possible for them, but it's been difficult."

"And you've included the copies of the letters that you wrote her?"

"Yes. We didn't know if they would be helpful to you, but Mr. March recommended we give you everything. We want to find our daughter, Mr. McCauley."

"We want to find her, too, Mr. and Mrs. Jacobs. Did you ever go to the post office in Burlington?"

"We did. We spent the weekend in Burlington three times and waited in the post office parking lot for hours. We hoped we might see the person who had rented the P.O. Box. No one ever came."

"I'll read the letters, and if I have additional questions I would like to talk with you again. If and when we get any information about Eliza's whereabouts, I will contact you. If she reaches out to you, will you call me right away?"

"We will. Here's Mr. March's number. We've given our

permission for you to talk with him. We want to know our daughter is safe, Mr. McCauley. Since you don't know her, you might call her Elizabeth. That's what the legal system calls her. They don't care that she had another life. Our daughter was a well-liked and respected counselor and midwife, Mr. McCauley. Her best friend Maria came to the prison on visitor's day but was denied access even though her paperwork was in order. They told her that inmates housed in Cell Block Z were not allowed to have visitors, that no one outside the prison staff got access there. We learned The Warden was within his legal boundaries about visitation, but he was not with in the legal limits regarding solitary confinement. One month of solitary confinement at a time is the legal limit. Our daughter was in solitary confinement for three years and eight months longer than she should have been."

"We are looking into her case, Mr. and Mrs. Jacobs. We know something is wrong here, and we want to get to the bottom of it."

"We're worried that she's missing, and we're glad the FBI is handling her case," says Arlene.

I give them my card and tell them they can call me anytime.

I am surprised that Elizabeth's parents have three years of letters from their daughter. Later that day we find out that a Craig Milligan rented P.O. Box 397 in Burlington. When we show the postal workers a picture of Brian Stafford, they confirm that Craig is Brian.

When Connor returns from his trip to the Canadian border, he reports that on seventeen May, a couple— Wendell and Wendy Falls—crossed the border. The border patrol man remembered them, said that Wendell told him they were going to Montreal to celebrate their anniversary at The Blue Goose. When this led to a dead end, Connor checked the airports in Montreal and Toronto. Wendell and Wendy Falls took a flight to Frankfurt on the morning of eighteen May. We located the motel they stayed in and learned they received two large boxes and a thick envelope at the desk at check-in. When the housekeeping ladies went to clean their room, they found two large empty boxes. The morning clerk remembered the couple leaving with two large suitcases. The employee at the airport luggage store confirmed that Brian paid cash for two large suitcases. Then their trail goes cold. The couple disappeared like they dropped off the face of the earth.

Although the investigation stalls on the international front, I am busy in the United States. I do not believe in coincidences. People do not go missing without a good reason. They leave by choice, either theirs or someone else's.

22 May 1989
Monday
Cape Vincent, New York
10:00

CONNOR
GREY

"Hi, Amanda. I'm Connor Grey, FBI."

"Hi, Mr. Grey."

"So you know why I'm here?"

"Yes. Mr. Drysden told me three years ago to expect a visit from the FBI."

"Did he tell you why?"

"He said the Elizabeth Jacobs case was controversial."

"Do you know what he meant by controversial?"

"That they convicted Miss Jacobs of murdering Lydia Garth, whose body was found burnt beyond recognition. He said that due to the extensive burning it was impossible to confirm that it actually was Lydia."

"Did he let you know that you might be in danger?"

"He did."

"Did you believe that?"

"I found it hard to believe, but then again, for a man to give up his whole life and disappear with his wife and two children, it seemed like serious business."

"You said on the phone that he left you files to give to the FBI?"

"Yes."

"How did you get them out of the office?"

"I didn't. After I typed everything into the Elizabeth Jacobs file and organized it, I gave it to Mr. Drysden. I never saw the file again. A week after Mr. Drysden left, Detective Valentino came to the office. He went through all the files and took some of them. The Elizabeth Jacobs file was missing after he was here, so I assumed he took it. When Mr. Drysden called, I told him about the missing file. He thanked me for letting him know about it and told me he rented a storage unit for the rest of his files, and asked me to pack them up and have them delivered to it. He rented two safe deposit boxes and told me the Elizabeth Jacobs file would be the only thing in Box three thirty-five. Box seven ninety-nine, which he gave to me, contained only the key to Box three thirty-five. He paid for the storage unit and both safety deposit boxes for seven years."

"Did this seem strange to you?"

"Yes, it felt like overkill until the storage unit got broken into. He told me this would probably happen and to not worry about it. He told me to report it to the police and then clean it out, take everything to the shredder. I did that."

"You were never threatened?"

"No."

"You never went to the safe deposit box?"

"No." She slides me an envelope.

"The key to your box?"

She nods.

"Can you tell me why you think Mr. Drysden went to all this trouble?"

"He told me this was an unfortunate case where justice was not served, that the law did not always work right. He was concerned for his and my safety. He talked to my husband Todd and me and told us that the less we knew, the better. Todd didn't like that I had a key, but I told him it was the least I could do, that I didn't want an innocent person being put to death."

"You think Eliza Jacobs is innocent?"

"Absolutely. No question."

"I'm going to take a trip to the bank. I may be contacting you again, Amanda."

"Will you close the box, Mr. Grey?"

"I can't. I don't have the authority to do that. Do you have any idea where Mr. Drysden is?" I've asked her this before, but I need to ask her again.

"No, sir."

"Have you had any contact with him since he left three years ago?"

"No, although at Christmas for the past three years I get a card from a Randall Clark. I don't know anyone by that name. I think it's Mr. Drysden letting me know he's alive and well."

"Have you saved the cards or the envelopes?"

"Yes. I brought them with me."

She takes a handful of cards and envelopes out of her bag and gives them to me.

"Did Mr. Drysden leave any other instructions?"

"He told me to close out the box after you made contact with me. I'll do that today."

22 May 1989
Cape Vincent, New York
Monday
13:30

ROBERT MCCAULEY

"Thank you for meeting with me."

"Didn't know I had a choice," says The Warden.

Ah, he's already defensive. We'll see where this goes. Do I ignore his attitude, or do I comment on what he said?

"Of course you had a choice."

"Well, then the subpoena," The Warden says dryly.

"Yes, there's that."

"So, you've interviewed all my staff." It's a statement, not a question.

I nod.

"I assume they've been forthcoming?"

"It seems so. What are you hearing?"

"That you're probing."

"That's my job, to ask questions."

"To trap people," states The Warden.

"To find out the truth," I say.

"Truth is variable."

"So, what's the truth about Elizabeth Jacobs?"

"The Prisoner killed a girl. She deserves to die."

"An eye for an eye?" I ask.

"My philosophy exactly."

"And what about your son helping her escape?"

"Did he? We don't know that. Unless you have some new information that I don't have."

"You're right. We don't know that for a fact. The facts are: The Prisoner and The Executioner are missing. They crossed into Canada and stayed at a motel in Toronto. They used the aliases Wendy and Wendell Falls. Then they flew to Frankfurt and stayed at a hotel near the airport. They had two boxes and a letter waiting for them when they got there."

"And then what? The newspaper has reported all of this. Do you have anything new?"

"We've lost their trail."

"Well, when might you find the trail? She could have killed him by now."

"You fear for your son's safety, Warden?"

"No, Mr. McCauley. I do not. What I fear is that my son has been taken in by this woman, this prisoner."

"Taken in?"

"Manipulated. Brian is susceptible to manipulation, particularly when a woman is involved. He's way too sensitive. Wears his feelings on his sleeve for all to see, has since he was a boy. Got that from his mother. He certainly didn't get it from me."

What I want to say is, *You seem to express your anger quite readily.* What I do say is, "So, what was Elizabeth

Jacobs, a woman, doing in Cell Block Z in your all-men's prison, Warden?"

"Waiting for her conviction to be solidified so the state could kill her."

"Why didn't she get housed in a woman's prison?"

"The decision was made for her to come here."

"Who made that decision?"

"Who do you think?"

"It doesn't matter what I think. Who ordered her to come here?"

"The paperwork should tell you that. Her file—"

"Her file does not tell me that, Warden. How she got here and who ordered that are missing." I don't tell him David Drysden's paperwork shows the governor ordered it, one small sheet of paper that I've only seen in Mr. Drysden's file.

"I don't know who ordered her to come here."

"You don't know? You didn't question a woman being sent to your all-men's prison?"

"No. I follow orders."

"Whose orders?"

He looks at me with hate in his eyes.

"I got orders."

"Written orders? A phone call?"

I pull out the paper and push it across the table.

"Where did you get this?"

I ignore his question. "Is this what you received, Warden?"

"I don't remember. If I did, it should be in the file."

"But it isn't in the prison file, Warden. The governor signed it." Silence. "Did you talk with the governor about it?"

"No."

Connor Grey is questioning the governor right this moment. We decided to do these interviews at the same time to see if there are any contradictions or other fallout. The Warden appears increasingly testy.

"Have you interviewed the governor yet?"

"My colleague is interviewing him as we speak."

He stares at me. This information sits like a large boulder on a piece of paper.

"So, I'm asking you again, did you receive this order from the governor?"

"I don't remember. If it's not in the file, then we didn't get it."

"So the governor called you?"

"I talked with him."

"He asked you if you'd take The Prisoner, the woman, Elizabeth Jacobs?"

"He told me he needed me to take her."

"Why?"

"He didn't say."

"Was the women's prison filled at the time?"

"I don't know. I didn't ask."

"So you were willing to take her not knowing if the women's prison was full?"

"I was willing to help him out."

"I've been told you had a private cell set up for her in A Block, but you ended up sending her to Cell Block Z."

"It didn't seem like a good idea to have her near the men."

"I hear she pissed you off."

"She had a smart mouth when she got here. She got cured of that right quick."

"Did you ever see her again?"

"A couple of times when I went to Z to do my biannual inspection, but we never spoke. She appeared to be sleeping every time I was there."

"Did you ever speak to her after you sent her to Z Block?"

"No. I had no need to speak with her. I got no reports that she was causing a problem."

"I heard that you did not let her parents come to visit her."

"People in solitary do not necessarily get visits. Visits are at my discretion."

"So if she was not causing any problems, why would you not let her parents visit her?"

"I do not feel that those who kill another human being deserve any extra rights."

"Yet you let men on death row have regular family visits, especially when they get near their execution date."

"Men are different than women."

"How so?"

"More predictable. Less emotional. I was concerned she would get upset, and I didn't want my men to have to deal with that."

"Do you know Dr. Peter Garth, Warden?"

"Just that The Prisoner killed his daughter."

"Lydia."

"Is that her name?"

"You haven't met Dr. Garth before?"

"I didn't say that."

"So where did you meet him?"

"I don't remember."

"Have you been to his house before?"

"Yes, for a fundraiser."

"You met his wife and daughters?"

"I did. But it was brief. I don't think I'd recognize them if I saw them on the street."

"That was the only time you saw them?"

"It was the first time I saw Mrs. Garth and their oldest daughter. I saw Lydia's picture in the paper when she went missing."

"Okay, Warden. I will most likely need a follow-up interview as we move forward in our investigation. If you think of anything that you would like to tell me, please feel free to call me."

"I want to know when you find my son."

"I will let you know when we find him."

22 May 1989
Albany, New York
Monday
13:30

CONNOR
GREY

"Good morning, Governor. I'm Connor Grey, FBI. Thank you for meeting with me."

"Good morning, Mr. Grey."

I put the tape recorder on the table and say, "Today is twenty-two May 1989. This is an interview with Stanley Warsaw, governor of New York."

"Do we need to tape this, Mr. Grey?"

"Standard operating procedure, sir."

"Well, for the record, I don't like being taped."

I'm sure you don't. "Most people don't, sir. But it is best to get your statement on tape, so no one is misrepresented." I smile at him. He does not smile back. "So, as you know, we are investigating the disappearance of Elizabeth Jacobs and Brian Stafford. We have some questions for you."

"Get on with it, son."

"When did you first hear about this case, Governor?"

He looks thoughtful. "Dr. Peter Garth contacted me when his daughter went missing."

"Had you met Dr. Garth before?"

"Yes."

"Did Dr. Garth file a missing person's report?"

"I don't know."

"You didn't recommend he do that?"

"I don't recall."

"Would it be normal to refer a person to the police if a constituent called about a missing family member?"

"It would be, normally, but when you have a prominent surgeon and pediatrician with a missing teenage daughter, I may not have done that."

"Why not?"

"He was upset and angry. He'd been to his daughter's school and had an unsavory experience there."

"What did he tell you about this unsavory experience?"

"That the school staff was not forthcoming, and he believed Elizabeth Jacobs knew more about his daughter's disappearance than she told him. He told me after Lydia saw her, Lydia disappeared, that Elizabeth Jacobs was the last person to see her."

"Did you know Lydia, sir?"

The governor pauses.

"Let me reframe the question, sir. Had you met Lydia before?"

"Yes."

"Where did you meet her, sir?"

"I don't remember."

"At Dr. Garth's house? At a political gathering? On the

street? At a club?"

"I met her at their house. Dr. Garth had a fundraising event there."

"Did you talk to Lydia?"

"I did. I talked to a lot of people that night. I met his older daughter, Isabelle, and his wife, MaryLou."

"You hadn't met any of them before?"

He hesitates slightly. "I may have met Lydia before. Dr. Garth was very involved in my campaign. He may have brought his daughter to some of the events."

"Which daughter?"

"Lydia."

"Not Isabelle?"

"No."

"Why Lydia and not Isabelle?"

"Isabelle has some developmental delays. She's a beautiful girl, but her intellectual faculties are less than normal."

"Dr. Garth was ashamed of Isabelle?"

"I don't know."

"Would you have been?"

"No."

A simple no.

"So, Mr. Grey, what does any of this have to do with Elizabeth Jacobs?"

"Good point, sir. After Elizabeth Jacobs was convicted of murdering Lydia Garth, did you sign an order committing her to the all-men's prison in Cape Vincent, New York under Warden Arthur Stafford?"

"No."

"Who assigned her there, sir?"

"The judge."

"Judge Corelli?"

"Yes."

"He tells me he did not assign her there."

The governor is quiet.

"If he didn't assign her there, then who could have?"

"I don't know."

"You were not asked to assign her there, sir?"

"No."

I take out the paper from David Drysden's file. "Is this your signature, sir?"

"What is this?"

"Is this your signature, sir?"

"Yes, but I never signed this."

"You've never seen this piece of paper, sir? Let me remind you. You probably don't want to perjure yourself."

"Where did you get this?"

"Did you sign this paper, sir, authorizing Elizabeth Jacobs to be put into the Cape Vincent Men's Prison?"

"I'm not going to say any more without my lawyer being present. Will you leave me a copy of this paper?"

"Will do. I'll be calling to set up another appointment with you and your lawyer. If you have anything else relevant to the case that you want to tell me, you can call me." He stares at me. "This isn't going away, Governor."

I call Robert after the interview.

"The governor stopped the interview after I showed him the order with his signature on it for Elizabeth Jacobs to be admitted to Cape Vincent Men's Prison. I placed it on the table. He looked scared, boss man."

"He should be. The shit's about to hit the fan and he's at the center of it."

"Looks like someone did not destroy this paper, much

to his surprise and dismay."

"Let's set up another interview with him and his lawyer and see what he's willing to tell us."

"How was The Warden?"

"Predictably belligerent. He's hiding something."

"They're all hiding something. I just don't know what it is."

"We'll get to it. Patience."

"It works every time."

ALICE

We sail through customs in Auckland, New Zealand. We rent a car and drive thirty-one miles to Waiuku, a town with 2500 people right on the Waiuku River in the Awhitu District. Waiuku reminds us of home, a small town on a river. We rent a room in a boarding house for a couple of nights so we can explore the area. In the morning the owner, Norma Lanson, makes breakfast for all the guests and we sit at a big round table. We have a normal conversation with the patrons who are mostly New Zealanders on vacation. They recommend places to visit.

That first day we find a green Subaru Forester and buy it. We make a trip back to the airport in Auckland and return our rental car. On the second day we go into the local realty office and see pictures of houses and land for sale. Three places look promising. The first two do not pan out.

Marcia, the realtor, tells us, "Hickory Farm went up for

sale today. Go take a look. See what you think."

After lunch we head out to Hickory Farm. When we turn down Hatton Road we see stunning views of Manukau Harbour with a distant view of Auckland. The farms are well tended and have abundant acreage. At the end of the dirt road we come to the mailbox with HICKORY printed on it, so we know we're in the right place. We drive onto the property, and a man, a woman, and a dog come outside.

"Lost, are ya?" asks the man.

"No," both of us say together.

Mason adds, "Marcia told us your place was for sale. She suggested we come and take a look."

"You're American?"

"Yes. We're planning to emigrate here."

"So you've been to New Zealand before?"

"No. This is our first time."

"And you're wanting to buy?"

"Yes," we both say together.

The four of us laugh.

And that's how our friendship with Austin and Lucy begins. They want to sell their house and property, and we want to find and buy a home. They invite us into their house, and we sit at their kitchen table. We have coffee, bread and cheese, Nutella, and honey.

"We already sold our cattle," says Austin. "We've bought a place in town."

"How long have you lived here?" I ask.

"Seventy years," Austin says.

"Your family owned the land?"

"My dad bought it when it was scrub land. He started with thirteen cows. I was two when we moved here. Lucy and I bought it from my parents when we got married. Raised our three kids here."

"Do you have children?" Lucy asks.

"No," I say quickly. I do not add that we haven't even had sex.

The talk moves to emigration and why we want to settle in New Zealand. They ask what we're planning to do.

"I'm a midwife. I hope to set up a practice." I don't say I'm a writer.

Lucy says, "Perfect timing. Allison Cooper has been our local midwife for years. She's been looking for someone to take her practice temporarily, maybe permanently. Her mother's dying, so Allison's moving back to the South Island to take care of her."

"No one's offered to take on her practice?"

"Not the last I heard. If they did, she must not have found them right. She and her husband are coming here today for supper. We thought you were them. Stay for supper. You'll want to meet them."

Mason and I sit at the table when Austin, Lucy, and their dog Sky go out to greet the midwife and her husband.

I say to Mason, "This is it."

"Yes," he says. "We've found our home."

He takes my hand, holds it, then brings it to his lips and kisses it. I don't know that Lucy sees this intimate gesture until later that night.

Before we leave Lucy tells me, "I'm happy you want to buy our home. You are the right ones."

"How do you know that?" I ask.

"I feel the love you have for our home, and the love between you and Mason."

So that's how it happened. When things are right, the universe aligns and everything falls quickly and easily into place.

23 May 1989
Tuesday
Cape Vincent, New York
19:30

PETER
GARTH

The Warden, The Governor, The Judge, The Detective, and The Accountant arrive on time for the emergency meeting that I set up the day before. I didn't want to meet, but I knew it was time. I called Eli and told him not to bring the girls on Tuesday, that I'd see him on Friday.

As we get settled in our seats, MaryLou brings us snacks and pours each man the drink of his choice. After she shuts the door, I quietly begin.

"I got three phone calls on Monday about the FBI's investigation of the Elizabeth Jacobs case. Leon called first and said there was a breach and that the FBI was looking into her case. Let's talk about what's going on."

The Warden and The Governor start talking at the same time. The Governor prevails.

"I'm pissed off that one of you didn't destroy my order

to send Elizabeth Jacobs to Cape Vincent's Men's Prison. We had an agreement to do that, but one of you didn't do it. When that FBI man pushed it across the table at me and I saw what it was I stopped the interview and told him I would not talk to him without my lawyer present. I don't have a fucking lawyer."

The Warden says, "They pushed it across the table at me, too, and it took everything I had to not turn over the table and hurt the FBI guy. Who didn't destroy it?"

"It would be nice to find someone to blame," The Judge says. "But at this point it doesn't matter. They have the document, and we need to come up with a joint plan to handle the situation."

Detective Valentino says, "I haven't been formally interviewed by the FBI. I gave them my file on Elizabeth Jacobs. I did everything by the book. My documentation is tight. I don't think we have anything to worry about. They think I'm on their team."

"How are we going to deal with this?" The Governor asks.

The Accountant says, "We need to hire different lawyers from the same law firm. I do the books for Parsons, James, and Williams. They're a reputable firm. I'll call them tomorrow. I think we should shut down The Club until the FBI completes their interviews and things calm down."

"Harry, I am not shutting down The Club," I say. "I am not going to be bullied by the FBI. I do not believe we are in any danger. Business as usual is the best plan. After I hear from you tomorrow, Harry, I will contact each one of you. I don't want any of you to do any more unplanned interviews."

Detective Valentino says, "I agree."

The Governor, The Warden, and The Judge agree to not participate in any more FBI interviews until they get legal counsel. They decide to not come to The Club until they have spoken to a lawyer.

I tell them, "I don't like your decision. There's no indication that the FBI has any knowledge of The Club. Business as usual is the best policy."

The Judge says, "We need to protect ourselves, Peter. Parsons, James, and Williams is a reputable firm, and they will give us the best advice. I'm ready to hire a legal team. It's likely we're going to need one."

After we make a plan, MaryLou comes in with a platter of meats, cheeses, and cookies, something to satisfy everyone. Her timing is impeccable. For the first time in a long time I feel a stirring in my groin for her.

As I listen to The Men talk and laugh, I want to ensure that my name does not come up. I have told myself that if Lydia, my little bitch of a daughter, is found, she won't talk. And whether she talks or not, when I find her, I will make her pay. I will kill her, but first I will torture her and destroy every inch of her femaleness.

After the men leave, I go to MaryLou's bedroom and have sex with her. I haven't touched her in a long time. It feels good to have her suck my cock and come in her mouth.

24 June 1989
Saturday
Waiuku, New Zealand
15:00

ALICE

After we put in our offer and the house is in escrow, we spend a week helping Austin and Lucy pack up seventy years of stuff, seventy years of life. We hear stories about their family and the land. We meet their daughter and two sons who drop in to see the Americans who are buying their childhood home. We take breaks and walk down to the harbor and swim.

Lucy takes me to her large, abundant garden. I plan to continue working this plot of land. I will add strawberries, potatoes, and more tomatoes. Lucy approves. She's happy for me, yet I sense her deep sadness.

In the evenings the four of us sit by the firepit and watch the lights twinkle across the harbor. We talk. They tell us they are selling their farm because Lucy is sick. She has a rare kind of cancer that has no known cause or cure. Lucy is dying. She and Austin are sad to leave their home, but they have weathered many storms in their long marriage and will now deal with their grief about Lucy's illness and leaving their land. They've known each other since they were fifteen years old.

Life is full of loss. I think about my parents, my brother and sister, Alexandria Bay, Cape Vincent, and the St. Lawrence River. Home for so many years. I think about prison and how when I was walking to my death, I was actually beginning a new life. Now, less than a week later, here I am. Here we are, in New Zealand.

We say our good-byes to the Hickorys as we prepare to explore the South Island for the next three weeks. We are taking a vacation, but mostly we leave to let Austin and Lucy be in their home and say their proper farewells. Austin doesn't feel like he needs that. He's the extrovert. Lucy tells me she wants to be there by herself, with her husband, and Sky.

Lucy says, "Sky won't like town. He needs to run. Would you be willing to adopt him?"

"Yes. We love him. Mason and I planned to ask if we could keep him here for you."

We stay at the boarding house in Waiuku for three more days and start the emigration process. We fill out paperwork and talk to officials. We tell them we do not like the political situation and the disintegration of the American family in the United States. I tell them I'm a midwife and a high school counselor, and that I oversaw the school's physical education program. Mason tells them he's a carpenter. We have skills. We can be of service to their country. I don't know if any of this matters. We don't know if filling out these papers will lead to permanent residency, yet we move forward. We act as if we know New Zealand is our home.

We say our good-byes to Norma and Kent, the owners of the boarding house. Norma prepares a delicious meal, and the guests celebrate our bon voyage. Norma gives me a journal that a Maori woman made and tells me to keep track of all our adventures. Kent gives us a homemade sign that says *The MacFarlands*. The generosity of these New Zealanders warms my wounded soul.

SECTION 2

EMMA

24 June 1989
Saturday
Santa Fe, New Mexico
10:00

EMMA

As soon as all the students take their seats, Professor Johnson reads us an article from *The New York Times*.

THE PRISONER AND THE EXECUTIONER:
THE GREAT ESCAPE

On May 17, 1989, prisoner Elizabeth Jacobs, a school counselor and midwife, missed her 11:00 a.m. execution at the Men's Prison in Cape Vincent, New York. At 11:10 a.m., a guard informed the warden, Arthur Stafford, that the prisoner and the executioner had not come to the death chamber. Immediately, Warden Stafford knew something was wrong because his son, the executioner, Brian Stafford, was never late. When a guard discovered an electrical outage in Cell Block Z, Warden Stafford called Sam Davis, a local electrician, who restored the electricity twenty-four hours later. When Mr. Davis and his son entered Cell Block Z, it was empty. Mr. Davis's son, who assisted his father, told us, "It was gruesome and eerie. Like a tomb, utter quiet with a lack of fresh air and daylight. All three cells and the glass guard station were locked. Two of the cells had bare mattresses on the floor. The third had a neatly made cot with a brown blanket and a pillow with a dirty white pillowcase. The bookcase was full of books by Camus, Thoreau, Emerson, Buddha, and Rumi."

Local Cape Vincent law enforcement and the FBI, led by Agent Robert McCauley, concur that Brian Stafford planned and carried out Elizabeth Jacobs's escape from Cell Block Z, an underground cell where death row inmates are usually housed two to four weeks before they are executed. New York law states that prisoners cannot be held underground for more than one month. In the thirty years that the prison has been in operation, no inmate has been housed in Z for more than thirty days. Ms. Jacobs resided in Z her entire incarceration of three years and nine months. Prison advocates have now taken on her cause, the injustice of her case.

Elizabeth Jacobs was convicted of murdering Lydia Garth, a fifteen-year-old girl and daughter of a prominent Cape Vincent surgeon and pediatrician Dr. Peter Garth, and his wife, MaryLou. Miss Garth's older sister, Isabelle, who says she misses her little sister, was at a residential school in Cape Cod for children with intellectual challenges when Lydia disappeared.

Limited and controversial evidence surround this case. Many people do not believe that Elizabeth Jacobs committed any crime. She is a known children's rights advocate who helped abused children. Dr. Garth believed

Elizabeth Jacobs had something to do with his daughter's disappearance as she was the last known person to see Lydia. He identified his daughter's burnt body by a chipped front tooth, and Lydia was cremated soon after his identification. Medical personnel tell us this female body was burnt beyond recognition. Detective Serge Valentino tried and failed three times to get a warrant to search Elizabeth Jacobs's house. Eventually, Judge Leon Corelli signed the search warrant and Charlie Thomas, a deputy with the Cape Vincent PD, found Lydia Garth's locket at the back of Ms. Jacobs's dresser drawer. They arrested and transported her to the county jail. Ms. Jacobs claimed she was innocent and had been set up. Her lawyer, David Drysden, believed his client was innocent. He visited her one time in prison and was scheduled to return. Instead, he and his family disappeared after he told friends and colleagues that he had been threatened. We do not know his whereabouts at this time.

Elizabeth Jacobs was this prison's first and only female inmate. The New York State Prison Board approved an emergency order to house up to five women in a men's prison if the women's prison was overcrowded. Governor Stanley Warsaw signed the order.

What is happening in Cape Vincent now?

Warden Stafford continues to run Cape Vincent Men's Prison. Judge Leon Corelli refuses to confirm that he signed Detective Serge Valentino's search warrant. Governor Stanley Warsaw denies that the emergency legislation he signed to put women in an all-male correctional facility has anything to do with the Elizabeth Jacobs case. However, The New York Times has documentation that there were available beds at the women's prison and that Miss Jacobs could have been housed there. Detective Serge Valentino states that his search of Elizabeth Jacobs's residence and her subsequent arrest was done by the book. He continues to work for the Cape Vincent Police Department under Police Chief Bob Bruce.

Lawyers we have talked to about the Elizabeth Jacobs case say her conviction is weak, especially for a death-row inmate. The FBI currently presides over this case and FBI Investigator Robert McCauley is unwilling to provide any information at this time due to the ongoing investigation. Ms. Jacobs's parents told us their daughter was railroaded and they do not know why. On her execution day, they were waiting in line to meet with her at 10:00 a.m. as the warden's secretary called them the night before and told them Warden Stafford approved a visit. Previously, Warden Stafford had denied their requests to visit their daughter even though Ms. Jacobs's parents had the appropriate paperwork.

Her parents told us it is not illegal for the warden to deny visitation to a family member, although it is unusual. On record, Warden Stafford has denied only one parental visitation in the past thirty years. That denial was due to a recent act of violence committed by the prisoner in question. At this time, Warden Stafford refuses to talk with the media.

Ms. Jacobs's parents have provided letters they wrote to, and received from, their daughter during her incarceration. The New York Times will publish them. They did not tell us who helped facilitate this correspondence, or how the letters got in and out of the prison. They are begging anyone who has seen their daughter to come forward. They do not know where she is or if she is still alive.

In a case where there is missing information as well as missing people, what is at stake here? We know Ms. Jacobs and Brian Stafford crossed the border in Vermont using the aliases Wendy and Wendell Falls, posing as a married couple. They spent the night in Toronto and got on a flight to Frankfurt, Germany on the morning of Thursday, May 18, just before electricity was restored to Cell Block Z. The Falls spent one night in Frankfurt, and now the trail is cold and their whereabouts unknown.

We are asking anyone who has any information to contact Craig Alden or Lisa Graves at The New York Times, *212-555-9675, or Robert McCauley at 202-555-7463.*

Professor Johnson looks up and says, "We have an interesting case here, folks. The lack of information regarding Elizabeth Jacobs's conviction is suspect. There are lots of loose threads. Throughout history, innocent people have been convicted and put to death. Sometimes, the real killer or the underlying reason for the innocent person's conviction remains unknown. It's been five weeks since the prisoner and the executioner escaped. We do not know if they are alive or dead. I've divided you into five work groups. I want you to develop a strategy of how you would proceed with this case. Papers and presentations are due in a month. Make sure you get a copy of the newspaper article as you leave."

I stay in my seat, stunned. I don't know how I was able to sit and listen to the entire article and Professor Johnson's words about capital punishment and a failed judicial system. In shock, I quietly watch my fellow students talk excitedly about the case—my death.

Claudia runs up to me. "We're in the same group,

Emma. This is a really interesting case."

I stare at her.

"Are you alright?" she asks.

"I've been better. I'll catch up with you later. I'm meeting my mom for lunch."

Claudia hugs me and walks away. She doesn't know that I was once Lydia Garth.

I walk quickly to the restaurant to meet my mom. I am overwhelmed. *I didn't trust anyone when I came to Santa Fe four years ago. Theo and Frank taught me how to trust. They took me in and walked me through many complicated situations. Theo shared her experience, strength, and hope, and Frank showed me how to develop plans and solutions so I did not stay stuck in the problem. Theo and Frank showed me that parents can be good. I love them.*

Miss Jacobs helped me. She saved me. She went to prison for killing me while I've been living my life as Emma Maxwell. She paid a big price. I am obviously not dead. Lydia may have died, but Emma has been transformed.

I get to Riva's and find an outside table. When my mom arrives, I hand her the article from *The New York Times.* As she reads it, she takes my hand.

She finishes the article and says, "I'm going to call your dad." She squeezes my hand and leaves the table.

When she returns, she says, "Your dad is on his way. He'll be here in half an hour."

"Mom, I didn't know Miss Jacobs was convicted of killing me. I'm not dead, Mom."

"Nope. You're very much alive."

"I need to do something."

"What are you thinking, Emma?"

"I want to call Robert McCauley and let him know I'm

alive. I have to. It's the right thing to do."

"Yes. It is the right thing to do."

"I don't want to go back to Cape Vincent. I don't want to see Peter and MaryLou. I don't want Peter to know I'm alive. MaryLou knew I was being abused and did nothing, Mom. She protected Isabelle, which I'm glad for, but she fed me to the wolves. It was so ugly."

My dad walks in and gives me a giant bear hug. "Oh, baby. I'm so sorry this is happening."

"Dad, what do you think I should do?"

"What have you and Mom been talking about?"

"I want to call Robert McCauley. I don't want to go to Cape Vincent. Can you call Mr. McCauley and see if that's possible?"

"Let's call him from my office."

When we get to my dad's office, he calls the FBI. Mr. McCauley is not there. My dad tells the secretary, Sally Reynolds, it is urgent and asks for Mr. McCauley to call him back as soon as possible. The three of us eat lunch and wait. Mr. McCauley does not call. I go home with my mom and leave a message for Claudia that I'm staying with my parents for the next few days. I'm anxious, so I take a hike.

Robert McCauley calls during dinner. My dad puts the call on speaker, and we introduce ourselves.

"I got your message that you have information about Lydia Garth."

My dad says, "My daughter's name is Emma Maxwell. She doesn't go by Lydia Garth anymore, hasn't for the last four years."

"You're telling me Lydia Garth is alive?"

"I'm telling you that Emma Maxwell, who used to be Lydia Garth, is very much alive."

Mr. McCauley pauses, then says, "I want to come to Santa Fe tomorrow and interview Emma on Friday."

My dad asks me, "Are you ready to meet with Mr. McCauley on Friday afternoon?"

"I'm scared, Dad. I want you and Mom to be there."

"Of course we'll be there, honey. The three of us will walk through this together. Mr. McCauley? Yes. Let's meet at my office at two o'clock on Friday."

He continues the call with Mr. McCauley while my mom and I make tea.

After my dad gets off the phone, the three of us sit down with our tea to talk.

"I never thought I'd ever have to go back to Lydia's life again. I thought I was completely done with her."

Mom says, "Sometimes we're asked to revisit an old identity again. You want to help Miss Jacobs. You have an opportunity to do that now."

"I want to expose The Basement Club. I've had dreams about doing that since I left Cape Vincent. These last few months I've dreamt about the abuse. I want to help other girls who've been harmed. I wish I was older and further along in my healing, but apparently the time is now."

"We don't always get to pick the time."

"You told me how confusing it was for you to be Charlene Stevens, Theo Sullivan, then Theo Maxwell when you married Dad. I've been Lydia Garth, Emma Walker, and now Emma Maxwell."

"Oh, my darling girl. I love you so much."

When I look at my father, he's got tears in his eyes.

24 June 1989
Saturday
Cape Vincent, New York
19:00

ROBERT
MCCAULEY

I call Connor.

"I'm off to Santa Fe tomorrow afternoon. Lydia Garth has risen from the dead. Her new name is Emma Maxwell. She's been living in Santa Fe for the past four years with her adoptive parents, Frank and Theo Maxwell. Frank's a lawyer, Theo's an artist. They're sexual abuse advocates, and over the years they've provided refuge to girls who've been sexually abused. They adopted Emma two years ago. I'll meet with the parents in the morning to confirm the conditions under which Emma will meet. I told Frank that she was nineteen and that it was her decision. His response was, 'If you want to talk with her, you'll agree to the conditions that she authorized me to formalize with you. She has a history of violent childhood sexual abuse. If you know anything about that kind of abuse, you know there is often stunting of the normal growth process. She's a young nineteen-year-old who's done a lot of work on herself. My wife and I will protect her the best we can from being re-traumatized. Our job at this point is to help her keep herself safe. Your call, Mr. McCauley. I will fax you her conditions. If you can't agree with them, she will not meet with you.'"

Connor agrees. "If what he says is true about her being a sexual abuse survivor, her parents are understandably protective. I like that. It seems like a normal response. It would certainly be what I would do if something happened to Ana."

"Things are opening up."

"We just got a big gift. I'll wait until you've talked with Emma to set up interviews with Dr. and Mrs. Garth."

"Sounds good."

"Have a good trip. Should be interesting to see Lydia rise from the dead."

"Yes. Talk to you tomorrow from Santa Fe. You can get my motel information from Sally."

25 June 1989
Sunday
Santa Fe, New Mexico
3:13

EMMA

I struggle as the noose around my neck gets tighter. I can't catch my breath. My breathing is shallow. Am I going to die?

I wake up drenched in sweat. My heart pounds. My bright red T-shirt with *tomboy* in white letters is sopping wet. I begin to shiver. I pull it off as I get out of bed and put on sweats and a different shirt. My sheets are soaked through. I strip the bed and go to the chair where I've put two extra sets of neatly folded clean linens. I don't want to disturb my parents. I don't want them worrying about me any more than they already are.

Robert McCauley arrives today. My dad wrote a contract with strict terms that Mr. McCauley said he would sign. This is supposed to keep me safe, but I don't trust it. I want to, but my old trust issues have surfaced, like fast-churning, roiling water where I can't find a place to put my feet, can't steady myself. I'm off balance, floundering.

I don't like this. Mom comforted me and acknowledged all the work I've done. *You are a sexual abuse trauma survivor. With this new information about Miss Jacobs spending three years and nine months in prison because she killed you, you are triggered, perhaps re-traumatized. How could you not be?*

I've stepped back into Lydia's body. I thought I had left this girl behind, the fearful one, the terrified one, the one who wore a mask because if she didn't she would be harmed. I was the prize possession. I made Peter lots of money. I can only imagine how angry he was when I disappeared.

I am wide awake. I am fifteen years old again. I am in Miss Jacobs's office. I silently put myself down for not leaving, as if a fifteen-year-old girl should be able to walk away from an abusive father and a neglectful, complicit mother. I tell myself someone stronger than me would have already walked away. But I have nowhere to go, nobody to go to. All I can envision is a life on the streets of New York City and I don't want that. I am young. I have skills to satisfy men sexually, to pretend to want to satisfy them, and to pretend I like them. Sex is like clockwork to me. Tick-tock. Tick-tock. I can make men come. I let them touch me any way they want. I witness what they do and what I do. I watch the scene from the ceiling. I act like I am present, but they don't care if I really am. They care that I treat them right and act like I care. But I don't care about them.

I fall back to sleep nestled in my dry sheets and cotton blanket. I wake up with a start. I hear Peter's voice.

Men are in charge. Women are lesser beings, Lydia. They

don't matter. Women are here to serve men. They have our babies. Men control the world.

But women are smart too, Daddy.

They can be, but their job is to make men happy. Women come second.

Can I make you happy, Daddy?

He pushes my head down and comes in my mouth. My training has begun.

My mom knocks on my door and asks, "Emma, do you want French toast for breakfast?"

"Yes, please."

"One or two poached eggs?"

"Two. I'm going to jump in the shower."

"Okay, honey. See you downstairs."

25 June 1989
Sunday
Santa Fe, New Mexico
7:17

THEO

As I make breakfast, I think about when Emma first arrived. At the airport we told her we lived in Santa Fe, about an hour's drive from Albuquerque. She was quiet and stared out the window.

That first day I oriented her to the house. I took her to her bedroom and showed her the bathroom. I showed her clean clothes in her dresser that she could wear and let her know that we would go shopping so she could pick clothes that she liked and felt comfortable in. She thanked me. I asked if she was hungry, and she said she was but wondered if she could take a shower first. I told her I would be downstairs in the kitchen making lunch. After lunch, I took her to the art studio and gave her dedicated space. I told her no one would enter her space unless she invited them. She thanked me for this space. I watched her sit and stare out the large window at the mountains.

I showed her hiking trails she could access right out

the back door. We hiked together the very first day. We talked about how the desert was a unique ecosystem and that it was important to carry an abundance of water, that it was a life-and-death issue.

Emma asked, *Is it safe to walk here alone?*

Yes, but in the desert I always keep aware of my surroundings. I'm mostly concerned about big cats and snakes.

Not people?

No. I've only run into one person out here, and that was many years ago. He was backpacking through these mountains and was as surprised to see me as I was to see him.

After that, Emma began to hike by herself. She waved good-bye to me when she left and let me know when she was home. She usually hiked for an hour or two. I didn't ask her about her hikes. I waited for her to take the lead on what she wanted to share.

People who have been violated have a great need for private space. I see this need in every girl who comes to us. They do not trust that their space will be sacrosanct, that they have a right to privacy, that they can say no, yes, maybe, or I don't know, I don't want to. Refusing to do something has not been an option. She reminded me of myself. I was a quiet kid, too.

Three days after she arrived, we went to the high school and enrolled her. She integrated into the school system in less than three months and always went to school. She was a trooper and a good student. Three months after being here, Emma approached me with some news.

I got invited to a party. I don't know if I want to go.

Why wouldn't you go?

Parties mean sex and drugs.

What kind of party is it?

Claudia's fifteenth birthday party. She's invited her family and friends.

Did she invite other boys and girls from school?

Yes, but she said it was mostly a family party. What's a family party?

Well, it could be her parents and grandparents and maybe aunts, uncles, and cousins, plus a few friends. People sit around talking, laughing, and celebrating an event together.

I wouldn't say Claudia and I are friends.

What is a friend?

She was quiet, then she said, *Someone I can trust.*

Do you trust Claudia?

As far as I know her. She seems nice, but how do I know if I can trust her?

Oh, honey, there's no knowing for sure.

The party goes from noon until five.

If you want to go, Frank and I can drop you off and come get you anytime. All you have to do is call us when you're ready to come home. I can also meet her mom or talk to her on the phone if you want me to.

Emma stared at me. *That seems like something someone younger would need. I'm fifteen.*

If you were younger, I would call the parents to check things out. At your age I can call or not call, your decision.

It's hard to know what to do.

It can be confusing.

What do you know about it?

I used to be Charlene Stevens. Then, for years, I was

Theo Sullivan. When I married Frank, I took his last name. I've been Theo Maxwell ever since. I was confused with all my name changes. The question I asked myself was, who am I?

You were taken out of your home?

I was. My father and mother were abusing me. Mrs. Gardner at my Sunday school helped me get out.

Emma looked at me. *How old were you?*

Thirteen.

Emma nodded and said, *I'm going to go work on my collage now.*

Sounds good. Can I bring you some lemonade?

Emma nodded.

At breakfast Emma tells me, "I had a dream about being in Miss Jacobs's office the day I left."

"What do you think about that?"

"Miss Jacobs was kind and gentle. She didn't push too much, but she didn't back off, either. She told me, 'Whatever is happening to you, whoever is hurting you has no right to do this. Adults have no right to harm or take advantage of children. An adult's job is to protect, guide, and steer a young person in the direction of the child's choosing, to be interested in what the child wants, and then, nurture, nurture, nurture.'"

"She was wise."

"Yes. She knew about abuse and wanted to let me know I had a choice."

"At some point the abuse can no longer be hidden."

"I'm glad you're my mom."

"Me, too, honey. Me, too."

26 June 1989
Monday
Santa Fe, New Mexico
13:30

EMMA

"Hi, Emma. I'm Robert McCauley."

"Hi, Mr. McCauley."

"You can call me Robert."

"I'm more comfortable with Mr. McCauley."

"Okay. I'm glad you called. That took courage."

I stare at him. *Courage? I don't know about that. I feel guilty that Miss Jacobs spent all that time in prison, in solitary confinement, on death row.*

"I'm going to ask you a lot of questions, but I am not trying to overwhelm you. I just want to understand your story. Please answer as honestly and completely as you can, and let me know if anything makes you uncomfortable. Your parents told me you learned about Eliza Jacobs's escape in your criminal justice class."

"Yes. Professor Johnson read the class *The New York Times's* article, 'The Great Escape.' They reported that Lydia Garth was dead. As you can see, I am not dead. No one here knows I was Lydia Garth. I am Emma Maxwell now."

"When did you stop thinking of yourself as Lydia?"

"Soon after I got to Santa Fe. All the people who helped me after I left Cape Vincent called me Emma. It took a bit of getting used to, but I was glad to not be Lydia."

"What was Lydia's life like?"

"I went back and forth between being a tomboy and a sex object."

"What do you mean by 'tomboy'?"

"At home I wore jeans, a sweatshirt, and red Converse tennis shoes or my LL Bean hiking boots. I played in the woods. When I turned ten, I started to hunt with Bobby. We were a good team. He taught me how me to shoot a gun and use a bow and arrow. I was a good huntress. I liked the silence, sitting together in the woods waiting for the deer to come. I loved shooting the bow and arrow. It felt like a fair fight, a duel, like the scale wasn't balanced for me to win automatically."

"You liked hunting?"

"Not really. I didn't like killing animals, but I loved being in the woods. I loved the St. Lawrence River. I could see it from my bedroom window. I loved Lake Ontario. I skated in the winter and swam in the summer."

"So you loved nature, and it gave you a chance to get out of the house?"

"It did. I loved being away from home. I don't know why Peter let me go, but I'm glad he did."

"And then suddenly you were in the desert?"

"Yeah. I was shocked when I first got here. I couldn't believe how hot and bare the land was. I'd never been in the desert before. I love Santa Fe now. There's snow in the mountains and the canyons are beautiful. The hiking is great. There's a couple of lakes nearby where we swim. The desert is my home."

"What about your family in Cape Vincent?"

"I love my older sister, Isabelle. I miss her. I always felt protective of her."

"Why?"

"She had some learning problems and Peter wasn't nice to her."

"How so?"

"He teased her and cut her down, told her he was ashamed of her. He told her so many times, 'Even though you have a good body, you'll never amount to anything.' She sat there and hung her head. He didn't have to slap her or physically touch her. He had complete control over her."

"What did MaryLou do about this?"

"She tried to protect her."

"Did MaryLou protect you?"

"No. She was completely focused on Isabelle and distracted when she was around me. It seemed like she had some kind of a bargain with Peter."

"What kind of bargain?"

"That he wouldn't touch Isabelle if he could have me."

"What do you mean by 'have'?"

I breathe a heavy sigh. "Peter began having sexual contact with me when I was five."

"What kind of sexual contact?"

I turn to my parents. "I've never told you in detail what Lydia endured. I feel protective of you. I told my two therapists, Christy and Jeremy, everything. I don't know if you need or want to hear the specifics."

Mom says, "I'm good to hear anything you want to say, Emma. Think about what *you* need."

Dad says, "We support you, honey. If us being here supports *you*, good. If us waiting outside is what you need, good."

"I'm embarrassed. I still find it unbelievable that someone could do this to their child, or any child, Mr. McCauley."

I look at Mr. McCauley. He sits quietly and looks me right in the eyes. I take a deep breath.

"Peter began grooming me—that's what the therapists call it—when I was five years old. From five to ten I learned and practiced sex with him. At ten I made my debut. Peter gave me a silver locket that night with a picture of him and me inside it. When he put it around my neck, he told me I had to wear it at all times, that it would keep me safe. He dressed me in sexually provocative clothes and put bright red lipstick on me that the men at The Club liked. I was the healthy ten-year-old sex toy. I knew what to do. Peter trained me well. From then on until Miss Jacobs helped me escape, I worked at The Basement Club."

"The Basement Club?"

"The sex club in the basement of our house in Cape Vincent."

"Tell me about The Basement Club."

"The Club entrance was at the back of our house. There was a circular driveway at the front and the back of the house that made coming and going easy. There was also a small parking lot in the back which made it convenient for customers, especially in the winter. The first thing you saw when you entered was a flashing purple neon sign that said, 'The Basement Club.'"

"Who came to The Club?"

"Lots of men came, but there were The Men who came almost every time."

"The Men?"

"The Warden, The Governor, The Judge, The Detective, The Accountant, and Eli."

"Do you know their names?"

"No. They went by titles only."

"No personal names were ever used except for Eli and Peter?"

"That's right."

"Did you ever talk to MaryLou about The Club? Surely she must have known about it."

"I tried to one time, but she wouldn't talk to me about it."

"Did MaryLou ever come into The Club?"

"Not when I was there. She stayed upstairs."

"How do you know she was part of the workings of The Club?"

"One time I got home early from school and heard her on the phone talking about a shipment of girls. She told me she helped girls come to the United States to further their education, but when I heard the word 'shipment' I knew she was helping Peter get more girls for The Club."

"Before you heard that conversation, you believed her?"

"Yes. Then I snooped around her office and looked at her files. The girls were enrolled in different schools, usually in pairs. A week later, Katya, Maja, and Misha arrived at The Club. They looked haunted."

"Were any other family members involved?"

"I don't think so. Peter didn't like his brother or his

family. MaryLou invited them to family functions, but Peter did not invite his brother to The Club. My aunt Cynthia, MaryLou's sister, did not have any involvement."

"Did MaryLou know The Men?"

"Yes. She knew them."

"So you had contact with The Men outside The Club?"

"Yes. That was a weird thing. The Men and the police chief would come to our family events. My birthday's in the summer. They'd bring presents. My uncle and his family would come, too. We played horseshoes and croquet and swam in the river. There wasn't any sex. But two nights later The Men would come to The Club and grope me. I had to make them come in whatever way they wanted. Eli never had sex with me or any of the girls. Nadia told me when The Accountant took her into the cave room she never got undressed. They talked about her life in the Ukraine. Nadia said no girls reported having sex with him. The police chief never came to The Club. I always wondered about that."

"Do you think he knew about The Club?"

"I don't think so, but I don't really know."

"Do you think any of their wives knew about The Club?"

"I don't know. I doubt it. None of their children were in the ring."

"When was The Club open?

"Three nights a week, Tuesday, Friday, and Saturday. Although sometimes individual men came on other days by special appointment for a one-to-one session."

"Did you have one-to-one sessions?"

"Sometimes, but mostly Peter wanted me for himself. I think the times he let other men have me were when he couldn't pass up the large amount of money he was offered."

"How much would that have been?"

"I heard ten thousand dollars one time."

"Where did the sex take place?"

"In the open, at the tables and on one of the two stages. If a man wanted privacy, he took a girl into a room in the caves."

"A room in the caves?"

"Yes. Cape Vincent has an extensive cave system. There was a door in the corner next to the bar where men could take you into the cave rooms."

"How did that work?"

"The men would pay Eli to use the private rooms in the caves. They paid a fee when they came into The Club which allowed them to drink and have sex in the open with any girl they wanted, except for me."

"Who's Eli?"

"The man who brought the eastern European girls to The Club."

"He drove them?"

"Yes. They came in a van. One time when I was running late, I watched them from my window. I was careful. Peter would have been angry if he knew I saw the van. It had a New York license plate that started with Z-Q-X-three. I can't remember more than that. I got spooked because I heard MaryLou in the hall. She probably thought I was gone. I was supposed to be at The Club before the girls arrived, but I wasn't. I got home from school late that day. I waited until I heard her bedroom door close. Then I went quietly down the back stairs right into the cave."

"How did other girls get there?"

"Some of them came with their fathers. Others came by cab. They always came with presents, like they were coming to a birthday party."

"How do you know the girls came from eastern Europe?"

"Nadia told me. She spoke good English. She told me she was Ukrainian and that the other girls were from Hungary, Czechoslovakia, Romania, Yugoslavia, and Poland."

"Would you recognize Nadia and the other girls if you saw them?"

"I think so. We're older now, but I think I would recognize them."

"Did the cab drivers know about The Basement Club?"

"I don't know."

"What girls went into the caves?"

"Any of us could go, but mostly the men picked the eastern European girls, especially the ones who didn't speak much English."

"Did Peter use the caves?"

"Not usually. He went into them the night before I escaped. He was really angry at Nicole, his favorite girl, a tall thin blonde with large breasts, an older girl who he treated like a wife."

"Did you see her come out?"

"Yes. She had on her plastic face and a bruise on her cheek."

"Plastic face?"

"She never showed any emotion. She kept her distance from the other girls. Most of us made some kind of contact with each other. Nadia and I talked at school. I liked her. We ate lunch together with Paula Langdon."

"You considered Nadia and Paula friends?"

"Nadia, not Paula. In a way, Nadia was the only friend I had."

"Why not Paula?"

"She wasn't there anymore. She couldn't handle the whole sex thing."

"I don't know what that means."

"She couldn't get with the program. We had to have sex with lots of men every time we were at The Club. It was difficult to deal with. It broke her."

"What happened?"

"She started coming to school with her beautiful, long blond hair dirty and stringy. She stopped talking. She had a breakdown at school on a Tuesday, the day before Miss Jacobs helped me escape. I imagine Paula ended up at The Pink Palace."

"What's that?"

"A mental hospital on the St. Lawrence."

"What happened at school?"

"She came out of the girls' bathroom naked with bright red lipstick all over her face and mouth. She ran into the lunch room screaming and talking gibberish. Nadia and I tried to comfort her, but she kept flinging her arms out to keep us back. She didn't calm down until the paramedics gave her a shot. They strapped her to a gurney and took her away. It was horrible."

"Did you and Nadia talk about what happened?"

"Yes. We met in the bathroom after the incident. Nadia told me this would be her last day at school, that she didn't have to monitor Paula anymore."

"Why was Paula being monitored?"

"Peter was afraid she might talk about The Club."

"So, Paula was gone and Nadia would be gone. That must have been hard for you."

"It was. Nadia took off the necklace her mother gave her and gave it to me. She told me her name was Cristina Floznikof, that she was from a small village in the Ukraine, that her parents still lived there as far as she knew. She told me to get out when I could." I take my necklace off and hand it to Mr. McCauley.

"What does this mean?"

"It's Ukrainian. 'Love conquers all.'"

"Were you surprised when she gave this to you?"

"I was. It felt like a good-bye present."

"You lost your friend."

"Yes."

"I'm sorry."

"Me, too, but the next day my opportunity came. Miss Jacobs sent me a call slip, and I went to her office. She asked me how I was doing after Paula's incident. We didn't talk directly about the sexual abuse, but she knew. Less than an hour later I was in a cab. The driver told me he was taking me to a train station in Westchester County and that I would be taken care of by another person after that. I've thought a lot about Nadia since I left Cape Vincent. She crosses my mind almost every day. I wonder if she made it out."

"Emma, what happened to your locket?"

"After The Club that last Tuesday night when I went back to my room, I took off the locket and put it in my nightstand. I wore Nadia's necklace to bed that night and to school the next day. I've worn it every night since I left Cape Vincent."

"You weren't scared Peter would find out you weren't

wearing the locket?"

"I wouldn't see Peter again until Thursday at dinner because he always was away on Wednesday nights. I was planning to exchange the necklaces again after school on Thursday so he wouldn't notice."

"What did Peter do on Wednesday nights?"

"He played poker with The Men."

"Where?"

"At a club in Syracuse. He was gone every Wednesday night. He stayed the night there."

"Did MaryLou like that?"

"We all liked it. Isabelle was home from school. It was one of the times the three of us spent time together and MaryLou actually seemed happy."

"What would you do?"

"Dance, make cookies, watch television. Sometimes Isabelle and I would read plays. MaryLou would be the director. It was fun. We laughed a lot and stayed up late."

"A girls' night."

I smile and nod.

"And then that Wednesday you escaped."

"Miss Jacobs walked me out the back door of the school and I got in a cab. The last thing she said was, 'You will be taken care of every step of the way.' And I was. The driver took me to the train station in Westchester where a woman met me. We took the train to JFK. A different woman met us there. She gave me identification with my new name, Emma Walker. We got on an indirect flight to New Mexico, stopping several times. At every plane change and airport someone met me. I was never left alone. People took care of me. One woman told me the people who helped me were part of a larger group who help victims of sexual abuse. They call themselves The Network."

"You've been living with Theo and Frank ever since?"

"Yes. I lived with them for a year and then they adopted me."

"You're glad to be adopted?"

I smile and look at Theo and Frank. "It's beyond my wildest dreams. I feel lucky. Should I tell him the story, Mom?"

She nods.

"When Theo and Frank wanted to adopt me, I asked myself, 'Why do they want me? Why am I so lucky?' When I didn't hear answers to these questions, I asked Theo, 'Why me? Why not the other girls you've helped?'

"She said, 'We don't know why.'

"'So it has nothing to do with me?'

"Theo said, 'I've tried to figure it out. I've tried to understand, why you, why now, why, why, why. It's a useless question. We heard: adopt her.'

"I said, 'Because you think it would help me?'

"She looked at me and said, 'We want to help you, yes, but we don't need to adopt you to help you. I can make up reasons and try to satisfy whatever you're looking for, but the truth is, Frank and I both heard a voice that said, "Adopt her." It was a surprise to us, too. Usually we take in girls for a year and then they move in with a different family who either adopts them or at the very least keeps them for a number of years. Frank and I are the first stop on the block. We deal with the escape—safety issues, feelings and thoughts about being out of an abusive situation, and the initial re-entry into the world. We create and provide a safe and trusting environment.

"'We were scared at the thought of adopting you, but we knew we needed it.'

"I found this hard to believe. I asked her, 'You were scared?'

"She told me, 'I never wanted to adopt. I never wanted the responsibility of saying "my daughter." You know some of my history. Like you, I was a pawn, my father's plaything and moneymaker. This does not engender trust.'

"I stood there, stiff as a board. I knew Theo understood, and that she would never adopt me if it wasn't right. My defensiveness melted away. I walked into her arms. We held each other. Apparently, she needed a daughter, and I needed a mom.

"She said, 'I'm going to call Frank. I want him to be a part of this.'

"I nodded yes, and that's the simple version of how I became Emma Maxwell, Mr. McCauley."

"Thank you for sharing this with me."

"Thank you for listening. I'm glad something good happened from this horrible abuse."

"I am, too. You are a strong woman to be able to start over."

"Yes, and I've had a lot of therapy, Mr. McCauley, a lot of help. When Professor Johnson read 'The Great Escape' I got triggered. I can't get the time Peter made an example of me out of my mind."

"What happened?"

"At The Club there were always lots of bright lights, noise, and young girls in various stages of undress. We entertained men and did a lot of public foreplay. Then a man picked one of us to have sex with. If it was on one of the stages, we had to watch the sex until the man came.

One time I turned away from watching a man and a girl have sex. Peter yanked me up into the center of the room, slapped me, and stuck his penis in my mouth. I could barely breathe. I thought I was going to die. He kept saying, 'You will never disobey me, you will never disobey me.' Then he came in my mouth. 'My daughter's going to be a good whore, gentlemen. Line up and take her for a test drive.' I never turned away again.

"I learned that usually it was safer when I had sex out in the open. When a man took a girl into a private room it often meant he wanted to do something violent that he did not want other men to see. The girl usually got hurt."

"Did Peter make examples of other girls?"

"Yes, but not like he did with me. Peter wanted me to know he was in total control."

"He told you this?"

"Sometimes, but mostly he showed it by his actions. He was rough with all the girls publicly; the other men were not. Peter would call me over and sit me on his knee. He bounced me and pushed my head down so I could suck him off. He pushed his fingers into my neck and sometimes I teetered on the edge of passing out. He is a sadistic son of a bitch. I once saw him shove a large fake penis inside a new girl, and when she screamed in pain, he shoved the dildo in harder. I saw her terror and watched her pass out. After that, Peter usually gave me drugs before I went into The Club. My only thought was, how can I make it through this and live?"

"Did any other American girls besides Paula Langdon go to your school?"

"No."

"Did her father bring her?"

"I don't know."

"How are you doing, Emma?"

"I don't like remembering any of this. Have you found Miss Jacobs?"

"No. She and Brian Stafford have done a good job disappearing."

"Do you have enough information to arrest Peter and The Men?"

"I'm going to call my office and have them fax me some pictures to see if you can identify any of The Men. I should get them tonight. I'll also have them fax me pictures of girls who we believe are being trafficked. I would like to meet with you tomorrow to show you the pictures and to tie up any loose ends."

"Okay."

"Will ten o'clock work for you?"

"No. I have my criminal justice class in the morning. It's an intensive summer course so I have a limited number of absences."

"How about two o'clock then?"

I look at my parents. They nod yes.

After the interview I go home with my parents. I am surprisingly energized. We sit around the kitchen table and talk while my mom makes dinner. We laugh. I beat them at Scrabble. I am glad they will be there tomorrow when I meet with Mr. McCauley again.

Before I fall asleep, I think about today's interview. It went well. I like Mr. "Call me Robert" McCauley. He's an adult, way older than me, so it would feel wrong to call him Robert. If I was going to call him anything besides Mr. McCauley it would be Mr. FBI Man, but even thinking about that feels disrespectful. I am glad he is here. Will he really help me? I don't know. What would help look like? Finding Nadia, Katya, Maja, Misha, the other girls. I care about all the girls. They matter to me.

26 June 1989
Monday
Santa Fe, New Mexico
18:00

ROBERT
MCCAULEY

I go back to my motel room and order room service. I call
Connor.

"What's up, boss?"

"I faxed you my interview with Emma Maxwell. She
identified a sex trafficking ring called The Basement Club
that operated out of the basement in the Garth house. I
don't know if it's still in existence, but I have no reason to
believe it isn't. Find a judge from outside the Cape Vincent
area to issue a search warrant. We need to get into that
basement. Emma identified a group she calls The Men who
went by title only, just like they do at the prison. I've asked
Sally to fax me pictures of New York governors, wardens,
judges, detectives, and accountants. I have to contact the
Bureau's Sex Crime Unit and have them send me pictures
of eastern European girls and their handlers. Apparently

MaryLou Garth was involved as well. When you've got the warrant for the Garth house, call her and set up an interview."

"A sex trafficking ring in Cape Vincent?" Connor says incredulously.

"Yeah. Makes some sense why the good doctor went after Elizabeth Jacobs. He must have thought she knew something."

"It was Serge Valentino who got the search warrant and arrested her."

"Emma said The Detective came to The Club. It could be Valentino. The police chief came to family functions at their house, but he wasn't involved in The Club. You might want to feel him out about Detective Valentino."

"Will do, boss. Sounds like a productive day."

"Yup. We're moving right along. Talk to you tomorrow."

27 June 1989
Tuesday
Santa Fe, New Mexico
03:13

EMMA

I wake from a dream. Peter and I are fencing. My arm comes up. I block him. He makes himself vulnerable. I am reluctant to go in for the kill. I continue to block and parry.

I hear, *A daughter should not go after her father. A father should be revered.*

I lunge at him and push his torso hard with my foil. I see surprise and shock on his face. He is disturbed. I do not like to disturb anyone. I am the mouse who watches quietly, then scurries into hiding. I am the one who learns the rules and seemingly abides by them.

Peter did not know I talked to Nadia, that we were friends. I wonder if I'll see her picture today. I hope she got out. *Get out when you can.* And I did. Did she have an opportunity? Or was she like MaryLou who didn't leave? I asked myself so many times why MaryLou did not take my sister and me and go. *Do you like being the doctor's wife?* I actually had the gumption to ask her that question. She replied, *Not particularly*. It felt honest, but I didn't know exactly what she meant. I was left with more questions than answers. Did she ever go into The Basement Club and look around when Peter was at work and I was at school? Did she wonder what went on there? How could she not? How could she give me to him? What kind of a woman does that with her child? I know so little about her. *Talk to Isabelle. Isabelle knows MaryLou in a different way. Learning problems do not necessary make for emotional deficits.* My sister was wise and had an uncanny ability to read situations, although we were not particularly close. *Not particularly.*

I wake up from a second dream drenched in sweat and my heart is pounding. I hear, *If you're going to ride a whale, don't sit on the blowhole.* I am on the whale's blowhole when he surfaces and shoots me up and out of a large body of water. I do two summersaults in the air, then land gently on my back in the middle of the water. My fear of sharks immediately rises up. I don't want to be out here with nothing but water all around me. I want to believe the whale will come for me. I want to be saved from my past, from my before, from my parents who didn't act like parents.

In my head and out loud, I don't call Peter and MaryLou mom and dad, mother and father, or my birth parents. It's first names only. I need to maintain a certain amount of psychic space where I have room to breathe, room where I can remember who I am. In the past four years, I have distanced myself from them. Now I am supposed to return to the scene of the crime, go back to my roots? Are you kidding?

The Voice says, *I'm not kidding. I'm offering you a*

deeper level of healing.

I argue. A father is someone who cares about his daughter and would never do what Peter did to me. I hate him.

Perhaps you will face him in prison, have a conversation with him through the glass.

I want to believe he will be convicted, but I don't know if he will be.

What would you say to him?

Why did you harm me? Why did you allow men to use me? Why do you hate women?

The Men were in the business of using and abusing girls. Systematic abuse.

Peter and MaryLou used me, betrayed me, could not do right by me, and could not do right by themselves.

What unrecognized wounds they must have to act like they did.

How can anyone put their child in harm's way over and over again?

I never got an answer.

In Santa Fe I desperately wanted to create a new life. I had no idea how to do this. In therapy, first with Christy, and then later with Jeremy, I talked a lot, cried a lot, was angry a lot. Both therapists told me, *feel, deal, heal.* I learned that intergenerational characteristics and patterns morph and grow, that some of them take root even when you do not want them to, that people find a way to grow in whatever conditions they find themselves. People do what they have to do to survive. They adapt. I adapted.

I used control and my will to focus. When that did not work, I persevered. Peter trained me to be diligent and vigilant, so I had that going for me. I lost myself when I tried to make something work that was unacceptable.

In therapy I discovered where I wanted to focus my energy. I meditated and wrote in my journal every day. Along with hiking and other movement, I developed a structure, albeit a rigid one at times. Rigid was an easier path than loosey-goosey. Later I learned about flexible structures and was able to sluff off some of my old patterns. I began to see when I was doing what I always did, even though I did not want to be doing it anymore. My deeply entrenched patterns have not died easily, have not transformed readily.

I systematically dealt with my past, a past I wish I did not have to claim, a past that is painful to look in the eye, and in many ways—naively, it seems—I thought I was done. And perhaps I was. Ride the whale. Sit on the plateau. Comfortable. Move forward with my life. Move in with Claudia. Move out from Theo and Frank. Be near them, but out. Do what normal nineteen-year-olds do.

I am not a normal nineteen-year-old.

I am a sexual abuse survivor.

All my therapy has not stopped me from wondering, why me? Why did MaryLou give me to Peter? Why didn't she protect me? Isn't a mother-daughter relationship supposed to be sacred? It is with Theo.

Now my old life, my childhood, is in my face again. I want to believe the timing is perfect. I am empowered by my dreams. I went in for the kill. I got Peter. I am clear that I need to testify against him in person. I want to stop him and The Men from hurting other girls.

Before school the next day, I go to my volunteer job at the childcare center on campus. I see the gamut of children—healthy, happy, sad, scared, social, quiet, energetic, talkative, timid, shy. Every week we meet to discuss the children's progress. Most of them are five and six, the same age as when I began my training with Peter. Right now, I don't see that any of them have sexual abuse issues. When a child is depressed, I go on high alert. At the last meeting I talked about Sarah. Others noticed a shift in her, too. Her parents have separated and filed for divorce. I chat with her mom and dad when they come pick her up. Sarah runs to each of them. She does not show the picture she painted to her mom. Sarah is quiet and obedient, and protective of her mom, who is distracted. Her mother tries, but she seems broken. With her dad, Sarah is completely different. She proudly shows him her painting. He swings her and puts her on his shoulders. She laughs and holds on tight. She lands safely. I love hearing her laugh.

I have thought about taking up fencing, but I've only gotten as far as going to the matches at school and talking to Louis about his experience in the sport. He has offered to teach me. I want to learn, but I'm hesitant.

MARYLOU GARTH

When the phone rings, I think it's my sister calling me back. "What's up, Cyn?"

"Um. This is Connor Grey, FBI. Sounds like you were expecting a call from someone else."

"I was."

"I'm calling to set up an interview with you."

"I'm packing right now. I'm going out of town."

"When are you coming back?"

"I don't know."

"How about I come interview you now?"

I pause and say, "Can't it wait?"

"No. I don't think waiting is a good idea, Mrs. Garth. I have some information about your daughter."

"Did something happen to Isabelle?"

"No. It's about Lydia."

I stop packing. "Is she alive?"

"Yes."

I breathe a sigh of relief. "Is she well?"

"She's well."

"Does my husband know?"

"Do you want your husband to know?"

"Not yet."

"Not yet?"

"I'm packing. I'm leaving."

"You're leaving your husband?"

"I'm going to my sister's house."

"Where does she live?"

"What does that matter?"

"We need to interview you, MaryLou."

"My sister just moved. I'm going to help her get settled in."

"Does your husband know you're going?"

"Yes, but he doesn't know Cynthia's moved."

"You don't want him to know?"

"That's right. I don't want him to know."

"Are you afraid he might hurt you?"

I pause. "He'll want to find me, and I don't want to be found."

"You're concerned about your safety."

"Not just mine. Isabelle's and Cynthia's."

"You think your husband's dangerous?"

"He can be."

"Do you think he's dangerous right now?"

"Yes."

"You've seen him hurt people recently?"

"Listen, I need to finish packing. I need to get out of here before he comes home. Can't this wait until tomorrow?"

"No."

"I'm heading to Syracuse. What about meeting there later today?"

"Okay. We'll pick you up."

"No. Tell me the address and time where I should meet you. I don't want my sister involved in this."

"Hold on, let me look up our office there... Two twenty-seven Broadway, Suite C, third floor of an old brick building in an industrial park north of Syracuse. It's a walk-up. Ring the buzzer that says Hiraeth Corp. Is three o'clock okay?"

"That will be fine. I'm concerned about Isabelle. She's at school."

"We've got her covered."

"You can assure me she's safe?"

"Yes. We've got a guard on her twenty-four seven until after we talk and come up with a plan for her and you."

"Okay. Will you let me know if Peter contacts her?"

"We will, but I don't have a number for you."

I sigh.

"I've got a search warrant, MaryLou. I'm waiting for it to be processed and then we're coming to your house right away."

"I'll leave the house unlocked."

"Will you leave the door to The Basement Club unlocked? Otherwise we'll have to break down the door."

"I don't have a key."

"Okay. I'll see you this afternoon in Syracuse."

"Good-bye, Mr. Grey."

"Good-bye, Mrs. Garth."

I finally got the dreaded call that was different than I thought it would be. Lydia is alive.

I look at my beautiful mahogany queen-size bed and the French doors that lead out to a balcony that overlooks green grass all the way down to the St. Lawrence. I finger the mauve comforter and the three-thousand-thread-count, soft, Egyptian cotton sheets. I love this room. I love the fine linens. I love being rich. I never want to be poor again.

However, the trappings of the comforter and the sheets no longer bring me peace of mind. I will miss this house, this land, the river. I pray, something I haven't done in a long time. *God, help me.* It's a simple prayer, nothing fancy. It takes me back to my childhood, going to church on Sunday where my family sat together in the pew. My father was scrubbed clean from his drunken stupor of the night before. My family appeared normal. I had a moment of solace.

But there is something else. I don't want to be a hostage in my own life anymore. Since Lydia's disappearance, the escape of The Executioner and The Prisoner, and now the FBI involvement, things are heating up. Peter and I have not talked about the case. Why would we? Since Lydia disappeared we have barely spoken. Peter is drinking more. Two nights ago I heard a girl's bloodcurdling scream. Usually the insulation works to keep the violence at bay, but it didn't work that night. I can no longer justify staying.

I made my decision to leave Peter. He's been on edge and is spending more and more time in The Basement Club. We have a long-term agreement that he doesn't touch Isabelle, and so far, he's abided by that. But I know my husband. I've been on the receiving end of his sexual predatoriness, his complete disregard and hatred for women. The last time he hurt me I didn't leave even though I thought I was going to die. I chose the money, the lifestyle, and the power that comes from being the doctor's wife. He hasn't hurt me in a long time.

The media is all over the missing prisoner and executioner case. Now that Lydia is alive, my husband will certainly be interviewed. He trusts I won't talk. He believes I am loyal. He has no reason to not believe this. I have stayed. I know all the players. Their wives don't know anything, at least they've never said anything to me. Some of them have asked me if I like having poker night at my house once a month—and sometimes more if The Men have necessary business to discuss. I've played it off as the servile wife who likes to take care of her husband and his friends. My role is clear. I am the doctor's good wife. I am a proponent of children's rights.

Peter got me on the board of an organization that raises money for poor eastern European girls to come to the United States to get educated. The organization really is a feeder system for my husband's sex trafficking ring. Does he think I'm stupid? Probably. I've played stupid. He asked me recently if the FBI had contacted me. I said no. *If they do, you need to let me know immediately.*

Since The Executioner and The Prisoner escaped and the article came out in *The Times* and then our local paper, a lot of men have stopped coming to The Club. I wonder what they're doing now to ease pressure. I can't imagine their well-put-together wives doing what those girls do for them. Peter is losing money, or at the very least, he's not making as much. There are a few die-hard holdouts, mostly the men who drink too much and like that they can drink as much as they want at The Club. Or they need the violent sex because, combined with alcohol, that's their primary way to alleviate stress.

I saw Ben Marcus at the gym yesterday. He was lifting weights and then he was running very fast on the treadmill. He nodded to me, and I nodded back. Apparently, his new way of alleviating pressure is working out. His thin, uptight wife joined him on the next treadmill. I imagine she has no idea what her husband's underbelly is like. Ben has not been to The Club since "The Great Escape" was published.

About a month ago, Peter had an emergency meeting on a Tuesday night with The Men. He called Eli and cancelled Tuesday night at The Club. After The Men left, he came up to my bedroom and wanted sex.

It had been a long time since Peter asked me to satisfy his sexual needs. I didn't want to suck his cock, but I did. He held my neck so tight that I thought I might pass out. When we first got together, I wore provocative clothing to flaunt my nubile body. I sat on his lap and fondled him adoringly. Then I'd feel his fingers at the back of my neck pushing my head down toward his penis. I learned the drill. When he asked me to marry him, I couldn't believe my luck landing a doctor, a man with status and money. I thought my life would be different. And in one way it was— no ramshackle house with a leaky roof, no drunk father lying on the couch while my mother went to work to try to keep food on the table for me and my sister. My mother did not know that my father touched me and made me touch him, and that I was desperate to protect Cynthia from him.

I thought if I married Dr. Peter Garth I would escape the abuse, that it was my way out, but it wasn't. It was another level of in, a sophisticated, supposedly nicer set of men, men with money, men who had power in society, not like my father, the blue-collar factory worker who drank too much and eventually became unemployed because he could not stop drinking. My mother died young trying to do right by us girls. We got out of the house, but I failed my mom. I am not a nice person. I am tainted. There is something wrong with me. My mom, at least, tried to protect both me and Cynthia.

I protected Isabelle, but I sold out Lydia. I could not save both of them and be the doctor's wife. I let him have Lydia. Maybe there's some redemption in the fact that when Lydia disappeared, even though I acted upset, inside I cheered her on.

At first people asked me how I was dealing with my daughter's disappearance. I played the grieving mother. When they found Lydia's burnt body, I went to see it. I could see no trace of my daughter. I knew it wasn't her, but we had a funeral anyway. After a while there was silence, and no one asked me about Lydia anymore. It was like it never happened. Life went on.

I listened to my husband's phone conversations. Serge told Peter, *It's done.* Peter said nothing. He quietly hung up the phone. Later Peter said something that made me think they came up with a body to frame that school counselor, that Lydia wasn't dead, but I didn't know where she was, and Peter didn't know, either.

One day I waited in the grocery store parking lot to talk to Elizabeth Jacobs. We exchanged only a few words, but I was assured that Lydia had escaped. I was glad she got out. Every day she's been gone, I have prayed she found a good home.

At one of The Men's meetings, I listened to Serge Valentino say they found Lydia's locket in Elizabeth Jacobs's drawer. He bragged about how he picked the bitch up and she was never going anywhere but the death chamber.

After the call with the FBI, I call Peter at work to let him know Cynthia is sick and I need to go to her. Calling him at work is the best time to tell him things because he's distracted and is usually agreeable to my need to go and take care of my sister. What he doesn't know is that this time, I am not coming back.

I have some compassion for these girls, but not much. I do have respect for Lydia, my rough and tumble and very smart girl. She got out. I'm proud of her in a way and pissed off that my daughter did what I could not do, but it isn't really a "could not." I weighed the odds and the odds favored me staying. I've got a pile of cash. I've got a lover. I'm set up to go when the time is right. And the right time is now. I've bought my sister a nice house in Rhinebeck. I paid cash for it. There's a cottage in the back that I can stay in when I'm around. It's a good setup for me and my sister.

After I call Peter, I call my sister, the only person I trust, and tell her I'm on my way, that I've gotten a late start, that I'll be staying at a motel tonight. Tomorrow I'll tell her that I have an interview with the FBI and that Lydia is alive.

I think the FBI will ask me if I knew that my daughter was in a sex trafficking ring led by my husband. I doubt anyone else will be that direct. I hope the reporters will not be able to find me because I don't want to be under public scrutiny. I am tempted to change my name so I don't have to deal with people. I lied about going to

Syracuse. I'm going to Rhinebeck instead.

I probably need to call my lawyer. There is no probably—I am culpable. I knew what went on in my basement. I snooped around. Perhaps I need to put off the meeting with Connor Grey until I talk to my attorney. Grey pushed me. I didn't fully cave, but I gave more than I should have, and if I don't come voluntarily, they will find me. I know that I do not have to testify against my husband, but I will if it keeps me out of prison. I will do whatever I have to do to not get locked up.

I see the black cars drive up from the upstairs window. I thought I'd be gone when the FBI arrived. I take my time going down the stairs when they knock.

When I open the door, the man says, "I'm Connor Grey, FBI."

He hands me the search warrant.

"Have you called Peter?"

"No. I'm leaving."

"I know. How do you get into the basement?"

"The main entrance is in the back."

"Is there another way?"

"Yes. There's a staircase that looks like a closet. It's the maid's staircase. It goes from the basement to the kitchen and then continues up to the second floor where the bedrooms are."

"Do you ever use it?"

"No."

"Did your husband use it?"

"Only when it was cold out and he didn't want to brave the weather."

"This is a crime scene now, Mrs. Garth."

"My bag is packed."

"We'll interview you in Syracuse tomorrow."

"Change of plans. I'm actually going to Rhinebeck."

Connor nods. "One of my men will follow you there."

"Do you have a picture of Lydia?"

"I do."

"Can I see it?"

He takes it out and hands it to me. She is beautiful. I hand it back to him.

"Thank you. I will see you tomorrow."

I see the cars and protestors at the prison as I drive out of town. They've been there ever since the escape a month and a half ago. There are more people today. I wonder when *The New York Times* will publish a second article. In my mind I see the headline splashed across the front page: *Lydia Garth Is Alive.*

I stop at a pay phone in Utica and call Suzanne Alstead, my divorce lawyer. It took me awhile to find her. I didn't trust that any local lawyer would not be in cahoots with Peter, but I found a good attorney in Rhinebeck.

"I got a call from the FBI right before I left this morning. I'm meeting with Agent Connor Grey tomorrow morning in Rhinebeck at nine o'clock."

"What's going on?"

"Lydia is alive."

"Where is she?"

"I don't know. He didn't tell me. He arrived at the house right before I left. He had a search warrant. They know about The Basement Club."

"So they know about the sex trafficking ring?"

"I imagine they do, although he didn't say that directly. I don't want to go to prison."

"We're a long way from there, MaryLou. Let's take it

one step at a time. I'll see you late this afternoon. I'll be with you tomorrow when Mr. Grey interviews you. No more talking to him or anyone else without representation. Drive safely."

I laugh. "No need to worry about that. The FBI is following me."

I feel less anxious after I get off the phone with Suzanne. I have someone on my side, on my team. It looks like I will have to involve Cynthia, which I don't want to do. I have that old feeling of knowing I have to save myself, Cynthia, and Isabelle. I also want to save Lydia in some way. I regret that I didn't even try to save her when I had the chance.

EMMA

As soon as I sit down for my second interview with Robert McCauley, I announce, "I'm going to testify in person. I've already told my parents."

"You want to come to Cape Vincent?"

"Yes."

"What changed your mind?"

"I had two dreams last night. I need to stand up for not only myself, but for other people who are being abused."

Robert McCauley does not look surprised, but he isn't an easy man to read.

"You want to testify in the hearings?"

"Yes. And I want to have face-to-face conversations with both Peter and MaryLou before I do any testifying."

"We can arrange that, though I don't understand why you would want to."

"I want to make sense of what they did. I don't know if that's possible, but I want to try. He was the active one.

She was passively complicit. Either way, the result was the same."

"And what result is that?"

"I was harmed. I want to see their faces when I tell them that a network of people helped me get out of their sex trafficking ring and that I have a good life now because of their help."

"And you believe you can identify the people who helped you and the people who harmed you?"

"Yes."

Robert McCauley lays out ten pictures of eastern European girls. And there she is.

"This is Nadia."

I point out three more girls who were in the ring.

Robert then lays out twenty pictures. I pick The Warden, The Governor, The Judge, The Detective, and Eli from the array.

I ask, "What are their names?"

"Arthur Stafford, Stanley Warsaw, Leon Corelli, Serge Valentino, and Eli Petrov. Did you have sexual contact with these five men?"

"All of them except Eli. And of course other men, too. I don't see The Accountant."

Mr. McCauley takes the pictures I have identified and gives them to another FBI agent.

"We'll fax these to our team in Cape Vincent now so they can get search warrants and make the accompanying arrests. We'll get the girls into a safe house."

Then he lays out pictures of people in The Network.

I am quiet. I recognize the cab driver and two of the women who traveled with me on the planes to Santa Fe.

"Do you recognize any of these people?"

"Yes, but I don't know why you want me to identify them."

"We know The Network exists, but we know very little about it. It's underground."

"Isn't it enough that it exists and helps people?"

"Perhaps. And if more people knew about it—"

"If more people knew about it, I wonder if it would be as effective."

"It could go either way."

"Miss Jacobs could have been prosecuted for helping me leave."

"Instead she was convicted of murder."

"Wrongly," I say.

"Wrongly," he repeats.

"What The Network does is controversial," I say.

"Yes. Many things that matter are controversial."

We sit there. What Mr. McCauley says is true.

"If I identify the people who helped me, what will you do?"

"We'll question them."

"Have you already questioned some of the people in The Network?"

"Yes."

"Have they given you useful information?"

"Some have, some haven't."

"Have the people who've given you information been forthcoming?"

"I would say they're careful."

"With good reason," I state.

"What reason would that be?"

"The government, the judicial system, does not necessarily keep people safe."

"We try, but no, we do not always, cannot always, keep people safe."

"Do you think I'll be safe to testify in Cape Vincent?"

"I think we can keep you safe."

"Can you assure me of this?"

"I can't be one hundred percent sure, Emma. What I can tell you is that every person you identified today is right now being faxed to our team in Cape Vincent."

"Did you find The Basement Club intact?"

"Yes. We went into The Basement Club this morning and found it pretty much how you described. With your identification of The Men who were involved in The Basement Club, our agents will now simultaneously pick up and take into custody The Warden, The Judge, The Governor, and The Detective. It's a coordinated effort."

"You're very organized. Has Peter Garth been picked up?"

Robert looks at his watch. "He's in the process of being picked up right now. My partner Connor Grey will call me as soon as Peter is taken into custody and is on his way to the county jail."

"What about MaryLou?"

"She talked with Connor earlier this morning. He'll interview her formally tomorrow morning."

"Will she be charged?"

"Most likely."

"For what?"

"For aiding and abetting sexual trafficking of minors and child endangerment."

"I'm going to wait on identifying the people in The Network, Mr. McCauley. If I do identify any of them, can I meet with them?"

Mr. McCauley looks at me. He seems surprised.

"They helped me, Mr. McCauley. I want to thank them."

"I can let them know that you would like to meet with them, however right now most of them don't know where you are or who you are, and they may not be safe if they find out either of those things."

Dad says, "Emma, you could send a note or card through Mr. McCauley."

"I can definitely take something written. Your deposition yesterday gave us the information we needed to move forward with our case. You are a very brave woman, Emma."

"Do you think this will come out in the newspapers soon?"

"I expect that today or tomorrow the press will be reporting on the arrests of The Men in The Club and asking you for interviews. They will find you sooner than later."

"What about Eli?"

"We're looking for him."

"Do you think he could find me?"

"We've got all the transportation centers covered in New York. We don't think he can get out of the city now, but he may have already left."

"And Nadia?"

"We know where she and the three girls you identified are living. Our people were waiting for your confirmation so we could pick them up and move them to a safe house."

"Can I see her?"

"I'll find out if she's willing to talk with you."

"Thank you."

"Emma, it's going to be overwhelming."

"I know, Mr. McCauley. I'm willing to do whatever it takes to shut down The Basement Club, and help any girl or boy who is a victim of sexual abuse."

"I'll be in touch with you and your parents as this process goes along."

"You'll let me know when I'm needed in New York?"

"Yes."

"If Nadia doesn't want to talk with me, can I give you a letter for her?"

He nods.

"And you'll let me know when you find Miss Jacobs?"

"Yes. She and Brian Stafford seem to have dropped off the face of the earth. I'm hoping with you surfacing that the two of them will come forward."

"I hope so, too."

"Any other questions?" He turns to my parents, who sit there quietly.

Dad says, "It'll be a shitstorm."

Robert McCauley says, "It will be."

Mom says, "I expect that the journalists will be parked outside our house very soon."

"They will be."

"It may be better for Emma to contact them and give one of them her story," Dad says.

"An exclusive interview is one way to go. Charlotte Higgins at *The New York Times* is a great writer and an advocate for women's rights. She's worked with the Bureau on several occasions and has always kept her word. She will handle your story candidly and respectfully, Emma. I can give you her number if you want it."

I turn to my parents. "What do you think?"

My mom says, "We know Charlotte, Emma. Not only is she a good writer, she has a lot of insight, expertise, and sensitivity around women's issues generally and around sexual abuse issues specifically. I trust her to tell your story honestly and to check with you about what details you want revealed and what ones you want to keep private. She will honor that, and if she feels like something needs to be said, she will talk with you about it and get your approval before she sends your story to print."

Mr. McCauley says, "I can put in a call to her now and give her your number. She will want to talk with you as soon as possible."

"Let's do it, Mr. McCauley. Will you let me know when Peter is in custody?"

"Yes. In fact, I'll call Connor right now and see if his arrest has been made."

"Thank you."

1 July 1989
Saturday
Cape Vincent, New York
14:30

CONNOR
GREY

We enter Dr. Garth's suite and show his secretary our credentials. We do not wait for her to let him know we are here. We want to get in and out quietly. We do not want to make a spectacle. No clients are in the waiting room.

Dr. Garth, however, does not go easily or quietly. He is not a man who is used to being told what to do.

"You have no right to storm into my office."

"We have a warrant for your arrest, sir, and a search warrant to go through your office and collect evidence that we deem relevant."

"What are you charging me with? Let me see that warrant."

I hand him the warrant. The first thing he does is look at who signed it.

He mumbles, "Vanetti," under his breath.

"Do you have a beef with Judge Vanetti, sir?"

Dr. Garth stares at me. "I'm not saying anything to you until my lawyer gets here and you are not going to search my office until he gets here."

I could tell him we are going to search his office whenever we fucking want to, but I don't. I don't want to push him over the edge. Yet.

"Tell Drew to get over here right now," he orders his secretary.

When she gets off the phone, one of the local policemen says to her, "Gather up your personal items, ma'am, and take them home. We're closing down this office, so don't show up to work tomorrow. This is a crime scene now."

Dr. Garth does not object.

The secretary gathers up her things and leaves.

Then we wait. The local police stand by the door. I sit in one of his comfortable chairs. He's not going to get out of the room and I'm not going to haul him out of the building in handcuffs in front of God and everybody unless I have to. I wonder if he really doesn't have any idea what's happening. He picks up the phone and calls MaryLou. I don't tell him that she is already gone. He leaves a message on their answering machine and slams down the phone.

His lawyer, Drew Stevens, arrives half an hour later. Peter thrusts his copy of the warrant in Drew's face.

"They have a right to search the premises, Peter."

"What gives them that fucking right?"

I wait to see what Drew will say. "They've charged you with sexual trafficking and sexual abuse of minor children. It's a felony."

"That's bullshit, and you know it. I'm not spending the

night in jail. Get me bail."

"I can try, but it's unlikely the judge will grant it."

"They have nothing on me."

I hand him a picture of Emma aka Lydia.

"Where did you get this?"

Not, *You've found my missing daughter. She's alive. I'm so happy. Oh, my God, she's not dead. Is she alright?*

"Where did you get this picture?"

His question hangs in the air.

"She's alive, Dr. Garth."

"Where is she?"

"She's safe, Dr. Garth. Unharmed."

He lunges at me. We cuff him and read him his rights. His lawyer stands there.

I say, "You'll be going to a county jail. Your lawyer can see you there."

"Where the fuck is she? You can't keep her from me. I'm her father." He looks at Drew and says, "I'm paying you a shitload of money. Do something. Get me bail. Call my wife."

I interject, "Your wife is gone, Dr. Garth. She left this morning. But you know that. She called you to let you know she was going to visit her sister."

"You son of a bitch. You have no right to talk to my wife without my permission."

"Peter," says Drew. "I'll meet you at the jail after I get some information from Agent Grey. I'm asking you to not say anything to anyone. You are formally charged and anything you say now can be used against you."

"I'll say whatever I want, to whoever I want. I'm paying you."

"And I'm telling you as your attorney that you need to

be careful about what you say."

"Fuck you. You're fired. You're a measly little nothing who can't even stand up to the FBI. You're no good to me. He's not my lawyer, boys. You can't give him any information."

I say, "We got it, Dr. Garth. No lawyer. No information."

"At least somebody responds to orders."

And then the deputies take Peter to the patrol car.

Drew says, "You played your cards perfectly, Agent Grey."

I smile. "Just doing my job, Counselor. Just doing my job."

After Drew leaves, my team begins to go through Peter Garth's files. I return to The Basement Club. Someone's turned on the sign and it's now flashing purple neon light throughout the room. Disco balls light the two stages. The bar is fully stocked with high-end liquor—Maker's Mark, Courvoisier, Johnny Walker, Grey Goose, some eastern European brands I've never seen. Everything is neat and tidy. Looks like business was thriving.

"Connor, got something you need to see."

I go through the door to the caves where there are small rooms with dirt floors, and each one has a bed and a thick wooden door. There are ropes and pulleys where women can be strung up. The techs are collecting evidence—fingerprints, semen samples, blood.

"Looks like a torture chamber. Let's leave the techs in peace and move into the house."

It's one of the original old mansions on the St. Lawrence. The staircase is heavy, dark wood and has wide stairs that lead up to the second floor where the bedrooms are.

"It looks like a scene from a Gothic novel, the regal staircase, the torture chambers in the basement. We're looking for pictures of the girls, a black book that gives names, dates, money taken in, a safe, clothing or jewelry that doesn't belong to Mrs. Garth. She left her safe open. Said she didn't know if her husband had another one. Go into every closet. Dr. Garth has a study on the first floor. Make note of anything that doesn't feel right."

"Looks like we got something, Connor."

And there it is, a box with pictures, an unidentified tall thin blond girl and Emma from what appears to be ages five to fifteen. She looks drugged in some of the more recent pictures. In the earlier ones she looks innocent, but I see the fear in her eyes. When I line them up from youngest to oldest I see how the light began to go out of her eyes. Ten years of abuse. It's beyond my comprehension that a father would—could—do this to his child. I think of my five-year-old Ana and her sweet innocence. I think of the depravity of human beings. What they will do is seemingly endless. The wreckage. The ravaging. Robert always adds "the resilience." Sometimes that's hard for me to add.

1 July 1989
Saturday
Cape Vincent, New York
15:15

PETER
GARTH

Connor Grey watches me as the cops put me into the back seat of a patrol car. I give him the finger. He nods at me with a look on his face that I don't like.

"Take these cuffs off. They're hurting me."

"I can't. You lunged at the FBI agent."

"Where are you taking me?"

"To jail."

"I know that. Which one?"

"Watertown."

It takes them a fucking long time to process me. Waiting. Waiting. So much waiting. They take my clothes.

I say, "I don't want to wear this orange jumpsuit. I want my own clothes."

"Everyone has to wear the orange jumpsuit."

"Why? I should get to choose."

One of the guards asks, "You've never been in jail before?"

"No. I'm a surgeon, a pediatrician in Cape Vincent. I went to Harvard Medical School. I know nothing about jail. Jail is for criminals."

"Well, they've given you some hefty charges, sir."

"None of which are true."

"I imagine your lawyer will be coming to see you soon."

"I fired my lawyer. I need to use the phone to make a few phone calls."

"That's not how it works here."

"I can't use the phone now? I have business to take care of."

"After we get you processed, a guard will take you to your cell. After dinner a guard will come around and ask who wants to use the phone."

There's a lot of hooting and hollering as the guard walks me to my cell. Men make comments to me that I don't like.

As the guard opens my cell, I tell him, "I need to make a phone call."

"After dinner," he says, then turns and walks away.

I say loudly, "I need to call my lawyer, now."

He doesn't respond.

In my cell there are bunkbeds. I walk around the cell and realize I have absolutely no privacy. I hope I don't get a cellmate. It is very clear that I'm in a confined situation. I pace until dinner. In the dining hall I sit at a table and an inmate tells me, "You have to move. This is somebody else's seat." I feel fury, but I get up and go to a different table. I sit alone. Two men sit down at the table and ask me if I'm new. I say yes. That's it. No more conversation. I am glad when dinner is done and I am taken back to my cell. I do not belong here.

Then I wait. I need a strong lawyer, one who will fight the FBI. When I met with Lance Wineberg a month ago, I didn't want to pay his outrageously expensive retainer, but now I'm willing to spend whatever it takes to get out of this mess.

When I finally get to use the phone after dinner just as the deputy told me I would, I actually reach Lance.

"I can meet with you tomorrow morning."

"I need you to come tonight." I'm not used to being put off, things going at a slow pace.

He tells me, "Even lawyers have to abide by the visiting hour rules except when we request special permission."

"So get permission."

"I can't do that."

"Why not? I'm paying you a shitload of money. I need to know that I'll be your priority."

"And you will be, Dr. Garth, once we meet and get all the t's crossed and the i's dotted tomorrow. My secretary has to draw up the paperwork."

"We've talked before. You know me."

"I know that you didn't want to retain me before because you thought I was too expensive. And now you're sitting in the Watertown County Jail and it's seven o'clock on a Wednesday night and I have other commitments to attend to. I'll be there first thing tomorrow morning."

"What time?"

He says calmly, "Nine o'clock."

I am in and out of sleep. The first time I wake up I hear rustling and men talking in their sleep, people calling out.

I am sweaty. In my dream my mother put a large object in my anus. It hurts. I haven't thought about my mother in a long time. I was happy when my brother tracked me down and told me she was sick and might die. I did not feel any need or desire to visit her in the hospital. I told him I couldn't make it. I haven't seen hide nor hair of him or my father. I don't know if she died or not. If I had gone to her funeral I would have spit on her grave.

When I left home, I went to college on a scholarship. Then I went to Harvard Medical School. My family did not come to my college graduation or my graduation from medical school. I never told them I was a doctor. I had nothing to do with any of them from the minute I left home. I went to friends' houses for holidays, or I spent them alone. Sometimes I slept with prostitutes. I could do whatever I wanted with them, no holds barred. I got out. I divorced my whole family. That was always my plan. I don't know how I ever was in that family. They were poor and abusive, although they did not abuse my brother. He watched both my father and mother abuse me. I'm sure he was glad it wasn't him. I was angry that he didn't protect me, that it was three against one.

The one thing my parents taught me is that having power was a good thing. Being a doctor brought me the power I wanted. Parents entrusted their daughters with me, and I was good at convincing fathers—poor fathers, usually—that they could make a lot of money and be able to take better care of their families if they let their daughters service men in power. I was surprised they gave their daughters to me. As one of my colleagues so aptly put it, *Men are pigs.*

It still sticks in my craw that Lydia left me and now

she's been found. I wonder how they found her. I couldn't locate her even though I hired a private investigator. That was a waste of money. I looked forward to that bitch, Elizabeth Jacobs, paying for Lydia's leaving, but she escaped from the maximum-security prison. We had a plan. Then The Warden's fucking son took her, and they both disappeared.

CONNOR
GREY

When I get back to the office, I learn that all The Men except The Accountant have been arrested and taken into custody. They are all sitting in different jails. I don't expect any of The Men to get out on bail. All of them know that Emma aka Lydia is alive and well. We showed her picture to each of them.

All The Men challenged the search warrants and their arrest. All of them had their secretaries call a lawyer. None of them called their wives. All of them went with varying degrees of anger and frustration. The only one who fired his lawyer was Peter Garth. All their attorneys are from the same firm, which leads me to believe that The Men had discussed and coordinated what they would do if something went haywire.

Eli Petrov, birth name Gregor Svetlof, has disappeared.

We brought Nadia Sklyar aka Cristina Floznikof to a safe house for questioning. She is not under arrest, but we are concerned about her safety. I am told when she saw Emma's picture, she smiled. Resilience.

I look at the picture of my wife and daughter. I decide to go pick up Ana from preschool. I need some time with her to remember that people can be good. I will see Robert tomorrow afternoon after I interview MaryLou Garth. We will interview Nadia together at the safe house and meet afterward to discuss the case. Getting our ducks in a row. Where are Elizabeth Jacobs and Brian Stafford?

Robert calls me from the airport right before I head out to see my daughter and then drive to Rhinebeck.

I tell him, "Dr. Garth and all The Men in the ring, except for The Accountant, are in custody. We don't have any idea who he is. Peter fired his lawyer this afternoon, and when I showed him the picture of Emma and wouldn't tell him where she was, he lunged at me. We had to cuff him."

Robert sighs. "He's a piece of work."

"He is that. Waiting to see who Dr. Garth hires to defend him."

"Should be interesting. He's in a lot more trouble than he realizes."

"I'd say that reality has come pounding at his door and he's in for the ride of his life."

"Emma told me she wants to come to Peter and MaryLou's hearings and wants to talk to each of them beforehand. She is willing to testify."

"So she changed her mind."

"She has. Said she had a dream that made her realize she needed to see them. She's a tough cookie. She asked if we could keep her safe. I told her our intention was to keep her safe, but I could not guarantee that she would be one hundred percent safe."

"She understood that?"

"Yes. She knows it's all a crapshoot, that nothing is for certain."

"She likes the truth."

"I don't know whether she actually likes the truth, but she wants to hear it. You'll like her. Reminds me of your Ana. Anything else?"

"Couple of things. We need to interview Detective Valentino and Judge Corelli sooner than later. I'm interviewing Mrs. Garth in Rhinebeck tomorrow morning."

Robert says, "I'll interview The Judge tomorrow afternoon. I'm going to call Emma now and let her know Peter's in custody and that MaryLou is scheduled to be interviewed tomorrow by you."

"I'll take Detective Valentino. Have a good flight, boss. Talk to you tomorrow."

2 July 1989
Sunday
Watertown, New York
06:00

PETER
GARTH

I wake up confused. It's noisy and stuffy. I don't know where I am. Then I remember I'm in jail and that I dreamt about my mother, Isabelle, and Daniel. Isabelle. Beautiful Isabelle. I resented her from the day she was born, not because she was a special-needs child, but because MaryLou spent extraordinary amounts of time with her. I got put on the back burner. I didn't like that. I began hiring prostitutes on a regular basis. When that stopped satisfying me I began to seek out girls, young, nubile, no breasts. I could control these girls. They were like budding teenage boys. I had my fair share of boys and young men. I liked their hard bodies and their dicks. I liked penetrating them. I did not like penetrating women.

Daniel. I met him at a medical conference. There we were, two young doctors sitting at the bar, shooting the shit with the bartender. I went to the opening conference cocktail party where many of the men were there with their young, thin, beautiful wives. I would have been there with MaryLou if the goddamn kid wasn't around. Her needs, her bottle, her, her, her. I felt uncomfortable and lonely.

Looks like we're the only two without our wives tonight. That's how the conversation began.

I learned his name later. We were both married, both of us had a young daughter, and both of us were at our first conference alone. I drank too much. I think Daniel did, too, because we ended up in his room and had the most incredible sex I've ever had, rough and gentle. I fell in love with his penis. I was already in love with mine, but I desperately wanted his pulsating large organ that he inserted in me. For the first time, it felt good. He moved slowly and gently at first. He was communicating something to me. He wanted to connect, which makes me think in retrospect he really had not drank as much as I had thought. I was caught up in alcohol and the passion of it all and his hard, beautiful, thin muscular body. Don't get me wrong, I liked MaryLou. She was beautiful, but she was eye candy. I liked that other men looked at her and I got to claim her as mine. That's what I liked.

Daniel and I spent that whole conference in and out of bed, mostly in. I couldn't get enough of him. I fell in love with him. Our relationship continued for a number of years. Actually, until Lydia was five. Then Daniel said, *No more.* He said a lot of other things before he said that. He told me he and his wife were separating. He asked me to leave MaryLou and join him. Over a six-month period he gave me every opportunity to be with him. The last time, that last conference, he did not come alone. Paul. I fucking hated Daniel and how he put Paul in my face. Well not literally.

We met that first night at the bar like we always did, but he told me, *No more, Peter. I've met someone else.*

What? You've got to be kidding.

No. I'm not. I'm in a relationship with him.

Come on, Daniel. You can't be serious.

Oh, I am. I've been telling you for the past year that I was changing my life and every step of the way I invited you to join me, but you didn't.

I couldn't.

Come on, Pete. Of course you could have, but you wouldn't. I don't know why, really, but I had to accept that you weren't going to leave her. I get it. But that's not about me. I had the difficult breakup with Barbara, and now we've got some sort of rhythm. I see Mandy half the week. I love being a dad, and Paul and I just moved in together. I'd like you to meet him.

No.

Come on, Pete. He's the only person who ever called me Pete. I never let anyone call me that. Too informal. Too intimate.

No. I can't meet him. I'm sorry.

I'm sorry, too.

Then he left and I sat there at the bar. I drank way too much that night and ended up having sex with some lonely woman. I caught a glimpse of Daniel and Paul the next day at a restaurant when I was walking to find a place to have lunch. Paul was a good-looking man. I wondered if he was a doctor. If he was, I didn't see him at any of the seminars I attended.

When I went home, I began training Lydia. I began having her play with my penis and quickly we moved to her sucking me off. It was good, great. I forgot about Daniel. Well, I tried.

4 July 1989
Tuesday
New York, New York
17:30

DANIEL

I learn about Peter Garth's arrest in the paper. When Paul comes into the kitchen, I read him the article.

"Fucking A, Dan. You dodged a bullet."

"Apparently I did."

"You got lucky."

"Who got lucky?" I tease back. We laugh.

Mandy calls, "Dad, are you ready?"

"I is."

"Paul, you'll be there?"

"At your service, my lady."

"And we're off. See you at the theater. Your ticket's on my nightstand."

"Normal," Paul says. "Think normal."

"Normal it is."

"What's normal, Dad?"

"You, sweetie pie. You."

5 July 1989
Wednesday
Cape Vincent, New York
15:15

CONNOR
GREY

"I'm Connor Grey, FBI. I work with Robert McCauley."

"I know who you are," says Detective Valentino.

"You know that you've been charged with sexual abuse of minor children and sexual trafficking?"

"Lies."

"You were the officer who arrested Elizabeth Jacobs?"

"You already know I was."

"I'll take that as a yes. How did you get involved in the case?"

"Dr. Garth reported his fifteen-year-old daughter, Lydia, missing. She'd been gone almost twenty-four hours. I went to Bob Bruce, my police chief, and talked to him about the missing girl. He asked me to follow up on the call and I did."

"Do you know Dr. Garth personally?"

"He's a member of the community. I'm a member of the community. I've seen him at some events."

"Did you ever go to his house?"

"Maybe one or two parties for his daughter's birthday?"

"Which daughter?"

"The younger one."

"Lydia?"

"Yes."

"Were you friends with Dr. Garth?"

"No."

"But he called you directly about his missing daughter after he left the school meeting with Elizabeth Jacobs and the principal."

"I don't know if that's true. I get a lot of calls."

"We've looked at your paperwork and you don't have much documentation about your calls with Dr. Garth. What else did he tell you?"

"That Miss Jacobs was not forthcoming about her conversation with Lydia."

"Anything else?"

"Miss Jacobs sent Lydia a call slip, pulled her out of class. No one saw Lydia after that."

"Do you know why Miss Jacobs pulled Lydia out of class?"

"She was concerned about how Lydia was doing. Paula Langdon had a breakdown the day before."

"Did you know that Nadia Sklyar did not return to school after Paula Langdon was taken away by the paramedics?"

"I don't know anything about that."

"You don't know that Lydia and Nadia were friends?"

"I don't remember Miss Jacobs mentioning a Nadia."

"Did Dr. Garth continue to call you?"

"He may have called a couple of times, but the next time I actively worked the case was when we discovered a girl's burnt body which turned out to be Lydia."

"Did Dr. Garth identify her?"

"He did. Said his daughter had a chip on her front tooth just like the one on the burnt body. Dental records confirmed Lydia Garth had a chipped tooth."

"Did Dr. Garth tell you anything else?"

"He said his daughter's locket was missing, that she always wore it, that it was special to her. He gave it to her on her tenth birthday."

"So you got a search warrant for Elizabeth Jacobs's house?"

"I did."

"Did you talk to Dr. Garth before you got the search warrant?"

Detective Valentino looks thoughtful. I wait to see if I'll catch him in a lie.

"Yes. I believe I did."

"Do you have documentation about this conversation with Dr. Garth?"

"It wasn't a formal interview. I just wanted to let him know that we got the search warrant and were headed to Miss Jacobs's house."

"Was it easy to get the search warrant?"

"It took some time."

"You went to three judges who wouldn't give you a warrant."

"I don't remember it being that many."

"What do you make of that?"

"Different judges. Different criteria. You know how it goes."

"I do know how it goes. Most judges wouldn't give a search warrant with so little documentation."

"Do you remember who signed it?"

"I can't remember."

"Vanetti? Corelli? Watson? Logan?

"I don't remember."

I push over two pieces of paper.

He reads, "Leon Corelli."

"Do you know that he's now incarcerated and charged with the same charges as you?"

"I don't know anything about that."

"You don't know that his lawyer is from the same law firm as yours?"

Detective Valentino is silent. He doesn't answer my question. I expect him to end the interview at this point. I would if I were him.

"When you went to Elizabeth Jacobs's house, were you looking for the locket?"

"Not specifically. We were surprised when we came upon it."

"Who found it?"

"Charlie Stevens."

"Were there pictures in it?"

"I don't know."

"You didn't look at it?"

"I did, but I don't remember any pictures."

"Did you tell Officer Stevens to search the bedroom?"

"I did."

"Had you been in the bedroom before he went in to search?"

"No."

"Did you interview Miss Jacobs after you took her to the police station?"

"Yes."

"What did she say?"

"That she didn't know how the locket got there."

"Did she know it was Lydia's?"

"No. Said she hadn't seen Lydia wearing it at school."

"Did that seem odd to you?"

"I don't know what you mean."

"Dr. Garth told you his daughter always wore the necklace, yet Miss Jacobs had never seen her wearing it."

"I didn't think about it."

I take out a picture of Detective Valentino on the lawn at the Garth mansion.

"Do you remember being at this party?

Detective Valentino looks confused.

"I don't."

I put down nine pictures of six men gathered under the same tree, a photo composition recreated over the years. "The Warden, The Governor, Dr. Garth, The Judge, an unknown man, and you. You've been attending Lydia's birthday parties since she was five, and these photos show you were there every year. You're telling me you don't remember that?"

"I don't. Maybe one or two."

"Do you remember Bob Bruce being there?"

"I don't remember."

I point to the unknown man. "Who's this?"

"I don't know."

"For nine years all of you attended Lydia Garth's birthday parties. You don't remember who that is?"

"It wasn't a big deal to me."

"No?"

"No. If I went it was a courtesy drop-by, part of my community building."

"Do you remember the pictures being taken?"

"No."

"MaryLou took them."

Detective Valentino is quiet. I almost expect him to ask who MaryLou is. He doesn't.

Then it comes.

"I'm done here," he says. "I want to talk to my lawyer."

"You got it."

20 July 1989
Thursday
Waiuku, New Zealand
20:17

ALICE

After our vacation, we return to Waiuku and our new home. A pile of *New York Times* and some other mail are on the kitchen counter. We decide to go through this in the morning. Austin and Lucy left their kitchen table and chairs for us. There is a blue vase on the table with red, white, and orange tulips with an envelope leaning against it. Inside is a photo of our new house and a handwritten note. *May you love this home as much as we have. May your family thrive here. Best wishes, Austin and Lucy. P.S. Call us and come to dinner in our new home when you're ready. Sky is waiting to be with you.*

I cry as I read their note. We walk through the house that is scrubbed clean. We plan to paint every room, but we haven't picked the colors yet. They delivered our new bed when we were gone, and Lucy made it up with our new flowered sheets that I bought in Waiuku.

That first night in our new home we make love for the

first time.

Afterward, I tell Mason, "I'm pregnant. We just made a baby." I don't know how I know, and I've never been more sure about anything.

He smiles and pulls me close. He doesn't question me.

In the morning Mason and I hold hands as we walk down to the water. He hums *This Land Is Your Land* and I sing the words. The land and lifestyle here are familiar to me—the dairy farms in Chateaugay, the casual get-togethers and the importance of relationships that happen in rural communities and get lost when you live a faster, busier life. I am glad to remember that I love the slowed-down life where I can remember my dreams, where time and space alone matter as much as conversation, where there is a balance, where the introvert in me can thrive and my creativity can blossom. We do not have to lock our doors here. Few people come down our road. Crime is virtually nonexistent. We love our land and our new home.

As Mason and I sit quietly looking at the bay I am reminded of my childhood where I thrived with this abundance of time and space and connection to nature. In my family, alone time was valued. My parents honored this in themselves and nurtured it in me. When my father came home from work, he would take me out for a walk while my mother made dinner, or he and I would make dinner and my mother would walk by herself, have a breather. We had game nights, movie nights, and family dinners. In many ways it was idyllic.

When my mom got pregnant the summer before I left for college, everything changed. At first she had a hard time accepting this unexpected pregnancy—with twins nonetheless—but she got used to it as she carried the babies for nine long months. Mari and Oliver were born when I was a freshman in college. When my mom went into labor I came home. I loved my little brother and sister. In a way it made my life easier when my mother was preoccupied with the twins. She no longer had time to feel anything about me leaving home.

When I was applying to out-of-state colleges, I told myself it was normal for me to want to leave home, to make a break, although by the time the twins were born I was planning to return to Cape Vincent after I graduated. I was lonely. I missed the north of New York, the St. Lawrence River, Lake Ontario, and my family. I can't say the long winters were the draw, although I do like winter. I missed the people, their friendliness, and the familiarity of community. I was happy to get a job in Cape Vincent so I could return and create a home for myself.

As we walk back up to the house we decide to go to the grocery store and the paint store in Waiuku and pick the colors for our bedroom, the first room we are going to paint. Consecrated space, the place where our baby was created. It's hard to believe I'm pregnant. My breasts are tender and have already begun to swell. How quickly the hormonal changes happen. I know this theoretically, but I have never been pregnant before.

We come home with food and paint in hand, and while I make lunch Mason goes through the mail.

"Anything interesting in *The New York Times*?"

Mason folds the paper and puts it at my place.

I look at him and walk to the table.

"You might want to sit down."

When I open it, I see "The Great Escape" on the front page.

"Breathe. They didn't put our pictures in the paper."

"It's only a matter of time before someone makes the connection."

The article states that the FBI is working the case and there is lots of talk about me being held in an all-men's prison and scheduled to die for a murder where the body in question was burnt beyond recognition. At the time this didn't seem to matter as they found Lydia's necklace in my underwear drawer. I told the police and my lawyer that I didn't know how it got there, but Detective Valentino scoffed as he handcuffed me. He put the cuffs on so tight that I had bruises for several months.

All of this seems like another life, a lifetime ago. Yet it's only been eight weeks since my escape, our escape, from the prison. We moved into our new life seamlessly, new country, new town, new home, new job, new friends. Click, click, click. Like Dorothy in *The Wizard of Oz*. Things have come together.

I'm startled when the phone rings. It's the first time it's rung since we've been home. The phone company must have given us a number when we were gone.

"Welcome home. Did you have a good trip?" It's Austin.

"We did."

"Wanted to let you know there's a potluck and community meeting tonight in Waiuku. Since you just got back Lucy and I can bring two dishes, so you'll be covered."

"We just got back from the grocery store. I'll make chocolate chip cookies."

He gives us the time and place and I hang up.

At the potluck Lucy and Austin introduce us to people in the community. I talk to Allison, and we set up a time to meet next week to begin to transition her practice to me. She has already told people about me, and they are feeling good about the new American midwife.

People in the community ask us a lot of questions.

"Why did you move here?"

"We needed a change. We wanted this lifestyle that's fading away in the United States."

"What about your families? You're so far away."

"Yes. This is the downside, but they will visit."

"Did they support you leaving?"

"Yes."

Mason and I dance around what we're doing here in New Zealand.

On the drive home we have a conversation.

"I don't like being dishonest. I hate telling people a partial truth."

"We're being discerning, Alice."

"We're lying, Mason. We're leaving out big chunks of our story."

"For now, only for now."

"I hope so. I don't want to live this way, like a fugitive on the run."

"But that's what we are right now."

"And I'm telling you, I don't like it."

"I don't like it either, Alice. And it's all temporary."

"You don't know that."

"Everything's temporary, Alice."

I want to lash out and remind him that I am Eliza Jacobs. But the truth is, I am not Eliza anymore. I am Alice. I'm a wife. I'm pregnant, for God's sake. My whole world is upside down. What I know is, I love our new house and land that goes right down to the water. I love sitting by the bay. I feel the energy of this earth.

My parents would like this place, and Mason says his mom would like it, too. We got three letters today, one from my parents, one from Mason's mother, and one from Terran, who's keeping us abreast of the investigation and would like to have our phone number when we have one.

6 August 1989
Sunday
Waiuku, New Zealand
09:15

ALICE

When Mason comes back from the mailbox he puts the unfolded *New York Times* on the table. In big black letters the headline reads: **Lydia Garth Is Alive.** I put on water for coffee, and we sit at the kitchen table. Sky is at my feet. I read, *Elizabeth Jacobs's conviction is overturned. No charges will be filed against Brian Stafford. Where are Brian Stafford and Elizabeth Jacobs? Where are the executioner and the prisoner? Come out, come out, wherever you are.*

Our pictures are in the paper, but it's hard to see the resemblance. Thank God.

All I want to do is blend in, be a part of this community, live a simple life, raise our child.

Mason breaks the silence. "Your conviction has been overturned. You're free."

"Free? I want all of this to go away."

"It will."

"Can we let it ride awhile?"

"We can, but I'm not sure how long we should wait to let people here know."

"I want to be more settled here. I don't want to deal with this now."

I see Lydia's picture. She looks good. I read brief snippets of her story, the skeleton, the bare bones. She is going to testify. Her father is fighting to avoid the death penalty, although he continues to claim he's innocent. The kingpins of a sex trafficking ring, The Men are dropping like flies—The Governor, The Warden, The Detective, The Judge. Powerful men.

I am in awe of Emma's path—to sit in the courtroom, give testimony, and watch lawyers question The Men and her parents. What strength! Later in the *New York Times*'s article, the FBI invited me to return to the United States to participate. Mason told me he would come and support me. Thanks, but no thanks.

Mason and I talk about his father.

"How are you feeling about your dad being incarcerated?"

"He deserves it."

"Yes, he does. But that doesn't have anything to do with your feelings about it."

"I lived in the shadow of my father for a long time. He was a large presence with an iron rule. I thought I could get him to love me."

"And he does love you."

"In his own way he does. He bent. He let me do spiritual counseling with the men on death row. He didn't like me doing it, but he didn't interfere. He allowed my protocols and honored them."

"How did he honor them?"

"Well, he accepted them. Honoring them may be going too far. He pushed my limit with you. He crossed a line."

"When he put me in Z?"

"Yes. He was not responsive when I challenged him about this. He wouldn't budge."

"Perhaps this is what set your plan in motion."

"Yes. Time to go. Time to save an innocent woman. Time to do what I couldn't do with my mother. I couldn't leave him. I couldn't walk away. He didn't want me to. He wanted to mold me, make me into something I wasn't and would never be."

"The Executioner."

"Yes. I kill someone and am not punished for doing that. How could I have let this happen?"

"Your father wanted you to do this job."

"But why did I accept that this was my job? Why did I agree to do it?"

I hear his pain. I wish I could fix it for him, but I know I can't. I listen.

"How can I justify that? I can't."

"You haven't been able to."

"I have to accept that I chose to be The Executioner. Was I that wounded and hurt?"

"You may have been."

"So I went along so I could get his love. It's sick. I'm sick. He's a sick motherfucker."

"Yes. He's a sick man."

"Love meant that much to me? To sell my soul."

Mason's flagellation continues. "I did what I did. Now I'm doing something else. I'm ashamed of my behavior, and I want you to punish me because I don't feel worthy.

Yuck. I deserve to be punished. Is that what it gets down to?"

I hold him as he cries.

In the afternoon, Austin and Lucy come for lunch. Afterward she and Mason walk the land while Austin and I run in Awhitu Regional Park on trails that Austin and Lucy helped create. They are orienteers, a sport that originated in Norway and is popular in Europe. We had heard of orienteering before, but we did not know anything about it. Both of us want to try it. Austin shows us some of the courses at the regional park and we use a map and compass to follow a set course across diverse terrain. Lucy cannot do these courses anymore, but she knows the land and the courses like the back of her hand. She gives me suggestions and talks me through the routes before I take off. I like getting to know Lucy and am inspired by how much she knows about this area and its diverse vegetation. It is an opportunity to get up close and personal with her and the land.

After dinner we play cards, talk, and laugh. We hope that Sundays will be a day we get together with this couple. It's good to have new friends.

We've been here two and a half months. Now that Lydia is alive and my conviction has been overturned, I can call my parents and receive mail from them without a secret go-between. Mason wants to call his mom, Terran, and Celeste. We talk about how we're going to handle this.

6 August 1989
Sunday
Santa Fe, New Mexico
07:13

EMMA

It is only a slightly better solution. Those are the words that come to me as I wait to get on the plane for New York. I have not been back in over four years. Theo and Frank are taking a different flight. I did not want to be on the same flight as them. I am not five. I am not fifteen. I am nineteen, inching toward twenty. To the best of my ability, I want to be my adult self, the adult Emma with the child and teenage Lydia deeply encased in me. Not forgotten. Forgetting is not the answer. I have questions. How does one leave home unexpectedly at fifteen? How does one move away from childhood sexual abuse? How did I leave everything external behind with my internal process still intact, solidified within my psyche, calcification surrounding my soul, a hard shell that I didn't recognize? I saw dark and light. I held a bit of hope that something could change.

I met Nadia when I was ten. I'm scared to see her now, but I want to. More than want to, I need to. She is my first stop. That's the plan. Robert McCauley will meet my plane at JFK. I am returning to the same place I left from when I was fifteen, but I am not the same. I am Emma Maxwell now. Until six weeks ago, I thought Lydia Garth no longer existed. Now the part of me that is and was Lydia feels fear, anxiety, and excitement. Such a close line between fear and excitement, a razor's edge. I am taking a nonstop flight. The safety factor. No one can get to me. Who's going to try? Peter is locked up and MaryLou is under house arrest. The Governor, The Warden, The Detective, and The Judge are locked up, too. The Accountant and Eli are missing. They think Eli has left the country, but they aren't sure. He did not have sex with me. I am not afraid of him.

I do not look the same. I have short hair and am taller, thinner, and more muscular. I have sunglasses and a green hat if I feel like I need a cover. When we got to the airport Theo reminded me, *Cover up, if you need to. There is no shame in this.* I have a motel room in New York City and will be there a few days. I have a pre-arranged meeting with Nadia at a café-bookstore combo. My kind of place. Federal agents will be there. I won't know them. The FBI hopes they can draw out Eli. They are concerned about Nadia's and my safety. Robert told me Nadia is not talking yet. He hopes she will talk after meeting with me. New York City is not my home, though, and I am not familiar with the streets. I studied the street maps I got from AAA. I memorized where I'm going: Café Oleander. It sounded like a quiet, peaceful place when I looked it up in the tour book. As I walk toward the café there is no quiet. This is New York City. Endless people and buildings, sidewalks and people walking. I'm grateful to be walking. Exercise. Movement. I look around. No one looks at me. No one pays any attention to me. I blend in. No one cares about a nineteen-year-old girl wearing sunglasses and a green hat who is carrying a backpack. I look like a student.

I see Nadia when I get to the café. Her brown hair is short, the long tresses she used to wear cut away, gone. She sits quietly at an outside table and orders a coffee. When she looks up, she recognizes me, disguise and all. She grins the same grin she always had for me. I move quickly toward the table where we hug each other, hold each other at arm's length, and laugh. As I sit down, I start to cry.

"I can't believe it's you," she says. "You look great."

"You look good yourself. You cut your hair."

"A few weeks ago. After the FBI transported four of us to a safe house. When I sat on my new bed, I realized I might actually have a chance to get out of the sex business. I decided to change my look."

"Short hair looks good on you."

"I like it. It reminds me of when I was a little girl."

I open my shirt and show her the necklace she gave me. I take it off and hand it to her.

She silently reads the inscription, *Lyubov peremahaye vse, Love conquers all,* and looks up at me with tears in her eyes.

"It's yours," I say.

She hands it back to me. "Not now. Maybe later."

"Why not now?"

"The Friday after you disappeared, Peter made all us girls stand up on the stage and strip off our clothes. He put his cold fingers around my neck and asked me where you were. I told him I didn't know. He didn't believe me. That night he took me to the caves. He was brutal. I had black and blue choke marks around my neck, and I blacked out a number of times. He kept asking me if you had spoken to Miss Jacobs on the day you disappeared. I told him I didn't know, that I never returned to the school after Paula Langdon had her breakdown. He questioned me about why I didn't come the Tuesday night before you disappeared. I told him Eli decided to take a new girl. I kept repeating the same thing. My story never changed. Eli was pissed that Peter hurt me."

I take her hand. "I'm so sorry."

"It was a long time ago, *moya podruha*—my friend. Later that week Eli told me your body had been found, burnt beyond all recognition, and that Miss Jacobs had been arrested for your murder. Eli said the Cape Vincent PD found your locket during a raid at Miss Jacobs's house. I figured the locket had been planted. I wanted to believe you had gotten free."

"Would you young ladies like to order something now?" the waiter asks.

At the same time Nadia and I say, "Yes." We start laughing again. Such a fine line between laughing and crying.

"Eli was at The Basement Club the Tuesday night before Miss Jacobs's scheduled execution. He told me Peter was jubilant, that he was drinking way too much, that he got sloppy drunk. All The Men were there. MaryLou prepared dinner for them. Eli always acted like he was a stupid Russian, but, of course, he wasn't. They recruited him when he was young. He was good looking and facile with languages. He wasn't some henchman. He never hurt the girls. All of them liked him. He was like a big brother to them as he had been to me. He's fifteen years older than me. I was seven when I met him for the first time at the airport. I thought I was coming to the United States to go to school, and I did go to a language academy in New York City. I also did The Basement Club and private parties. My parents wanted something better than the poverty and communism in the Ukraine."

I ask her, "What's your life like now?"

"I have a four-year-old daughter, Tasha. She's living in Connecticut with my parents. I live part-time with them and part-time in the City."

"You're still in the ring?"

"I was until a couple of weeks ago when the FBI came and picked us up. Even when Connor Grey showed me pictures of you that seemed real, I didn't trust that you had identified us and that you were still alive."

"But you came today..."

"Yes. They transported me here. FBI agents are everywhere."

I look up and don't notice anything unusual. "Which ones?"

"The man and woman sitting at the table behind us."

"Long blond hair and a beret?"

"Yes. And the guy standing by the lamppost reading the paper."

I look over. He looks normal, like he's waiting for someone. "How can you tell?"

"Years of being in this life. Numerous raids and chats with law enforcement. All of them have a certain look and feel about them. A few months before they moved me to the safe house they told me I was on their radar. They knew about my daughter, my parents, and my house in Connecticut. They were fishing for information about Eli.

I didn't give them anything. I told Eli they were asking questions."

"Do you still go to The Basement Club?"

"No. I stopped going to The Club when Tasha was born. Eli got me out of there, but every weekend he still makes the trip up to Cape Vincent. That club is for men who like young girls. I do adult parties in the City and in Westchester County, bachelor parties, a man's last hurrah before he gets married. It's rarely brutal, but men are men and when they've been drinking, they can get mean. But for the most part it's easy."

"Do you see Eli often?"

She stares at me, then quietly says, "Eli is Tasha's father."

The waiter brings our lunch.

"They tell me they won't send me or my parents back to the Ukraine if I testify. They told me they'd put me and my family in Witness Protection. I'm afraid I'll be killed if I talk. And the weird thing is I feel guilty, like after all Eli has done for me I would be doing him wrong. When I was pregnant, he arranged for my parents to be brought here and he got me out of The Basement Club. He's taken care of me. He's a good father to our daughter."

I want to say, *He has used you,* but I don't. Nadia has only been in a safe house, in protective custody, for a few weeks. She has not had therapy and she has been trafficked for more than half her life. Whatever her feelings and thoughts are about her relationship with Eli have helped her survive. He has been her connection to her roots, to her country.

I hear her say, "I'm like a mother to these young girls. I have a soft spot for the Ukrainian girls, but I love them all. I've learned a lot of languages so I can talk to the girls in their native tongues. This helps in their transition."

"You are helping these girls feel like they have a home, a safe place."

"Yes. When a Ukrainian girl arrives, I'm desperate to talk to her. I want to hear about this place that I left so long ago. The girls teach me expressions that are new to me. I like learning them. Recently, a girl came from my village. She used to know my parents. She told me they disappeared one day, and no one knows what happened to them. I have a brother and a sister I've never met. She went to school with them. Eli has been trying to get them out. Right now, they're living with my aunt and uncle. My mom was relieved to hear that. My parents were taken in the dead of night and had no idea where they were going or what happened to my brother and sister."

I look at Nadia. She's beautiful. "How have you been able to keep doing it?"

"I have to support my daughter and my parents. We live in a Russian section in Connecticut. There's a community. My family is doing well. My mother takes care of Tasha when I'm working. Eli visits regularly. I love him, Lydia. But you don't go by Lydia anymore, do you?"

"No. My name is Emma Maxwell. Did you marry Eli?"

"Not legally, but I'm attached to him. We have a daughter and a beautiful home. He brought my parents here. He transports girls to sex clubs, but he also takes them to school. He did the same thing with me, but underneath all of that, he's a good man, a good father, a good son-in-law."

"Are his parents here?"

Nadia looks at me strangely. "No."

I don't know if I believe her, and I don't know if it makes any difference. We sit in silence.

"Would you like another coffee?"

"Yes," she says.

We are quiet until the waiter brings the coffee.

Nadia asks, "Are you wired?"

I look at her, surprised. "No. Why would you think that?"

"Eli's parents are here. I don't want to lie to you, Emma."

She's scared, and why wouldn't she be? Her whole life is crashing down. It may be a fucked-up life, but out of something horrible she's made something good. She's a mother. She has a daughter. Her family is here. Eli and she have forged a connection.

"Do your parents know what Eli's business is?"

"No. They have no idea what either of us do. Right now, my mother thinks we're on a business trip. I call her every night and talk to her and Tasha."

"Do you know where Eli is?"

"No. The FBI's deal is, if I help them find Eli, they will relocate all of us."

"Are you going to help them?"

"I haven't decided. Did they tell you anything about me?"

"No. Nothing. I asked to meet with you. I made this part of my agreement when I agreed to testify. I owe you my life."

She shakes her head.

I say, "Yes," and take her hands. "When you gave me your necklace and told me to get out when I could and then the next day the opportunity came, I had the courage to go. You gave me the courage, Nadia. Every day I've worn your necklace. Every day I've thought of you."

I start to cry. I hand Nadia a box. When she opens it, she looks up and stares at me. Her eyes are full of tears. It is a silver replica of the necklace she gave me.

"I had it made for you, for our visit."

"Thank you. I love it." She puts it on and takes my hand.

6 August 1989
Sunday
New York, New York
14:37

NADIA

"Emma, I'm going to the bathroom."

I call Eli from the phone booth next to the bathrooms. I'm not surprised when I see the woman with the green beret come into the bookstore. She looks around. I know she's looking for me.

"Eli, I have to get off the phone."

"Nadia. Be calm. You are not a prisoner. I doubt she speaks Ukrainian."

"I feel like a prisoner. I have to be careful."

"Being careful is a good thing. We are all here, safe and sound. We are looking forward to seeing you. How's it been with Lydia?"

"Good. She goes by Emma now. She's agreed to visit my parents and Tasha in Connecticut. I don't like lying to her. I told her about us."

He is quiet. "You trust her."

"I do. She brought me a replica of my necklace. She

offered me the original that my mother gave me, but I feel better about accepting the copy. Love Conquers All."

Eli sighs.

"I asked her if she was wired. She was shocked."

The woman with the green beret is close to me now. I say, "Mom, I'll see you later."

"Get to Grand Central Station," Eli says.

The woman looks at me as I hang up the phone.

I say, "I'm all done. Do you need to use the phone?"

She shakes her head and goes into the bathroom.

I remind myself I am not a prisoner. This is not the Ukraine or Russia. I am not in a sex club. This is not The Basement Club. Somewhere I got free. Did it begin when Lydia disappeared? Having a baby? Falling in love? I see the changes in Lydia. She flinches when I call her Lydia. I need to call her Emma. She has always been strong. When her father allowed all those men to take her, one after the other, she never broke. Afterward, he put her on his lap and made her suck him off because that's what Peter liked. That time in the caves he made me do it, too. He didn't like to have sex with penetration, at least not with girls. I always wondered about that.

I hear Eli's voice in my head, *Get to Grand Central Station.*

When I return to the table, I ask Emma, "Do you want to go to Macy's?

"Sounds good."

When we get there I say, "I need to go to the bathroom. Will you come with me?"

"Of course."

When I come out of the stall, I watch Emma do a double take.

"I can't go back to the safe house, Emma. I'm going out the other way, through the employee section."

I open my shirt and show her the necklace she gave me. "Will you wait in here ten minutes before you leave?"

"Yes." We hug each other.

"I'll let you know when I'm safe."

"God speed."

EMMA

I wait in the bathroom for at least ten minutes. When I leave, I stop at a sale table that has picture frames and high-end knickknacks. The woman with the green beret determinedly walks by me heading to the bathroom. I say nothing to her. When she comes out, she is walking quickly. I divert my eyes and focus on the sale items. I feel her eyes on me, but she doesn't stop or say anything to me. We don't know each other. I think about what Nadia said: *There are all kinds of prisons. I do not want to be in any of them. The question is, what is freedom?* I told her, *Coming and going as I please without fearing that someone will harm me.* She asked, *Do you know who the good guys and the bad guys are?*

When I turn around the woman with the green beret is gone. A man lingers at a table with stoneware. He looks slightly out of place. Is he part of this law enforcement system that is supposed to keep me safe? I don't like not knowing who is and who is not part of the system. Why are they even here? They can't keep me or anyone one hundred percent safe. There is something freeing in this line of thought. I got what I wanted here. I connected with Nadia.

6 August 1989
Sunday
New York, New York
16:15

NADIA

When I get to Grand Central Station, I go to locker 131. I get the valise and ticket to Montreal. I walk to the bathroom, go into a stall, and change my appearance again. I keep on the black pants. Off with the black flats, on with the stylish black boots. I put on a different shirt and jacket. I remove the blond wig and put on a wig with long brown hair. I wear a hat and large black professorial-like glasses. I carry the black valise with my new identity, my passport to freedom. Since no one is in the bathroom I bury my shirt and jacket in the bathroom trash bin. I know exactly where I'm supposed to put my shoes and the blond wig. I don't waver from the plan. Even though my heart is pounding—which I don't understand, because this is what I want, have wanted, have been dreaming of for a long time—I go from bin to bin dumping the last remnants of Nadia. I walk away from a life I never wanted to a life I think I want.

I get on the train and am relieved when it pulls out of the station. I watch New York City disappear. I don't know when Emma will find my letter. I wrote two, one if we connected, the other if we didn't. I ripped up the not connecting one and flushed it down the toilet. Either way I wanted Emma to know that I was grateful to see her, glad she sought me out. I heard about her new life and the only thing that makes me happier than that is me going to my own new life.

It's my turn now. It's been a long time coming. I'm ready. I have a mission. I hated not telling Emma the whole truth. *Do you swear to tell the truth, the whole truth and nothing but the truth, so help you, God? I do. All in good time, my pretty. All in good time.* When I read *The Wizard of Oz* to Tasha, I couldn't believe that my throat closed up and tears rolled down my cheeks. Tasha asked me, *Mommy, what's wrong? I repeated, All in good time, my pretty. All in good time. Something about those words makes me sad.* Tasha said, *Mommy, love conquers all.* I held my baby girl. Eli came to the bedroom door. I nodded to him that I was alright.

On the four-and-a-half-hour trip to Montreal I think about my life. When I first arrived in the United States, I lived in a house with girls from different eastern European countries. Ukrainian house parents took care of us. Eli had his own room in the house and would take all of us to school. None of the girls in my house went to the language academy, only me. The rest of them went to various public schools. There were always at least two girls at a school, so they had each other to talk to. I was alone. I was no longer Cristina Floznikof. I was Nadia Sklyar. My school went Monday through Thursday. The focus was languages, the arts, music, and writing. I thrived. When I started going to The Club on Tuesdays, I had to miss school. I didn't like it, but that's just how it was. I didn't have a choice. Eli kept me out of the Tuesday rotation for as long as he could.

Lydia and I did our debut on a Tuesday night when we were both ten. They put us up on stage together, the blond American girl and the Russian girl. They never understood that there was a difference between the Ukraine and Russia. I pretended I did not speak English or any other language. I was supposed to gather information, listen to conversations, and tell Eli everything.

My mind drifts to my new job, a good job, I think. I hope. I have a few weeks before I begin work. I will be part of a team who finds safe homes and schools for girls who have been trafficked. I will be a translator for these girls individually and in their support groups. I want these girls to not feel so alone. I worry it is too soon to work with victims of sexual trafficking, that I have my own recovery to deal with, but the opportunity came when it came. Love Conquers All.

Nothing is ever as it appears. But as soon as I think that, I know it's not true. Tasha, my beautiful, beautiful girl, is the love of my life. She is already fluent in French, English, and Ukrainian. She has a chance, an opportunity to break the cycle of poverty and abuse, to remain a thriving normal child. Eli and I are finding our way as a couple and as parents. Both of us have been traumatized.

Years of sexual abuse has made me a master at working with my thoughts. If I hadn't been able to do this, I would have gone crazy like Paula Langdon. My resolve got stronger when I watched her being led away, strapped to a gurney, seeing the last fluttering of her eyes as she went into a drugged sleep or at least a place of temporary rest from her demons. I wanted to visit her, but I never did. Maybe Lydia and I can do that one day. I want to stop calling her Lydia. That's her old name, her old self. Nadia is my old self. I am now Cristiane Solier. I got as close to Cristina, my birth name, as I could.

Eli and I put our escape plan into motion when he returned from The Club and woke me up to tell me that Lydia Garth was alive. That night I got on the train to Canada with my parents and Tasha. We got to Canada safely and moved into a house in Montreal. My parents will take care of Tasha until Eli and I move there. My parents will do well in Montreal. Both of them speak French fluently and their new house is in the midst of a Russian neighborhood. Eli's parents have been living in Canada since he was a student at Magill University. They are happy we are finally coming to Canada to live. They want more contact with Tasha.

Eli and I bought a house in a village outside the city as we moved closer to getting out of the sex trade. We want Tasha to be brought up in a small town like we were. Both of us had fond memories of the Ukraine. We loved the land, the people, the friendliness. We did not love the poverty, the hunger, the rigidity of the government, and the fear. We did not like having to be careful. From a young age I had to watch my words or something bad could happen to me or my family. I had to hide that my family spoke French. My mother sent me to the food lines because she knew I could handle it and it was safer for me than for her. She was an educated woman, and she and my father believed that soon educated women would be targets. I did handle it. I gave up my childhood for the greater good. Being careful follows me. I have gone halfway around the world, and I am still watchful.

When a second article came out in *The New York Times* that Lydia was coming to New York to testify, I insisted that Eli leave immediately. I am glad I did because the next day they came and picked four of us up and moved us to a safe house. I've been in the safe house for over a month. The people in charge don't like me going out because they're afraid I won't be safe, although I have been able to take walks when I can't stand being cooped up. I soothe myself by remembering my family is safe in Canada.

I never wanted to be in a safe house. I pretended I was considering protective custody, but I would never abandon Eli and take my daughter away from her father. I feel glad that the other three girls who Emma identified from The Club have a chance now. They can choose a different life on their own or through Witness Protection. Do they want out? What a stupid question! We all want out. It's how can we accomplish that.

When Emma wanted to meet with me, I knew this was my opportunity. I gave her my old address in Connecticut where an elderly Ukrainian couple live with their granddaughter who looks a lot like Tasha. They took over the rental once my parents were safe in Montreal. It's weird. We crossed the border the same day as Elizabeth Jacobs and Brian Stafford. We did not plan it that way. We thought Miss Jacobs would be executed. We had no idea The Prisoner and The Executioner were going to escape.

Four and a half hours later I breathe a sigh of relief when I cross the border. Our plan is complete. I am now officially Cristiane Solier. I speak French. I have always had an easy time learning languages. It was one of the reasons I got recruited into the sex trade. Nadia is dead. My new life begins. I rub my necklace. I will get my mother and my daughter a replica of this necklace, and we will be three generations of love conquering all.

As I disembark, I see Eli and Tasha. He must have told her I would be dressed up like for Halloween. She recognizes me despite the wig and runs into my outstretched arms. I am home. We swing her as we walk to the car. Tasha chatters about some kids in the neighborhood she plays with now. She is happy to have friends. I am happy for her.

6 August 1989
Sunday
New York, New York
22:30

EMMA

After I meet my parents for dinner and a play on Broadway, we return to the motel where we have connecting rooms. The door between us is unlocked. As I'm getting ready for bed, I find a letter in my jacket pocket.

My dearest Emma,

I have no idea how our visit will go today. If I leave this letter with you, all went well. If not, you will get a different letter.

I am sorry I could not say more of the truth when we talked at the café. The bottom-line truth is, I am escaping—leaving New York, going to Eli, our daughter, and my extended family. I am getting out of the sex trade because my opportunity is now. It's that simple. I was able to use you and our meeting as a springboard. I decided to follow my own advice: Get out when you can.

I am sorry I drew you into this, but your reappearance and asking to meet with me made me believe I could get out.

I will write to you in Santa Fe. I hope you will come to visit me when things settle down. You are welcome anytime.

Please destroy this letter. I am sorry I put you in the middle, but I did not want to deal with the authorities.

I am grateful you are in my life again. Always remember, love conquers all.
    Cristiane

I cry as I read Nadia's letter. She has a journey that I know something about, but only partly. She goes to a husband and a daughter, her parents and his, and a community. Her freedom looks different than mine. Finding Nadia and talking with her is one stop on my journey. Tomorrow my parents and I will go to some art museums and see another play. We will meet with Robert McCauley and Connor Grey in preparation for my visits with Peter and MaryLou.

I read Nadia's letter again. I want to sear it into my brain. Then I tear it up and flush it down the toilet. I write her words about freedom and imprisonment in my journal, part of my random jottings. If anyone ever read my journal they would never know they are her words. I miss her more now than I did before I came. How can this be? Our connection was instantaneous. The trust was right there, two women who met as girls and came out together at The Basement Club. We went through a traumatic series of events together and bonded like veterans of war. We supported each other. We connected at school. We kept our distance at The Club. We did not want them to find out we were friends. The code was: the eastern Europeans stick together, and the Americans do the same. No crossover. Except there was.

I cry myself to sleep.

7 August 1989
Monday
New York, New York
10:00

EMMA

My parents and I meet with Robert McCauley and Connor Grey at ten o'clock. I like Connor immediately.

"How are you doing this morning, Emma?" Connor asks.

"Good."

"I assume you know Nadia's missing."

"I heard."

He smiles. "When was the last time you saw her?"

"In the bathroom at Macy's."

"Did you see anyone else in the bathroom?"

"A woman with a green beret came in and out."

"The girls in her safe house are freaked out that she didn't come back last night. Do you think someone got to her?"

I want to say no, but instead I say, "I don't know."

"You don't seem upset that she's gone."

"No. We had a conversation about freedom and

imprisonment. I wouldn't be surprised if she walked away."

"Why would she do that?"

"She felt like a prisoner in the safe house."

"She told you that?"

"Yes."

"You two were close."

It is not a question. "Yes. We did our debut together at The Basement Club when we were ten years old."

His eyes widen. He nods. "I'm sorry."

"Me, too. But the good news is we got close. She started coming to my school and we became friends. She was the only friend I had."

"It must have been good to see her."

"It was great to see her. I got to hear about her life. She believed that soon she would be free of the sex trafficking."

"I'm glad for you and for her."

"Thank you. Me, too."

"So. Let's talk about your upcoming visit with MaryLou. As you know, she's been transferred from house arrest to the women's jail."

Connor talks about the jail setting and walks me through every step. "I'll be there with you all the way to the interview room. There will be a table and two chairs. You will have the chair that is nearest to the exit. There's a button under the table that you can push at any time. If you push it a guard will come and ask you what you need. MaryLou will not be chained or in handcuffs."

"Will anyone be able to hear our conversation?"

"No, unless you want to wear a wire."

"Why would I do that?"

"We might possibly get more information about her

part in The Club."

"Hasn't she already admitted that she was bringing girls into the United States under the guise of being foreign exchange students?"

"Yes. But we've discovered that all the girls went to school, too. They learned English and got an education."

"At the same time as they were being sexually abused." I feel this fact will get lost if I do not state it directly.

"That's true. What we don't know is how much MaryLou knew about The Club."

"She knew she was recruiting girls. She gave me to Peter, who gave me to other men. My parents sold me to the wolves." I am angry, angrier than I want to be.

"We know she gave you to The Club. I am sorry for this."

I want to say, *Leave your sorrys for someone else who needs them,* but I can tell he is sincerely sorry. "Do you have children, Connor?"

"One daughter. She's five."

"What's her name?"

"Ana."

"I like that name. I was five when Peer started grooming me and a hell of a lot younger when MaryLou gave me to him. Can you imagine Ana living like that?"

"I don't want to imagine it. It's horrible, beyond comprehension. I want to get these guys as much as you do, Emma. Believe me."

"I'll wear the wire. I want girls and boys to be safe from sexual abuse and trafficking. I'll do whatever it takes."

Connor doesn't say anything. I feel like saying, *That's why I'm majoring in Criminal Justice and then going on to law school. I'm going to get the bad guys one by one.*

"What made you go into law enforcement?"

"My father was a mean drunk and he took it out on my mother. My sister and I finally got her to leave him after he beat her to a pulp. She was lucky to get out before he killed her. Needless to say, I wanted to get the bad guys."

"You and me both."

"I can tell you that everyone in this business, everyone who's really, truly in, has a story. We all have a mission. That mission varies but it runs along these same lines: *I want to make the world a better, safer place.* Glad you want to join the club."

I smile. "Some clubs are worth joining."

8 August 1989
Tuesday
New York, New York
13:30

EMMA

"Thank you for meeting with me, MaryLou."

"Lydia—"

"My name is Emma. Lydia died over four years ago."

"Okay. Emma."

"I've got a bunch of questions, MaryLou, so I'd like to jump in."

"Okay."

"Why did you give me to Peter, MaryLou? Why did you allow him and the other men to abuse me?"

I watch her face contort. It's probably pain, but right now it is not her pain that I care about, it is mine. Perhaps later I can care about hers. I don't say, *You fed me to the wolves.*

"I could not protect both you and Isabelle."

"Why not? You could have left."

"I couldn't."

"You could have, MaryLou, but you didn't."

"I couldn't go back to the poverty."

"Poverty? What does poverty have to do with it?"

"As a child I lived in a ramshackle house with a leaky roof. I was always hungry. I escaped from that life when I married your father."

"Peter. I call him Peter. I need you to call him that."

"Okay. Peter."

"So having your daughter abused and being rich was better?"

"I thought so at the time."

"And now?"

"I was mistaken."

"Did you ever look for me?"

"No. I prayed every day that you had found a better place."

"You prayed? I don't ever remember you praying." As soon as I say it, I have a vague recollection of her and Isabelle and me going to church, sitting in a pew, MaryLou's head bowed.

"When I was a girl, my family went to church together every Sunday. We sat together in the family pew."

"We stopped going to church when I was five."

"Yes. Your father—sorry—Peter, would not allow it."

"Why not?"

"He wanted control. He didn't want anyone to know about our family. He was afraid I might talk to the minister, not purposely, but in a moment of weakness. He was afraid I might say something that he did not want known. In the end I decided I couldn't go anymore, Emma. I couldn't face the minister. I couldn't face myself."

I am quiet. I understand not being able to face myself.

"So Peter knew what he was doing was wrong and he was afraid you would blow his cover?"

"I don't know if Peter thought he was doing anything wrong. He had odd ideas and thoughts about what was normal in a family."

"Odd? What does that mean?"

"Unusual."

I wait. MaryLou looks like she's having difficulty finding the right words.

"Unusual? How? What?"

"Like how a parent takes care of their children. Peter was not taken care of by his family."

"Come on, MaryLou. He went to a good college and then he went to Harvard Medical School, one of the best medical schools in the country. You're telling me his parents didn't take care of him?" I'm surprised how aggressive I feel.

"That's what I'm telling you, Emma. Just because he left home and went to school and became a doctor does not take away that he was harmed."

"Harmed? How?"

"His father physically assaulted him, and his mother sexually abused him."

"He told you that?"

"Yes."

"I don't remember you guys talking about anything, ever."

"Early on we talked, when we were dating and when Isabelle was little. Mostly I listened to him talk. I was a safe refuge for him. That had all pretty much fallen by the wayside when you were born."

"What happened?"

"I think it was the stress of having a child, and a child with special needs to boot. It brought out the worst in Peter. He had never been patient, but after Isabelle was born he got agitated and demanding. He was used to having all my attention, and Isabelle required a lot of my time. He didn't deal with this very well."

"What did he do?"

"He got more demanding. I was afraid he would hurt Isabelle. I stopped leaving her alone with him even for short trips to the grocery store."

"Did he hurt you?"

"Sometimes. He was unpredictable, that was the scary part. He wasn't like my father. My father's behavior was like clockwork. Every drink he took I knew what came next. I could prepare for it."

I am shocked by MaryLou's honesty about her relationship with her father and with Peter. I know Peter's unpredictable, erratic behavior and his lapses into violence, but I resist the temptation to commiserate with her. I will not share details of my experiences with MaryLou. She is not my friend or part of my support system. I do not want to talk about myself and my feelings with her, and I do not want to give her the power that knowledge would provide. I don't trust her. She did not take care of me.

After my dream when I got clear that I needed to meet with MaryLou and Peter, I met with both Christy and Jeremy, my therapists. We talked about what I hoped to achieve in these meetings. I am here on a fact-finding mission. I want to put some of the pieces of my life in place, pieces that have been hanging out there with nowhere to go. I want to make sense of my situation even though I know that applying logic doesn't make my situation understandable. *One meeting at a time.* That's my mantra. I use it to stay focused. The truth is, I don't know if I will have another meeting with Peter or MaryLou. This might be a one-shot deal. *One meeting at a time.* It's a good mantra, a good reminder. It takes some of the pressure off.

"And you? Did you, do you, have distorted ideas about what is normal in a family, MaryLou?"

"I did. I probably still do. I don't know what normal really is."

"But you know what normal isn't?"

She sighs. "Sometimes. Then I forget. I go on autopilot and I'm back to my old ways of thinking, old ways of surviving. I don't have any real friends, Emma. I just have my sister. She's the only person I trust, the only person who really knows me, although I hide things from her, too."

"Why?"

"I guess I'm still trying to protect her. Old habits die hard."

"What were you protecting her from?"

"My father."

My stomach tightens. "What about your father?"

"He was an alcoholic and he sexually abused me. I was able to keep him from abusing my sister. It became my job."

"What was your mother doing?"

"Working. All the time she was working. Trying to make enough money to put food on the table, clothes on our backs, and keep a roof over our heads."

"You didn't tell her what your father was doing to

you?"

"No. I needed to protect her."

"Just like you needed to protect Isabelle and not me?"

"I believed you could take care of yourself."

"I was five, MaryLou."

"It's not logical, Lydia."

"I'm Emma. Please call me by my name."

"Emma, what I did is not right. I was wrong. I chose Isabelle and myself over you."

"Why?"

"It was part of the bargain."

"The bargain?"

"What I had to give up to keep living in the house."

"You thought he would divorce you?"

"No. I never worried about that. But if I kept Isabelle from being abused, I had to do certain things."

"So it was a negotiation?"

"Of sorts."

I am quiet.

"You loved Isabelle more?"

"No. I believed she needed my protection more than you did. You were my feisty girl, full of energy. Strong. You spoke your mind. When you didn't come home that night when you were fifteen, I was happy. I hoped you had gone to a better place. I needed to believe that."

Again I am quiet. MaryLou is honest. It is hard to hear her truth, but I appreciate her saying it to me. She does not justify. She does not sugarcoat any of her behavior. We are two people having a conversation, with the caveat that she is my estranged birth mother, and I am her adult daughter.

"I was wrong, Emma. I am sorry. I don't know how to

make it better."

I look at her. "It is my job to forgive."

"I don't know how you would do that."

"In the last four years I've learned that I can only recover from this sexual abuse and trauma if I forgive. Coming to visit you, talking and hearing your story, is part of my healing process."

"What I've done is not forgivable. My own mother would be aghast at what I did."

"Why do you say that?"

"She did everything in her power to take care of my sister and me."

"And still, you were abused."

"She had no idea my father was sexually abusing me. I never told her. She had enough to worry about. I believe if she had known what he was doing to me, she would have tried to protect me. Instead, I took on protecting my sister."

"So you protected your sister and my sister, but you did not protect me?"

"No. I did not protect you. I told myself I couldn't, that your father was my ticket out of poverty. I had no idea that the abuse would continue with him."

"Peter was abusing you when you were dating him?"

"Yes, but I only saw it in hindsight. With my history it was normal that men took sexual liberties with girls and women, that it was their right to do so. I got pregnant with Isabelle while Peter and I were dating. I never told him that. I wasn't sure what he would do, how he would react. I had no idea what I was going to do. All my confusion went away when Peter asked me to marry him. I felt lucky. He was a doctor; he had money. I thought everything would be different when we got married."

"But it wasn't."

"No. It was the same except I had a beautiful home, nice clothes, a car, all the trappings of what I thought would make my life different."

"You were naïve."

She gives me a half-smile. "Sadly, tragically, I was."

"But then you got on the Board and helped him get girls for The Basement Club. Why did you do that?"

"At first I thought it was a normal board. I worked with schools and couples to give poor, eastern European girls an opportunity to go to school in the United States and have a safe place to live."

"But at some point you must have known that something else was going on. The Club was in our basement, MaryLou."

"Yes, at some point I knew."

"When?"

"When I watched a good-looking, dark-haired man open the van door and eight girls got out and walked into our basement."

"You didn't question what was going on?"

"I did. They were all carrying presents. I thought it was some kind of party for you."

I am stopped in my tracks. My debut. "Some kind of party?"

I hear MaryLou's voice in the background. "It doesn't make sense to me now, Emma."

"That was over four years before I got out."

"I did a lot of thinking after you disappeared. I never believed you were dead. I didn't know where you were, but when Peter came home from the school meeting with Miss

Jacobs and the principal, he was absolutely convinced that she helped you leave. He set a plan in motion to get her convicted of killing you. We never talked about it, but I heard him on the phone hobnobbing with his friends, and I was in and out of the room the night the men devised a plan to entrap her."

"So you knew they were going to make it look like Miss Jacobs murdered me?"

"Yes."

"Did you ever think about going to the authorities?"

"No. I thought I had too much to lose, and I didn't think they would believe me."

"So you went along?"

"I went along, thinking things would get better because he could no longer harm you."

"But you didn't know where I was, and you said you didn't look for me."

"I didn't look for you, but I did talk with Miss Jacobs one time."

"What? What did she tell you?"

"She didn't tell me anything specifically, but she conveyed that you were safe, never to be found again unless you chose to be found, Lydia."

"Please don't call me that. I'm Emma. I never want Lydia's life again."

"Yet here you are."

"It's the right thing to do."

"You always wanted to do the right thing."

I stare at her. "What does that mean?"

"When you were a little girl and your father and I fought, you tried to make things better. Your father loved you—"

"Stop, MaryLou. I can't listen to you talk about Peter loving me. I've had enough for now. I need to go."

I get up to leave. She stands up as well.

"Thank you for meeting with me, Emma. If you want to visit again, I will be glad to see you. If you want to write to me when I'm in prison, I will write you back."

"Thank you for meeting with me, MaryLou. Thank you for your honesty. I don't know about visiting you or writing you. I'm on overload now. I need to leave."

When I get through the clinging and clanging of the gates, I see Theo and Frank. I run to them. They hold me as I cry.

We spend the rest of the day at the hotel. We order in and watch movies on television. My dad cancels the afternoon meeting with the FBI. I am glad he stepped in and told them I needed a break. They didn't push it. Tomorrow morning I will meet again with Connor Grey and Robert McCauley. We will talk about my upcoming visit with Peter. Then my parents and I will drive up to Cape Vincent. I want to show them around. I want them to see the river and the lighthouse, and I want to visit the library. I wonder if Mrs. Malone, the librarian, is still there. Four years is a long time in one way, but in another, it is just a blip on the radar. We plan to go swimming, and I will see if my parents can find the exact place where the St. Lawrence meets Lake Ontario, Cape Vincent's claim to fame.

9 August 1989
Wednesday
New York, New York
03:13

EMMA

I wake up early hearing the words, *Do not meet with Peter now. It is not the right time.* I breathe a sigh of relief. A full breath. I didn't know I was breathing shallowly. I don't know if I will ever visit Peter, although I will see him in the courtroom at his trial. I don't know if I will attend his hearing. Everything's up for grabs. I thought I had a plan. Now I am being asked to stay present and make my plans as I go. No future planning. Am I disappointed? No. Well, maybe a little. I had no idea how hard it would be to sit in a room with MaryLou and stay present. I was fraught with barely contained emotion. I hear my therapist Christy's voice: *It is difficult to truly forgive.* But there is something else that I experienced yesterday. I had to guard against being sucked into the vortex of MaryLou's pain, of Peter's painful history, new information to me. I had to remember that I was on a fact-finding mission. I kept repeating in my head, *fact-finding mission.* It took work and endless repetition of this mantra so I could stay grounded and present. Then I hear Jeremy's voice: *It takes work to have boundaries, and when your parents do not have boundaries around sex, the lines are murky.* I think, more than murky—grey, non-existent. I became the sex object. I had to, so I could survive. And then I hear: Betrayal, Abandonment, Abuse. *BAA*...I say it out loud. I bleat like a wounded sheep.

I call Jeremy and he picks up the phone.

"Jeremy, this is Emma. I hope I didn't wake you up."

"Emma, what's going on?"

"I met with MaryLou yesterday and I woke up crying for my perpetrators."

"MaryLou and Peter?"

"Yes. Except it was for my mother and father." I can hardly breathe.

"Breathe, Emma. Long, slow breaths."

"BAA," I bleat and laugh.

"What does BAA mean?"

"Betrayal. Abandonment. Abuse. BAA." I laugh wildly.

"Having a sense of humor is a good thing, Emma."

"Is it?" It's a rhetorical question.

"I'm smiling," he says. "Bigger issue is, you acknowledged MaryLou as your mother and Peter as your father."

We sit in silence on the phone for several long moments.

I say, "I want to hide. It's like I'm peeking out from a dark closet."

"And you called me from that closet."

"Yes. I don't like being in the dark, alone. Did I actually say my mother and father?" My throat constricts.

"You said, *my perpetrators, my mother and father*."

"My perpetrators, my mother and father."

"Betrayal. Abandonment. Abuse. BAA," he says.

I start singing. "Baa, baa black sheep..."

He laughs.

I feel his love. He's got my back. There is no betrayal here. But Jeremy knows all about betrayal. He's a sexual abuse survivor, too.

"It goes on," I say.

"It?"

"This healing. These knowings. This gut-wrenching pain."

"Yes. It goes on. Gifts with thorns."

"Gifts with thorns?"

"Gifts that keep on giving."

"Sometimes the pain feels like too much."

"Sometimes it does, Emma. But, I'm a believer that we never get more than we can handle."

I nod even though he can't see me. I used to debate him about this, but no more. I know what he says is true. I may not feel ready to handle something, but that does not mean I can't handle it.

"Chunks," he says. "Another chunk."

"A chunk of cheese," I say.

"A wedge."

"Smelly brie."

"Rotten cheddar."

I laugh.

He laughs.

"I'll see you when I get home."

"See you when you get home. And Emma, if you need or want to talk again before you get to Santa Fe, call me."

"Thank you."

SECTION 3

ALICE

9 August 1989
Wednesday
Waiuku, New Zealand
10:13

ALICE

I call my parents and leave a message on their answering machine. I leave my phone number and address. When they call me back there is a lot of crying and relief that I am safe. I tell them I am pregnant.

And then the letter writing begins, just like in prison. Except this time, I get to be in touch with my brother and sister, too.

Oliver writes:

I got into Harvard. Mari did not. We both got accepted to the University of Vermont in Burlington. She wants me to go there, so we can be together, but I want to go to Harvard. Mom and Dad encouraged me to go where I want to go. I told Mari that I'm going to Harvard. It was hard to see her upset and disappointed. She told me that we'd never been apart, and she wanted to be together. I told her perhaps it was time to be on our own. She kept repeating she did not want to be separated. She talked about how great it was when we were at camp together, how we talked every day. I agreed that it was great but that now it was time for something different. Now we are apart, and I feel free.

Mari tells me a different story:

Oli got into Harvard. I didn't. I cried when Mom and Dad took me to my dorm at the University of Vermont and left me there. I was so afraid, Eliza. I feel like everyone's leaving me. My roommate, Shelly, is nice. She's from a small town in northern Vermont and goes home most weekends. I go with her. Her parents and younger brother are great. I've become like another member of their family.

I think it's home I miss. I don't really know. Mom hasn't visited me since they dropped me off at school. The last thing she said to me was, "Sink or swim." I think Mom's glad to be free of me, maybe of us. I get it, but it hurts. I need something. Dad has visited and taken Shelly and me out to eat. The three of us took a boat ride on Lake Champlain, and I had fun, but I wished Mom had been there, too. Dad said she was busy. I don't understand why she doesn't want to visit me.

I write my sister back.

Mom's tired. She's had a lot to contend with. I

don't think it has anything to do with you, Mari. I'm sorry you are hurting.

Underneath it all, I think what my mom thinks and had the guts to say—*Mari, sink or swim.*

Mom writes:

Oliver is happy and easy to be around. He loves Harvard and is completely engaged in the academic life. Mari's transition has been difficult. After I told her to sink or swim I knew I had to back away. I hurt her and I do not want to do any more harm. Your dad has taken her on. He's working with her on how to be in the world. I'm taking a memoir class and am writing my story. I've identified two themes: independence and self-sufficiency. I realize that having the twins late in life was a stretch. I don't think I would have felt that way if I had not had you. Raising children for so long took its toll on me. It was so hard to let you go, Eliza. Yet with the twins I feel relief.

I am so happy you are pregnant. You will be a great mom. I am looking forward to being a grandmother.

Dad writes.

All is well here. Your mother and I are enjoying the freedom of the empty nest. The Basement Club trials have begun. I am following them closely. I am busy at work and am looking forward to seeing you at Christmas. I miss you and am glad you are safe and sound in New Zealand. Mason is a lucky guy.

In late January after all our Christmas guests are gone, Mom writes:

> *We got home safely. The twins are back at school, and your dad and I are getting back to our lives. Strange to be in snow and cold weather after having spent two weeks in summer in your new home.*
>
> *The biggest news is that Oliver gave a school tour to Emma Maxwell and her parents. Strange, but true. Now they are dating. He is smitten with her. She has transferred from her community college in Santa Fe and will do her next two years at Harvard. He tells me her plan is to apply to Harvard Law School. He is happy to have a girlfriend. Your father and I are thrilled. We're going down to Boston in February to meet her and take in a hockey game, Bruins vs Red Wings.*

When Mason gets home, I tell him about Oliver and Emma.

Mason says, "I think we should visit your folks and my mom."

"I'm never going back."

"Why?"

"Because I don't want to."

"Why not?"

"I like it here. New Zealand is my home now."

"I know it's your home. It's my home, too."

"But...?"

"You're expecting everyone to come to you."

"Yup. That's how it is, Mason. I'm not going back to a country where I got locked up, and not just locked up, falsely accused, and condemned to death."

He is quiet. This is where I always go when we have this discussion.

I remind him, just like I've reminded him all the other times, "I lived underground for three years and nine months. You got to leave every day and run in the woods, visit Celeste, have a beer with Terran. I did not have those privileges."

He backs off.

17 May 1990
Friday
Waiuku, New Zealand
11:56

ALICE

On 17 May 1990, Cora is born one year to the day I escaped from prison. With her birth my heart opens in some way that I do not understand. My heart opened when Mari and Oliver were born, but my mother never talked about her heart opening. She and my dad had me when they were young, and I was raised as an only child. I was away at college when the twins were born, and it was like two separate families. I felt more like their aunt than their sister. I lived at home the first summer after college when they were infants and helped my mother take care of them. I got my lessons in changing diapers and feeding newborns. My mother said they were easy babies and told me I had been an easy baby, too. *But somehow these two, well, they have each other, don't they? They don't need me as much as you did.* I questioned my mom about this. She was struggling, although she kept a stiff upper lip, and the twins thrived.

The twins slept together in a big double-wide crib. Every night I looked in on them before I went to bed, and every time they had moved right next to each other, rump to rump usually, or if they were on their backs one of them had their arm flung onto the other one, always touching, always connected. They were never alone, had never been alone until they went to different colleges.

Now I have my own baby, Cora Marlene MacFarland. Cora's middle name honors Mason's mother, Marjorie, and my mother, Arlene. Mason and I stare at Cora while she sleeps. My mom and dad are coming to New Zealand for the month of August. The twins will be working and will not be coming this time. Oliver attends the Basement Club trials regularly with Emma and does not want to leave her while she is dealing with this. My mom offered to come and help me take care of the baby when she was born. I told her I would be fine, that I'd see her in August.

When I got pregnant, Mason wanted to immediately make contact with our families. I said no. When the article came out in *The New York Times* that my conviction was overturned and there would be no charges brought against Mason, I told him I needed a few days before I reached out to my family. I felt raw and vulnerable. I was living in New Zealand. I was a midwife with a full practice. I questioned being free. When I got pregnant, I talked with Lucy, who had birthed three children who were now adults. She became like a mother to me. Well, maybe more like a big sister, something I would have liked but never had. There are good and not so good things about being raised as an only child. There was a lot of aloneness and a lot of loneliness. I craved to be alone, juxtaposed with the desire to be with people. This issue consumed me until Cora was born. She is our little, bright-spirited girl who was born free.

"So, I think we should take Cora to visit her grandparents, aunt and uncle, and extended family."

"No. Not now. She's too young."

"You don't want Cora to meet her family?"

"Of course I want her to meet them."

"So..."

"What I am not interested in, Mason, is visiting the United States."

"So when do you begin to move on?"

He challenges me, which he's never done before.

"I've moved on, Mason. I'm here in New Zealand. I have a daughter. I'm a midwife in this community, my community, our community. I have friends."

"But you don't want to leave and visit family and friends."

"No. I don't want to leave now. I don't know if I will ever want to leave. If you want to go, go. Have a great visit, then come home."

"I don't want to go without you."

I want to say, *That's your problem, not mine.* I've said this before, early on when we debated what free meant, what freedom actually is.

"Freedom is not being run by fear," he says.

And although I theoretically agree with him, I cannot embrace that now.

"I will not put my daughter, our daughter, in harm's way."

"So you won't let me take her?"

"Not now."

"When?"

"Maybe when she's five."

I go out to hang the laundry.

I think about the twists and turns in my life. I try to find a way out of my circular thinking. I worked on this in The Tomb, the dungeon with grey concrete walls that sometimes dripped with water as though they were sweating. I'd pull the collar of my dark blue sweater tighter around my neck. I'd hear my mother's voice, *Pull up your collar, Eliza. Keep the chill out. You don't want to get sick.* As a child I bought in. I believed her. I rarely got sick. No missed school days. Always layers of clothes, taking them off and putting them on, not staying warm too long, not staying cold too long.

I listened to PG One and Two talk about The Tomb. Josh Candry did not like working below the earth in a cave. He left as often as he could and always sighed when he returned. When he got a tape deck, he'd go right to the music. When I was still talking, I never asked him what music he was listening to. I could tell by his tapping on the desk and the moving of his shoulders that it was something with a strong beat. I imagined it was rock and roll. That's what I would have listened to. I was envious he had a way out even though he was in The Tomb. He was happy when his shift was done and eager to leave. When he took his summer vacation, he came back tan and relaxed, but quickly his shoulders tightened. PG Two, Kevin, was a quieter, more contemplative guy. He liked doing crossword puzzles and he hummed tunes I knew and tunes I had never heard. I liked his humming. I hummed in my mind, maybe even sometimes out loud. I can't believe I am thinking about all of this. I don't want to be.

I jam the wooden clothespin onto the line. One clean sheet touches the ground, and I am angry because there is dirt on it. My anger is like a volcano heating up, ready to burst.

Mason comes with Cora to where I am hanging the clothes.

"Maybe it's time to see a therapist."

"For what?" I shoot back.

"The trauma, sweetheart."

"I'm dealing with it."

"I'm not saying you aren't."

"Really. Then why are you bringing it up?"

"I'm concerned. You're edgier than usual."

"And you don't like that?"

"I didn't say that, Alice. Maybe talking about your experience might be helpful."

"I lived it, Mason. I don't want to relive it."

"But you are reliving it."

"You have no idea what I'm doing."

"I think I have some idea."

I shoot him a look.

"But you're right, I probably don't really have any idea. I'm going to take Cora to town, give you a break, and visit Austin and Lucy."

"I don't need a break."

"I do."

This is how these discussions end. I am normally self-satisfied that he's admitted he doesn't know anything. But right now my self-satisfaction has worn thin. I am hanging laundry, something I like to do, because I like to see the colors blow in the breeze and I love to look at the bay, but I am miserable. The jig is up. I can no longer pretend I can work through this on my own. It is seventeen October 1990, a fall day in Cape Vincent, but here it's a spring day heading to summer. Cora is five months old. I finish hanging the laundry without dropping any more of it in the dirt. I walk into the house and take the card that Lucy gave me out of the drawer. I call Ellen Glasco, a therapist. She sounds nice enough. I've heard this same answering machine three or four times, but I've never left a message before.

I sit at the kitchen table after I put on the kettle for coffee. I feel the first shred of hope that I can actually get free, whatever the fuck that means.

I take out the letter Emma wrote me.

Dear Miss Jacobs,

I am so sorry you spent three years and nine months in prison. I don't say almost four years and I don't say three-plus years because I know how important time is. I know exactly how many days I've been out of The Basement Club. It's all due to you. Thank you. These two words seem hollow and minimal, yet underneath them I have immense gratitude for you walking me out that door and putting me into a cab. I have never forgotten your reassuring words—you will be taken care of. And I was, I am, every single day since I escaped from the abuse.

I have deep sorrow that you were imprisoned in The Tomb. Your sacrifice enabled me to get free and have a life.

I am majoring in Criminal Justice and plan to

go to law school, all because of you. You gave me this chance.

As you know, your brother and I are dating. If you don't mind, I would like to visit you. I could come on my own for a few days, and then maybe Oliver would come so we could visit you together and also tour New Zealand. I am ready to take a break from the trials.

Again, thank you.

Peace and love,
Emma Maxwell

When I first read this letter, I cried. I was in the garden with Cora, who was quietly sleeping. My tears fell onto the pumpkins I had planted. They don't celebrate Halloween here in New Zealand, but we will carve a pumpkin because that is my tradition. Mason never carved a pumpkin with his father, but he did get to celebrate Halloween with Celeste and Cal and Derrick. Some things don't die, they get reborn.

I want Emma to come for a visit. I want to talk with her about freedom, something I can't seem to get a firm grip on. Perhaps that's how it is with freedom—there is no firm grip. Strange, because I am tied to Mason, Cora, Austin and Lucy, Waiuku, Hickory Farm, this land, and the bay. I am also tied to my family and Cape Vincent. Everything I've ever wanted is right here, right now. For the first time in my life connection does not feel like suffocation, strangulation, and ultimately death. A change has come over me. I am no longer Eliza, the one who struggles with connection and space. I am Alice. I take space when I need it and embrace connection when I need that. I am married, and it does not feel like a yoke around my neck. I feel more free than I ever have. I have the structure of a home, a family, and a community.

Further, I have come clean. I talked with Austin and Lucy first, and then I got up and spoke at the town meeting. I told my story. People cheered. They asked questions. I answered them as honestly as I could. At the end I read Emma's letter and talked about how this girl, now a young woman, is living a life she never knew she could have. I ended with my own *thank you*, those two small words that say it all. Afterward I talked with John Taylor as we ate Lucy's delicious brownies. He is an editor and he encouraged me to write my memoir, said he would help me edit it and get it published. Sandra Collins, an advocate for victims of abuse, suggested we host an international conference on healing from sexual abuse and trauma. This community's love and support warmed my heart. My pregnant mothers hugged me and held my hands. We cried together. Everyone accepted me and Mason and Cora. Not one person turned away from us.

Ellen Glasco calls me back and I schedule an appointment for the next day.

That first session she tells me, "If you do the work, you can heal. You will never forget, but the trauma will not run you anymore. You will have freedom of choice."

"My life is in upheaval. I can't stop my crazy thinking. I'm like a hamster on a wheel who can't get off the wheel, the two seem to be glued to each other."

"What does the wheel say to the hamster?"

"Get off."

"Then what happens to the wheel?"

"It's rolling down a hill, rolling to freedom, except I start going too fast and feel out of control. I end up in a rock pile, stopped, because I got off track, off the trajectory that would take me where I want to go."

"Where do you want to go?"

"To a place of acceptance, to a place of peace and balance."

Ellen says, "In every dream, in every image, you are that image."

Therapy is going well. I am less edgy and caustic with Mason. I no longer pretend that I wasn't harmed, and I am more accepting of the wrongs that were done to me before and during my incarceration. Detective Serge Valentino has been convicted and sentenced to fifteen years in prison. I think it should be more, and I vent my fury with Ellen.

"I want to slam him against the wall and hold him there by the throat and castrate him. Then leave him there to bleed to death."

Ellen doesn't flinch.

"I feel the same way about The Warden."

When I get home I talk to Mason about my fury.

"I hate Detective Valentino."

"I imagine you hate The Warden, too."

"I don't like him."

"That's quite an understatement. My father's a bastard and a mean son of a bitch. He's a pawn in the system."

I listen. Ellen and I talked about how Mason has to deal with his father, that I need to stay out of it.

"No. He's more like the rook or the horse." I go with Mason's chess metaphor.

He says, "Peter Garth's the king. The Governor's the

queen. The Judge is the rook. The Detective is the horse. My father's the bishop. MaryLou, Eli, and the girls are the pawns."

"What about The Accountant?"

"He's gone, disappeared. No one knows his name, and The Men are not saying."

"The chess analogy doesn't totally work."

"No, but it does give us a way to talk about this."

"Yes. A game where I did not know the rules, and I got caught up in something way bigger than me."

In therapy, Ellen reminds me, "And you got free."

"I escaped. I want to be free."

"What does free mean to you?"

"Able to say the truth."

"Check," she says.

She's right. I can and do say the truth now. Mason and I have disagreements, but they do not last long, and when my rage is like hot lava, I walk away and take space. Take Cora or don't take her. Visit Lucy. Take a walk. Write. Call someone. I have increasing numbers of women whom I can reach out to. I do not have to be alone any longer. If I need a listening ear, all I have to do is pick up the phone, which used to feel like a hundred-pound weight. No more.

"How things change," says Ellen.

"Yes. Always there is change."

"So when do Emma and Oliver arrive?"

"In July. School gets out in May, and Emma is scheduled to testify in June. Then they're coming for a month. They'll stay with us and also go travelling on their own. I'm looking forward to their visit. Emma is coming by herself first so she and I can spend a few days together before Oliver arrives. She wants this, and I do, too."

3 June 1991
Monday
Watertown, New York
09:17

EMMA

I am in the courtroom waiting for Peter Garth to be brought in by one of the deputies. Oliver is sitting next to me, and Mom and Dad are on the other side. Oliver's parents are behind me. Connor Grey and Robert McCauley are sitting in front of me. I am surrounded by people I trust. Even so, my heart is pounding, and my face feels hot. I have not seen Peter since I left Cape Vincent over six years ago. When he enters the courtroom there is a hushed silence. He looks thin and old. His hair is grey. I see his eyes scanning the courtroom. I am glad Connor is in front of me. I don't think Peter can see me.

After Peter says he will tell the whole truth and nothing but the truth, the deputy seats him. Peter's eyes keep wandering all over the courtroom. I see him stop at Connor Grey. He gives him the finger. Connor does not move an inch.

Then I hear Peter. "I know you're here, Lydia. Come

out, come out, wherever you are. You don't have to hide from me. I want to see you, Lydia."

I want to scream. I feel Oliver's arm tighten around me.

"Mr. Garth, you need to control yourself."

"It's Dr. Garth, Judge. I want to be called by my rightful title."

"Dr. Garth it will be."

"I want to see your face, Lydia. I want to look at you. Why are you hiding from me? I know you're here, but I can't find you."

"Dr. Garth, I need for you to stop talking out of turn."

"Come out, come out, wherever you are. No need to be hiding, Lydia."

"Counselor, if your client cannot control himself, he will have to be removed from the courtroom."

And then he sees me. Connor bent down to get something, and I am visible.

"There you are, Lydia. You've gained some weight. You were nice and thin when you were with me."

I can't stop staring at him even though I do not want to be looking at him. My cheeks are hot, and my neck must be red because it is itching.

"Ah, that lovely flush on your neck, Lydia.

"Counselor, control your client."

I start to rise up. Oliver squeezes my arm, and my mom reaches over and takes my hand.

"You betrayed me, Lydia. A good daughter does not betray her father. You will rot in hell."

His voice is thunderous, and then Peter lunges at me, but he can't get by Connor Grey. The deputies cuff him as he continues to spew his venom at me.

As they remove him from the courtroom he continues to shout. "Why did you betray me, Lydia? Why did you abandon me? I loved you. Look what you've done to me."

And then he is gone and there is a recess.

My mom says, "Breathe, honey. Long, slow breaths."

I do what she says. I didn't know I was holding my breath.

I look at Connor, who has tears in his eyes.

"Did you sit in front of me to protect me?"

"Let's just say I wanted to ensure your safety."

"He was going to have to get through you if he wanted me."

"Protect and serve," Connor says.

"Thank you."

"Thank you, Emma. Your courage is inspirational and a testament that people can change their lives."

"I've had a lot of support. Can I hug you?"

He opens his arms. I walk into them and close my eyes.

When I open my eyes, I am surrounded by my parents, Oliver, Oliver's parents, and Robert McCauley.

"A circle of love. Thank you." And then I begin to cry.

1 November 1991
Friday
Waiuku, New Zealand
10:00

ALICE

I tell Ellen, "In three weeks, the conference starts. Oliver is flying over with Emma and Theo and Frank the week before. They'll stay with us until my parents get here, then they will go to Norma and Kent's boarding house. They're putting up a lot of the out-of-town guests who are presenting at the conference. She'll feed them well and give them the lay of the land. Mari is not sure she's coming, but I hope she does. I don't want her to feel left out."

Ellen says, "Yet, maybe she needs the separation, on her terms?"

I look at Ellen and nod. "That could be."

"How are you and Mason doing?"

"We're good. I feel lighter. When we have something going on and he wants to hug me, I usually let him. I don't feel like screaming. I'm not suffocating. Images of strangulation and death don't dance in my head. So there's that."

Ellen laughs. "You've done a lot of work. It's good to see you reaping the benefits."

"I never would have been able to help make this conference happen if I hadn't."

"Who is coming?"

"Theo and Frank Maxwell will do a workshop on providing a safe home for abused girls. My mom and dad are going to lead a parenting group along with Eli's and Cristiane's parents. Billy Williams and his wife, Su. He's doing a talk about the importance of changing your name and your identity for safety purposes. Robert McCauley and Connor Grey, the FBI agents who broke the case. Emma is the keynote speaker on Friday night and Cristiane will do the honors on Saturday night. Theo will tell her story on Sunday morning after breakfast. She will close out the conference. Celeste, Terran, Mason's mother, and Mrs. Teasdale are also coming."

"Aah, the Marjories."

I laugh. "Yes. Robert Bruce, the Cape Vincent police chief, and his wife. Eli, Cristiane, and Tasha. Girls who escaped from The Basement Club and other sex trafficking rings. The Network folks."

"Your whole crew from the United States."

"Yes. Twenty-six countries will be represented. There may be more."

21 November 1991
Thursday
Auckland, New Zealand
Aotea Centre
16:30

ALICE

"Welcome to the First International Trauma and Sexual Abuse Conference. I am Alice MacFarland, one of the team members who has worked on and organized this ‵conference. I am originally from the United States. Two and a half years ago I emigrated to New Zealand. Happy Thanksgiving to all. In the US, Thanksgiving is a holiday that focuses on gratitude. I am happy to share a traditional Thanksgiving dinner with you. We are all here to welcome you and hope that this conference brings you many gifts. At the dessert table you will find traditional holiday desserts from many different countries. You can read about what the dessert is and which country offers it, or you can talk with a person from that country who will tell you about their food. As we eat dessert, Maori women and men will do a welcoming ceremony. At the conclusion of this ceremony we will open the twenty-four-hour-a-day meeting room that provides a supportive, safe space that will remain open throughout the conference. There are suggestion boxes in every conference room, and there is an information booth that will be staffed throughout the day. We have professionally trained therapists available if you need this kind of support. We would love to hear from you about what is working and what is not working. Team members will be wearing purple shirts with our conference logo on the front and the back. Please feel free to talk to any of us at any time."

When everyone has gotten their dessert, I introduce Emma, tonight's keynote speaker.

As Emma walks toward the podium there is a hush in the room.

"Emmuh."

"Cora."

"Wov you."

"I love you, too, Cora-Bora."

My mom takes Cora out of the room.

"Welcome everyone. I am so happy and honored to be here. I am Emma, a survivor of sexual abuse and trafficking."

"Hi, Emma," says a chorus of voices.

At the end of Emma's talk every person in the room stands and people begin singing *We Shall Overcome*. The harmonies are strong and beautiful. Then women come to the microphone and sing songs from their countries about hope and love. They teach the group the words, and the women and men form a circle and hold hands.

Mason and I drive home to Hickory Farm after Emma's talk. Cora sleeps in the back seat. Emma and Oliver wore her out today. Tomorrow Lucy and Austin will watch her for the day and the Marjories will take her on Saturday night. I can tell she is loving all this family contact.

6 March 1995
Monday
Waiuku, New Zealand
10:13

ALICE

I sit at the kitchen table and open the card from Emma. It's an invitation to her graduation from law school on seventeen May 1995, Cora's fifth birthday. There's another card, a wedding announcement. Oliver Jacobs and Emma Maxwell invite you to their wedding in Cape Vincent, New York on nineteen May 1995. *We hope you will come. We love you.*

I sit at the kitchen table with my hands folded and look out the window at the bay.

When Mason gets home, I push the envelope toward him.

He picks it up and reads it.

"Well?"

"Well what?" I play my part.

"You know what."

And I do.

"Are you in?"

"I'm in."

ACKNOWLEDGMENTS

I have deep appreciation and gratitude for the many people in my life who helped me birth this book. Thank you for supporting me and loving me. It takes a community to bring forth these stories. I could not have done it alone.

To Lori, my partner of 33 years, for being there for me through thick and thin, and giving me time and space, support, grounding, and truth telling.

To Heather, my editor, for taking on this project, loving my story, and helping me make it the best it could be.

To Grace, Leigh Ann, Helen, Claire, Robert, and the Idyllwild Writing Group, all my writing buddies, for writing to and reading prompts. I'm a better writer because of you.

To Gin-Gin, my sister-in-law, with whom I went through the pandemic. I wish you were here to celebrate my new book. Your love, support, and stories enriched my life.

To my Imagery Group for supporting my imagination and storytelling.

To my recovery family for your on-going love, support, and acceptance and our sharing experience, strength and hope. Change is!

To my mom and dad for modeling and teaching me about focus, patience, and determination.

To my children, Emmett, Robin, and Heather for your love and support and believing in me as a writer. I am grateful to be your mom.

To Maxx and Mya, my grandchildren, for helping me to remember how wild and lovely imagination is. I am so happy you both love books.

And last but not least, to my Muse for her generosity in giving me stories.

ABOUT ATMOSPHERE PRESS

Atmosphere Press is an independent, full-service publisher for excellent books in all genres and for all audiences. Learn more about what we do at atmospherepress.com.

We encourage you to check out some of Atmosphere's latest releases, which are available at Amazon.com and via order from your local bookstore:

Twisted Silver Spoons, a novel by Karen M. Wicks

Queen of Crows, a novel by S.L. Wilton

The Summer Festival is Murder, a novel by Jill M. Lyon

The Past We Step Into, stories by Richard Scharine

The Museum of an Extinct Race, a novel by Jonathan Hale Rosen

Swimming with the Angels, a novel by Colin Kersey

Island of Dead Gods, a novel by Verena Mahlow

Cloakers, a novel by Alexandra Lapointe

Twins Daze, a novel by Jerry Petersen

Embargo on Hope, a novel by Justin Doyle

Abaddon Illusion, a novel by Lindsey Bakken

Blackland: A Utopian Novel, by Richard A. Jones

The Jesus Nut, a novel by John Prather

The Embers of Tradition, a novel by Chukwudum Okeke

Saints and Martyrs: A Novel, by Aaron Roe

When I Am Ashes, a novel by Amber Rose

Melancholy Vision: A Revolution Series Novel, by L.C. Hamilton

The Recoleta Stories, by Bryon Esmond Butler

ABOUT THE AUTHOR

Catee Ryan retired in 2011 after 35 years as a marriage and family therapist. She has dedicated her life to writing since then. She spends her days in her home office in the Coachella Valley, down the street from her wife of 33 years. She enjoys strong coffee, expensive chocolate, and falling asleep on the couch to foreign language murder mysteries on Netflix. Catee's book of short stories, Diving Home, was published in 2017.